BROKEN VOWS

SOPHIA KARLSON

Cover Art: Qamber Designs

Editing: Zee Monodee

Proofreading: Meg Chronis

Dear Reader,
This one is for you.
*Don't do this type of sh*t at home, and if you do,*
remember the ER is for real medical emergencies,
NOT your type of dilemma.

PS: corks pop out easier than other stuff.
They're kinda made for it, you know?
Yep. Here's looking at you, Fred.
😆

FOREWORD AND TRIGGER WARNINGS

This is the second book of the *Il Consiglio - A Mafia Dynasty* - Series.

These books **can't** be read as standalones (well, they can, but I don't want you to get lost here). Please read HATED VOWS, the first book in the series, before you read BROKEN VOWS.

This is a dark Mafia romance and has elements of suspense. Other trigger warnings include: on-page violence, gun violence, gore, references to domestic violence, scarification, and torture. Please read with care.

1

GIGI

The Trapanis sure know how to throw a party. Here on our yacht, anchored off the coast of southern Italy, we're a world apart from the rest of humanity.

Lights blink on the shoreline, a golden line dividing the dark ocean and star-littered sky. A warm breeze wraps its fingers around my hair, bringing with it that sweet-salt smell of the Mediterranean Sea.

I turn my back to the railing to have the wind in my face and watch my sister, Carla, whose eighteenth birthday we're celebrating. She's laughing with a bunch of girls her age. They're all dressed as if they just walked off some catwalk at a prêt-à-porter designer fashion show. Nobody here is in a dress priced under five thousand euros. They're slipping into a giggling fit, and boys are looking on, champagne flowing from several bottles and splashing on the deck.

What a waste.

And someone is going to have to clean that up.

It's not only the luxury of this yacht and being out at sea that underlines the sharp divide for me. It's the mix of company on the boat tonight: mostly Carla's friends from boarding school. Rich, elite, entitled. In the shadows, the people who serve and clean up after them. Waiters. Chefs. Mixologists. *Bodyguards.*

When I turned eighteen ten years ago, I didn't celebrate in such flamboyant style. I wanted to jump ship from this privileged life to one that lets you melt into the shadows.

I wanted to disappear, and not only because my mom had died of cancer earlier that year. I wanted nobody to notice me, unlike Carla, who's living her best life in the limelight of the European young, rich, and beautiful. Let's hope this abundance of zero caution isn't going to bite my little sister in the ass.

Carla is of age now, and in the world we're part of, turning eighteen comes with serious hazards. So far, Don Trapani hasn't said anything about her future, but my stepdad—and her biological father—is progressive and has allowed us more freedom than I've ever imagined. For now, Carla seems safe, but I know better.

I was eighteen once and almost forced into marriage. I stood my ground and fought tooth and nail for what I wanted—a life free of the Mafia and the obligations that came with it. I'll be forever grateful for my stepfather who bowed to my wishes and let me be.

A server approaches me with a fresh tray of filled champagne flutes, and I shake my head. I'm heading to London for an art auction in the morning. Now that the toasts are done, I can sneak off to my cabin, but the DJ has turned up the volume, and I might struggle to sleep.

With champagne, I can never stick to just one glass, and I can't be hungover on the job tomorrow. Red wine, on the other hand, is a whole other ballgame.

"I'll have some wine. Bring me a Merlot, please."

The server nods. That will knock me out in thirty minutes flat.

As he walks off, my stepdad, Don Mario Trapani, puts an

empty glass on the server's tray and comes to take my hand. His fingers are warm, his skin soft, his hand a safe haven for the young girl I once was. It's still a strong, firm hold but gentle at the same time. He's never raised a hand to me in anger or in malice, but I'm not naive—this hand must have blood on it, but it's never been mine. Don Trapani has proven himself to be an unexpected protective shield against this world we live in.

"Gigi." He steps away to look at me at arm's length. After a few intense seconds, he swallows, his face pained. "You always look so beautiful. Just like your mother did."

"Thank you, Papa." I'm the spitting image of my mom. A walking reminder of her to this man who took us in and loved us. With the way he looks at me and the emotion playing over his face, it's as if she's here tonight. I blink away the swell of tears. "It was a lovely speech."

He squeezes my fingers as he raises them to his lips for a peck.

"Walk with me, *cara*," he says.

I let him guide me down the main deck towards a quieter spot away from the party crowds.

We take a wide berth around a couple smooching. They're either too drunk or too high to notice or care that their elderly host is strolling past them, because they don't stop.

"Quite a party, isn't it?" I chuckle. We all know how *that's* going to end.

"They're young and carefree." My stepdad smiles and winks at me. "Let them enjoy it while it lasts. As for Carla, let me spoil her while I can."

We're spoiled, for sure, each of us in our own way, but the way he says it makes my heart clutch. At seventy-two, my stepdad looks fit, but his eyes are tired.

Mom was Don Trapani's second and last wife, and when she married him, he adopted me as his own, surname and all. Don Mario Trapani is mostly a good man and a good father, but all the love and devotion from this man could never wipe my memories clean. My first experience of a father—and men in general—is forever tainted. Men have this switch in them which they could flip on and off without warning. As a child, I've been on the receiving end of that flipped switch too many times.

I shrug off my dark thoughts. Ever since Don Trapani married Mom, I've had little reason to fear men on that level.

To think my stepdad has three kids, each from a different decade as we all have ten years between us. My stepbrother, Vincenzo Trapani, is the only offspring from his first marriage and also his only son. For some reason, he couldn't be here tonight, and I've been so relieved it's almost comical. Vincenzo might never have raised a hand at me, but he has a mean streak and makes my skin crawl.

We walk in silence until we reach the other side of the yacht where the party is less of a distraction, my mind wandering to memories of Mom and the unrelenting passing of time.

I know why he is cornering me. Now that Carla is eighteen, we should split our inheritance. "About the Swiss—"

"Now's not the time, Gigi." My stepdad sighs as he lets go of my hand, and we lean on the railing to look out to the sea.

"No? But Carla's share—"

"I've always wanted for you what your mom wanted," Don Trapani interrupts. "Freedom from family obligations, from this spiderweb we're caught in. God knows, after decades of trying to leave the Mafia, my son is dragging me back in."

Deep in my gut, unease stirs. What did Vincenzo get involved in this time? He's been Don Trapani's headache for years, on and off, always poised to turn into a full-on migraine.

"What's happened?" I ask, reminding myself I'm my own person, with my own thriving business, unattached and unbound to the Trapanis' Mafia affairs. This shouldn't affect me. In fact, I *won't* let it affect me.

For ten years, I've worked to extricate myself from their web as I'd vowed to Mom I would. I plan to take Carla along as soon as I possibly can. When she was born, a chamber opened in my heart shaped just like that little baby girl, almost as if she were my own. Over the years, this space has expanded and grown with her. I'll never leave her behind.

"The world is changing, *cara*. I am no longer able to keep up with it...or with your brother."

"He isn't my brother," I whisper, because in my gut, I sense where this would go if I don't nip it in the bud. Vincenzo is my stepbrother and no blood of mine. We share the same surname, nothing more.

"In this, he sees you as his younger sister."

And a pawn. I fist the railing and clench it hard, anything to contain the anger rising in me. Anger that smells of fear.

"I have my own life, my own business." I owe him nothing. I need him for nothing. I plan to keep it this way. To be honest, Vincenzo Trapani can go fuck himself.

"Which you built and found success with by using the Trapani name and connections. Don't think you would've gotten this far without it, *cara*. And don't snub your origins. They will always be part of you."

I push down on the anger, which is morphing into panic in my chest. It's all true. More than a century of Mafia blood runs in me; rivulets gathered from all over Italy into my veins. I might not be Don Trapani's own daughter, but I'm from old stock, too. I'm a product of my past, but I refuse to give it a future by bending to anybody's will. Least of all my stepbrother's. "I've built what I have, and nobody will take it away from me."

"This isn't about your business, Gigi."

No, it isn't. It's about how fragile this wall I've built around me could prove to be if Vincenzo decides I'm handy in the bigger scheme of his plans—it's about how fragile *I'll* prove to be if things come to a head.

Don Trapani sighs, and in this moment, he's no longer my stepdad but a Mafia Don. I sense the change in him, in his stance and the bow of his head.

"I've given you all this freedom, Gigi, sending you to boarding school in Switzerland, allowing you to study in England and France. In retrospect, maybe every one of them was a delusional decision on my part. I thought I'd be able to protect you forever, but I can no longer promise that. I'm too old for this game." He shifts on his feet and lowers his gaze. "You know how this works, *cara*."

I do. And it's the type of knowledge that keeps me up at night, worrying if I've done enough, if my fort would hold. I've seen more of the machinations of the Mafia than I ever cared for. Every vow I made to Mom on her deathbed, every truth I held myself honest to, surges up in me.

"What about Carla?"

I'd promised to keep her safe, to make sure she has the same exit from this life as me.

"She's Vincenzo's half-sister. They share the same blood, but when it comes down to it, she'll be in the same boat as you are."

Over my dead body. I won't see my sister bartered and married off to secure some new alliance Vincenzo must be forging with another crime ring. I will protect her with my life.

Don Trapani's words might be subtle, but I read their true meaning between the lines: under the dark water of this underworld we hail from, monsters are stirring.

My heart rate has been escalating with each minute of this conversation, and now it pulses in my temple as fear shoots up to settle in the form of a stress headache.

I have time. I've always been ready. My business has kept

me travel fit and I'm ready to run without much notice. I'm not so concerned about myself, but Carla is innocent and naive, and living in a bubble that can pop at any time.

"Now that she's done with school, she'll need a permanent bodyguard," I venture aloud.

She's no longer protected by the confines of a very exclusive boarding school in Switzerland. It's the same school I went to, but beyond our education, the only difference between me and Carla is the first decade of my life where I got to know the 'real world' firsthand. Those ten years are making all the difference in our perspectives on life. Where Carla is still happy to go with the flow, I make sure not to get caught in the tide in the first place.

"You too, *cara*."

"I'm fine."

For almost a decade, I've lived under the radar, not attending any events as a Trapani daughter, a *Mafia princess* for the taking. I've stayed as far away as humanly possible, made myself vanish in a way, and surely, this must pay off now.

"One day, I'm going to insist, Gigi, and I won't take no for an answer."

I close my eyes, refusing to believe my own ears. Things can't be this dire?

"Can you talk to her about the bodyguard?" Don Trapani says, not giving me the gap to counter him. "She isn't going to be happy."

Trust me, no eighteen-year-old is happy to be watched twenty-four-seven by some random guy who'd take a bullet for her.

"I will."

Now my whole body is tensed up, my shoulders hitched to my ears. I've been walking on eggshells for decades, and it's exhausting. Now, I'll have to get it into Carla's head that the freedom she knows is like a carpet. Ready to be ripped right from underneath your feet by the people you trust the most.

I'd hate for her to learn this lesson the hard way.

2

STEPHANO

Sweat runs from my brow and temples into my eyes and down my cheeks. I force myself to ignore the sting that comes with it. To keep my focus even beyond this discomfort. My body is drenched. The ref rings time, and I back off. He tosses me a towel, and I wipe down while I hop on my feet. Another round and this guy will be out for the count.

The bell rings again. We bump fists and start to circle each other. I go for him, grappling at his hands, wrestling until I get my arm around his neck. He is just as sweaty as me, and it's hard to get a solid grip. We've been at this for thirty minutes, give or take. We call it *the death spar*, or until you're so physically exhausted you want to die.

I'm not sure how this type of cage fighting evolved, but being a Scalera, I created what I wanted. What I needed. A form of mixed martial arts where everything goes except fists. You can kick a man to death, but you can't punch him in the face.

Let's just say, it hasn't hit the mainstream yet. Not that I care. This is my gym, and I make the rules. Fist fighting on its own is allowed, and I will hit a punching bag for hours when I feel like it. It's this *feel like it* part I need to keep under control. I've always been happy to hand out punches. Too happy.

I knee my opponent in the stomach, and he folds into me. I feel his grunt vibrate against my chest, but he isn't out yet. He tries to flip me, and we fall, roll over each other until I have him pinned. He struggles, but I gain inch by inch. Eventually, I have my legs in such a way that I could choke him if I wanted to.

"Fuck it, Steph, what pissed you off?" my opponent grunts.

Life in general.

"Tap out," I huff, squeezing his chest with my thighs.

"Jesus." He taps, and I roll off him.

For a moment, we're both on our backs, and then I laugh as I glance at him. "You'll do better next time."

As I sit up, I spot my brother Matteo where he's walking past some of the boxing rings. He's in his usual suit, so obviously not here to sweat.

I spit out my mouthguard and stand as he toes the edge of the ring.

"Still running your version of Fight Club down here?" he says with a cocked brow.

"You should try it out some time. The rules are simple, you'll get it."

"Fuck off, Fanny," Matteo says with a grin. "This no-fists thing doesn't do it for me."

I hate this nickname but don't bother to tell him off. I roasted him first.

"*No fists* is the ultimate control challenge. Any man can use his fists." Keeping them out of a fight makes you master a lot of other things. Yourself, foremost.

He shrugs. "Do you have time?"

"Sure." It's not often that Matteo walks into my gym at midday wanting to have a talk.

I collect my water and towel and give my opponent a handshake. "Same time tomorrow?"

"Maybe in two days' time. It's intense, but fuck—" He cuts off as he shakes his head with a grin.

I get it. This is why I do it, too.

As I pull on a T-shirt, Matteo stands idle, hands shoved in his pants pockets. "Aren't you going to shower?"

"I'll take five at home," I say, feet digging into Adidas slides.

I lead the way out of the gym and around the corner to the small lobby of the four-story apartment block. Our bodyguards are hovering on the periphery, but we both ignore them. A bodyguard is always in my vicinity when I'm out, one of the perks of being in *Il Consiglio* and a Scalera—or *not*. Being in the Mafia means someone always wants our blood, but we're the Scaleras and are usually the ones to draw blood first. I like some distance between me and my bodyguard and can get away with it. Matteo, on the other hand, needs more eyes on him. He's the firstborn, the heir to the throne.

As we scale the stairs to the top floor, he sighs. "Fucking dump. I don't get it. Why?"

"Because I like it." I punch in the code for my apartment's door and swing it open. "I don't get why you have an issue with it."

"You can afford a freaking penthouse," he says as we walk inside, "yet you choose to live here."

I glance over the space. It's old redbrick on one full wall, floor-to-ceiling windows on the other overlooking a park that gives the sense of space. It has only one bedroom in the loft, but I don't need more. I have my office, an open-concept kitchen, dining, and living room, plus a man-cave for my TV and computer games. One full bathroom and a guest washroom. With the high ceiling, it feels massive for a single guy who doesn't spend all his time here. Most important of all: it isn't an intimidating space. It's welcoming.

"Not all of us are the future face of *Il Consiglio*, Matteo."

And thank fuck for that. I don't *need* my living space to

intimidate and impress. I like to help people, not rule them, and when they come here, I need them to be at ease.

"Thanks for the fucking reminder," he grunts as he makes his way to the fridge, opens it, and leans in.

It's a touchy subject, his ascension to the throne.

"Help yourself. I'll be back in five."

"Rub-a-dub-dub, have a good scrub. You sure as fuck need it."

I smirk as I take the stairs to the loft. In moments like this, I see hints of my brother and not the Don he is becoming. I strip and step under the cold shower, soap down quickly but take time to read the words inked on my inner forearm, done in such a masculine gothic font you can't read it at first glance.

It's in your blood.

Then I went and proved it to myself by almost killing a boy my age once. I was only fourteen. Fucking young to start for a Scalera. Now I prove it to myself again every day in the gym, but with the iron fist of control over every move I execute for the two hours I work out daily.

The slogan has a double meaning. I might not be the head of *Il Consiglio* any time soon, what with Matteo and Dominic in line before me, but being a Scalera means only one thing: there isn't an out for the likes of us. This life is in our blood. Even if I could get out, I've done things that have entrapped me in the safety net that comes with being in *Il Consiglio*.

I step out of the shower, roughly dry, and get dressed in some wash-worn jeans and a T-shirt. I'm not working until much later and won't bother with a full suit like Matteo does.

When I walk into my living room, he's sitting at the kitchen island, a beer in hand and some of my housekeeper's home-cooked chili in a bowl. Not exactly Italian fare, and we might be hundred percent Italian by bloodline, but we've grown up American. He's dished up some for me too, along with a cold can, and I slide onto the stool next to him.

I take a deep chug of beer, waiting for him to speak up.

"Here." He pushes sour cream and grated cheese in my direction. "It's good."

"You're not here to taste-test my chili." I douse my bowl with condiments. "What's up, bro?"

Matteo tilts his head in a small nod and swallows his last bite down with beer.

"The Don has cancer."

I lean back to look my brother in the eye.

"What?" *Cancer*. Of all the things to take the old man out. "He's dying?"

He hitches his shoulder. "Prognosis is four months."

Fuck. *Four months.* And just like that, the man who started it all, who is the last living custodian of my secret, will be dead.

"He's taken his sweet time to get to this point, and now, he's going to make us wait four months?" I have a strong bond with my four brothers—one rooted in our mutual hatred for Don Guiliano Scalera, our father. The head of *Il Consiglio* and a complete psychopath.

"He's not done." Matteo wipes his mouth with some paper towel and looks at me. "He's left me in charge of wrapping up dirty business."

Ah, fuck. Never mind the news about the Don, I knew this wasn't a social call. *Dirty fucking business.* I suppress a sigh. "Okay. Need some help?" My brother already has my *omertà*, he doesn't need to ask for it.

"You're not going to like it, Steph."

As if I've ever been given the option. I steel myself. "I'm not touching his mistresses."

"No," he sighs. "It's nothing like that." He rakes his fingers through his hair and then settles his hands on the counter, fingers splayed. "He wants me to ruin the senator's daughter. The final retribution."

"But we're quits. Two for one—"

"I know it's fucked up. Alex died, and the senator paid for it when the Don killed his wife and son. But he owes us money, and for twelve years, he hasn't bothered to pay up."

"So? Kill him and leave Tasha Armstrong out of it."

Matteo meets my gaze, and I blink at the cold glare in his own. "We both know it isn't about the money."

"No."

Anything around Alex will always trigger Matteo. His trauma is laced with guilt and the burden of not having been able to save our brother.

He will also step into the Don's shoes, by the sound of it sooner than any of us anticipated, but handing out a double dose of revenge isn't how we normally operate.

I bet the Don is using this to test Matteo one last time. Every fucking day, the Don tested and groomed us, each one of us primed for a specific role he saw us taking up in the organization. Every Scalera son has earned his seat at the table the hard way. We never talk about it, but none of us needs to fill in the blanks to know how fucked up we are.

I swallow hard on the chili that doesn't go down with ease. Even now, I can still feel my dad's fist clenching around my throat. I squeeze my beer can, as if the reciprocal move could wipe out memories.

Nothing will wipe my slate clean. There are always the Don's expectations, and sometimes, no level of revenge is enough. Especially when it comes to Alex.

Sometimes, it's just this fucked-up need for violence.

It's in your blood.

"We both also know that if we don't do it, the Don will hire someone else," Matteo grunts. "I won't let anybody else deal with our dirty laundry."

"No." We can't slip up on the Don's final requests, and none of us will hand Tasha Armstrong over to another organized crime ring. I can just imagine what they'd do to the senator's daughter, and when it comes to women— "So, what's the plan?"

"A virgin auction, offshore."

I toss my spoon into the bowl, and it clinks in the silence. "I'm not running a virgin auction for anybody who hasn't signed up for it herself."

"Told you you're not going to like it."

"How the fuck do you even know she's still a virgin?" Rebellion is stirring up in me. This isn't how I roll. I might have many vices, but I have my limits.

"Conjecture. Listen, I don't like it either, but it's going to be the easiest way to give the Don what he wants."

"Someone raping this woman? The girl lost her mom and brother thanks to us. So yeah. Sounds about right for the Don's *Il Consiglio*."

We should just kill the fucking Don ourselves and end this feud. There's no love lost between him and any of his sons, least of all Matteo.

"You've vetted your client base," he says, stopping me from talking treason. "You know most of the men on your list on a first name basis, Steph. I'm asking you because with you arranging it, it will be easiest for her."

I push my half-eaten chili out of the way and drag a hand down my face. Matteo wouldn't ask this of me if he didn't have his own agenda for revenge. Alex's death catapulted us all into the reality of what it means to be in the Mafia, but *Alex died in Matteo's arms*. No man recovers from seeing his brother's lifeblood run out, seeing it drench his shirt and dry to the extent they had to cut the fabric off his body.

I was there when they brought my brothers in from the shooting. Matteo wouldn't let him go. Even unconscious, he clung to Alex's body. Those images are branded on my mind, flashing smoldering red at times when I need it least.

The Don didn't weep when he saw his dead son's body. He

was already plotting his revenge. But I don't care about the Don. I care about my brothers. But still—

"You need something to keep your mind busy, Steph. This existence, where you go all Fight Club for two, three hours a day, overseeing our clubs at night, running some of the online stuff, draining yourself to a point of no return... I can't watch you do this anymore."

I crunch my empty beer can in my hand, not wanting to go there. I know he's right, but it's this mindless routine that keeps me in control.

"I need to eliminate another target in Sicily first," Matteo says. "That will need planning, too."

"Who?"

"The Sicilian."

"Don Emilio Randazzo?" I repeat, stunned. "You have to take him out? For real?"

"Yes."

He sighs, and I grunt. Our old man is losing his mind.

"This auction will happen offshore, and it will involve a lot of planning. All I need for you to do is go through the motions as if she's signed your usual contract," he continues. "We can work both missions together. It will take your mind off Tatiana and everything that's happened."

I dip my head, not wanting my brother to see the red flush heating my face. It doesn't help when he reminds me of what happened to Tatiana. How the woman I deeply cared for was brutally raped and left for dead. Yes, she was a prostitute and went willingly with Greg Fucking Martinez, but no woman deserves that.

"It's as if she's already gone," I say, not wanting to take this conversation any further.

"She was never yours, Stephano."

I lean back and slap my hands down on the counter. Does

he really want to go there right now? "It doesn't matter. I'm going to kill the fucker that did this to her."

"Yes. You will. We will make it happen. But Steph—"

"No. No more." I stand. "Now you're just trying to pick a fucking fight, Matteo. Let me warn you, I'm still pumped from earlier at the gym." And I'll beat him to a pulp. Matteo is in shape, but he doesn't war with himself every day like I do. He has his own battles, plus he is going to be the Don of *Il Consiglio* soon. I'm his brother, and he will always have my loyalty. Now's the time to show it to him. "I'll do this virgin auction for you, provided she is one. But understand this clearly: I'm doing it because *you* asked, and not for the Don."

"Thank you. Teamwork makes the fucking dream work." He picks up his phone from the counter as he stands. "I'll keep you posted."

3

GIGI

Monte Carlo is packed, and although I love it here, I prefer it less congested with tourists. It's the beginning of summer peak season, and the taxi is battling to get ahead to the restaurant where I'm meeting Carla. I don't know what the hold-up is but as a last resort, I make the driver stop. I tap my card to pay and hop out, bracing myself to walk the last two hundred meters in heels not made for walking.

By the time I get there, I'm wilted. Thank God for air conditioning. Carla waves to me from where she's already seated, and I spot her bodyguard sitting unobtrusively at the bar, nursing an espresso. We make eye contact, but he doesn't acknowledge me.

"Hey." I lean in to kiss my sister on the cheeks. She's in a white strapless top, tight around her breasts. Her skin is sun-bronzed, and with her long mahogany tresses framing her face and brown eyes, my little sister looks seriously grown up.

"Traffic's a bitch, isn't it," Carla says as she stands to hug me, but I wave her to sit down.

I'm too hot for hugs.

"Yes. Don't use that word."

She rolls her eyes but reaches for the carafe and pours me some water. "How long are you here for?"

"Three days. I have an auction in Cannes tomorrow, and I'm meeting a client in Nice later this week."

"Don't you ever get tired of it?"

"What? The art? I'll never get tired of the art, or the auctions." There's the thrill of the chase, the buzz when I find a real treasure. The happiness when I make a deal for my clients. My work is a bit of a trip without the nasty addiction that comes with drugs.

"No, I mean the travel. You're forever flying from one corner of Europe to the other, never standing still. Even that bolt hole in London isn't much, and it isn't as if you spend a lot of time there."

A waiter hands me a menu, and I glance through it, trying to delay a response. "I'm so used to it, I hardly notice."

But I do. I've been running all over Europe since my business found its feet, and the last three years have been grueling. Most important, though, is the fact I'm fit and ready for the day I really need to run. After the talk with Don Trapani at Carla's birthday bash two months ago, I've made a point of making sure my exit plans are oiled and ready to be put into action at a moment's notice.

"In any case, I'm always welcome at home or Lake Como. And there's the yacht," I throw out, trying to appear careless.

Carla glares at me from under her thick lashes. "You only go to any of those places when Vincenzo isn't around. I've noticed, you know."

Yep. When it comes to my stepbrother, I prefer *out of sight, out of mind*. But I don't want to dwell on it. Not here, and not with her. Especially not after the talk I had with Papa on her birthday. That conversation has been eating at me like a worm, tarnishing a perfect-looking fruit from the inside out.

"What are your plans for the next few weeks?"

She's hanging out with friends in Monaco for now, but at some point, they'll all move to the yacht and chill. It's not as if these kids need to work to make money or be ready to disappear to avoid an arranged marriage. None of them is in this situation, except Carla, and this fact hasn't sunk in with her yet.

"Trying to give my bodyguard the slip?" she mutters. "Fuck, he's irritating."

With a sigh, I lift my gaze to where the man is sitting. He's studying the diners as if he's bored, but I know better. "You know the rules, *cara*, so don't even think about it. Please. It isn't safe."

I bet Don Trapani didn't have the same little talk with her like he had with me. Carla is going through life with blinders on, ignorant as to what could happen to her if someone decides she's a handy pawn or good for ransom money.

"I don't understand why I need to have someone attached to the hip when you can go gallivanting around Europe on your own without a bodyguard. You're just as much a Trapani as me!"

"Keep your voice down," I say as I put my hand on hers in warning. "This exact attitude is why you need a bodyguard. You're young, pretty, and rather naive if you think you can go through life as a Mafia princess and not be snatched," I whisper the last words, close to her ear. "You're not the only one in your friend group with a bodyguard, so cut it out. I'm not coming to identify your body if you get kidnapped and something goes wrong."

I retract my hand, not knowing how else to get the real danger of our situation into my little sister's thick head. "In any case, I'm not sure why you're complaining. At least he's something to look at."

Carla rolls her eyes at me. "Have him, then. I don't care."

I hitch my eyebrows as my jaw goes slack. My nonexistent sex life is none of anybody's business. "I really hope you don't go about selling your bodyguard like a sexual favor to your friends."

I don't know him, but I know Carla and the type she's hanging out with. I know *me*, and I'm a product of the same system. Swiss finishing school alumni. English boarding school girls, where the yearly school fees could make a normal person want to vomit a little. Sated, spoilt, privileged to the point where they have no concept of reality.

"Can you stop mothering me for a minute, and be like...I dunno? A sister? A friend?"

This puts my back up. Ever since Carla went to Switzerland for the last two years of school, it's as if she's left, and I don't know how to find my way back to her. I've seen her whenever I can, but this crevice between us is cracking open wider each time we see each other.

"Sorry," I mumble, but I can't help myself. Where I've fought for every inch between me and the Mafia, Carla hasn't realized yet she's the bull's eye. "Let's just order."

I shove my face into the menu, and for two minutes, there's a strained silence between us. When my phone vibrates in my purse where I have it hooked over an extra chair, I reach for it.

With an exasperated sigh, Carla reaches for her own phone where she's placed it face down on the table. There goes my rule, but I need to take this. It could be my client.

"Hey, Papa," I say, looking at Carla.

"How're my girls?" Don Trapani answers.

"I didn't know you knew I was meeting Carla today." I bet my movements are being tracked.

"She told me. I'm glad you're in Monte Carlo. I have a favor to ask."

"Sure, what can I do for you?" I indicate to the waiter to come take our order. My afternoon is open, but I suspect I'm going to have to run an errand now.

"I have guests on the yacht. They're sailing from Sicily and will be in the Cannes marina at around four this afternoon. I need you to go meet them."

I blink. This is a bit last minute. "I—I—"

"I know you're supposed to be in Cannes tomorrow. Surely, you can make this work, Gigi. In fact, you *must* make it work."

"Papa, I'm in Monte Carlo."

"So? It's an hour's drive—"

"You haven't seen the traffic—"

He sighs into the phone. "I don't care. Make it happen, *cara*. Go meet them. Charm them. Make new friends."

"Why? Who are these people, anyway?"

"Friends from America. And you know why. We might need them."

This. Everything is about scratching each other's backs.

"Who are they, then? I assume their business is *not* the same as yours?" My subtle way of prodding to see if I'm stepping into another crime-riddled Mafia ring.

"No. The Scaleras are from Boston. You'll see for yourself. They're good people to know."

"What business are they in, Papa?" I insist. I'm not going to smooth the way for the 'Ndrangheta or Cosa Nostra from America into Europe. Plus, I've never heard the name Scalera before.

"Honestly, Gigi. They own security companies in the US. Top of the range and latest technology like we don't know here yet."

I exhale slowly, forcing myself to calm down. If Don Trapani is making connections with security companies in the States, to the extent where he allows them to use our yacht, things are worse than I anticipated. If you're getting a company from the States to come and upgrade your security, it only means you don't trust anybody locally anymore.

We're in deep, deep trouble. And I bet Vincenzo doesn't know anything about this Scalera visit.

"I'll go meet them," I say, my eyes focusing on Carla's flawless face, her makeup done to perfection and doing nothing to hide her youth.

"Thank you, *cara*. We'll talk tomorrow."

We ring off, and I revert to the menu, but my appetite is gone.

4

STEPHANO

I'm pacing the St. Chalamet presidential suite. Waiting is the worst. Two months of planning, and now, time drags. My body is buzzing with unspent energy and a nagging worry about Matteo I can't shed. The only word I got was a quick message stating *it's done* after he killed Randazzo.

My phone vibrates in my jacket pocket. This better be my brother. I groan in relief when Matteo's shitface shows on the screen.

"Fuck, Matty," I say as I answer the call. "Are you okay?"

"Hey." He clears his throat. "All good."

"Bro. I'm sitting here on pins and fucking needles waiting to hear from you." I sweep my gaze over the ridiculous luxury of the space. 'Pins and needles' isn't exactly right. The two-bedroom suite exudes class, money, and style. It has magnificent views over the white sandy beach of Cannes's La Croisette, currently packed with umbrellas, deck chairs, and vacationers. The sunlit ocean beyond is such a bright blue, it's almost blinding.

If I weren't so fed up with this virgin auction, I would've

relaxed on the balcony and enjoyed the services that come with of this level of luxury.

Matteo laughs, if a bit drily. "I'm good. Made a fine escape on Don Trapani's yacht, I'll tell you this much."

He might be cruising in style, but now I'm sensing again things didn't go exactly as planned. "So the Don made the right call?"

"Yeah. And with our jet already in France, it will be harder for someone to trace our tracks."

I sigh in relief, but I won't feel at ease until I've seen him in person. I can't wait for all of this to be over. Up until my arrival in Cannes, I'd been going through the motions, mindless, forcing myself to make the necessary arrangements for this auction. With my twin brother Luca, we've done hundreds of virgin auctions, but the women always come to us, wanting to auction off their virginity for whatever reason. Student or medical debts for family members, wanting to fund their travels, buy a home for their ailing parents, anything. If you can think of a reason, it's been used.

Our clients are men with so much money they don't care to throw it around for a bit of *innocent* pleasure. With every woman who applied, asking us to arrange her auction, I've vowed it would be the last time. Yet every single time, I figured better us than another party with fewer scruples and measures in place to ensure the girls aren't brutalized in the process.

"What time are you arriving in Cannes?" I ask. The clock is ticking, and this show needs to get on the road.

"We're about to enter the marina. Should take another half an hour, I'd say."

"Seriously?" I want to strangle him. The whole freaking day, I've been waiting to hear from him, but he's ignored my calls, messages, everything. Something's up, and with what has happened in Sicily, it could be anything.

"You didn't get shot or something yesterday?" Panic grips my chest. Things can go wrong—things did go wrong that night with Alex twelve years ago. For all I know, Matteo got hurt and is keeping it to himself so we don't freak out.

"No, Burley's got a bullet in the butt and arm, but I'm fine. Listen—"

"Fucking hell, Matteo!" I yell into the phone, pacing the room. "It was supposed to be a clean fucking job."

"It was fucking clean." His tone is cold and clipped. "But if that psycho's estate is torched, don't come ask me if I doused it with fuel. Randazzo had more maggots coming for him than a piece of carrion."

I sigh as I rub my forehead. Reading between the lines, it was a close call. "Okay. So what did you do today other than ignore me?" I'm not buying it. Something is so off, I can smell it from here. There's a beat of silence on the other side of the line, and I wait, giving him the opening he needs.

"Caught up with some work I've been neglecting," he replies, brushing over my question. "Are you ready for us?"

In that moment, he sounds so tired, I wish we could all just get the hell out of here and fly home. Skip this whole virgin auction part that's been destroying me like some flesh-eating fungus. "I'm ready. Party packs and all."

I glance to where our exclusive party packs are stacked in a pyramid on a console table, each containing everything a man could need for a perfect sex fest: condoms, lube, toys covering a wide range from handcuffs to cock rings, candles for wax play, chocolate body paint, you name it. For her, some Plan B, wipes, sanitary products, thrush and UTI meds. Painkillers.

If we were in the States, we'd include some recreational drugs, but I wasn't going to fly that shit in for anybody because I don't want to extend my stay in France for drug trafficking. I'm counting on our guests to bring their own.

"Steph, I—" He breaks off.

"What?" I swear he is pacing like a caged bear.

There's a long beat of silence and then he sighs, but it's more a grunt than anything else. "Just meet us at the marina."

"I'm on my way." Once I have seen him face to face, I'll know exactly what's up.

I kill the call and stride through the suite one last time. The virgin auction side of our online business has a certain standard to maintain or exceed, and this evening will be no exception. I might not condone what will be happening here tonight, but I have a reputation to uphold. For the first time ever, I have a live stream going too. I've set it up in the foyer for now but will have to change the camera's angle as the night progresses. Fuck Don Scalera for getting this creepy on his deathbed.

Flower arrangements give the place a homey, feminine vibe, but the bar is set up with a wide selection of some of the most expensive whiskeys in the world. An off-white circular sectional stands center stage, and on the coffee table, climate-controlled boxes of Cuban cigars await the bidders. Waiters will serve dinner, snacks, and champagne or wine. There's no limit on the spending here tonight.

I might have gone over the top with this one to soothe my own conscience. Funny how I seem to still have one.

With a sigh, I pocket my phone and check my appearance in the bedroom's floor-to-ceiling mirror. Stone-colored suit, white shirt, brown leather boat shoes with hidden socks. All very Côte d'Azur. I'll blend right in.

"Let's go. Party's starting," I say as I walk into the living room where my two bodyguards have been killing time.

Fuck it. I don't know when that slogan got ingrained in *Il Consiglio's* business affairs, but it's become our umbrella term for anything from *Shit's going down* to *Bring more beer*. You always need more context to read between the lines. In this case, it means *I need to collect the merchandise*.

We take the elevator and exit the hotel's main entrance. My driver has been waiting in the porte cochère.

Ten minutes later, as we approach the marina, I spot the Trapanis' yacht. We can drive all the way to their berth, but I need a moment to get a grip. I haven't had what I call a *proper workout* since arriving in Cannes, and it isn't a good space to be in, physically or mentally. My body is buzzing with unspent energy, and I'm feeling caged, but since arriving in France, the business at hand has taken up all my time.

"We'll walk the rest."

The driver parks, and I get out with my bodyguards, strolling along the marina and eyeing the ludicrously expensive yachts lined up. Most names are passable; some are so pretentious, they trigger my gag reflex.

The Trapanis' *Onda Maestosa* towers over some of the other moored boats. As I crane my neck to get in the full picture of the yacht, rushed footsteps draw my attention.

A dark-haired brunette is high-heeling it down the marina in a navy sundress splattered with red poppies, chiffon skirts so light, the breeze etches out her thighs. She's so focused on the yacht, she doesn't see me.

And then she trips, her ankle buckling as her heel hits a small hole in the pavement. Our bodies almost collide, but I steady her with a hand on her arm. Our gazes connect for the briefest moment before she stiffens.

"*Merci*," she mutters as she shrugs loose but then continues down the dock as if nothing happened.

Close call, angel.

She seems to be rushing to the next yacht, and for a moment, I appreciate the visual of her ankles in those sandals, the length of her legs culminating in the perfect, rounded ass any man would want to sink his fingers into. Her scent trails in the air. Expensive floral perfume to match the dress.

"*Ciao*!" the brunette calls out and waves as she looks up.

I follow her gaze, and alarm bells go off in my head.

Tasha Armstrong, the senator's daughter—the *merchandise* as we labeled her if only to distance ourselves in some way from the Don's last, manic request—is standing at the railing, looking down at us as Matteo steps up from behind her.

Fuck. Whoever this unknown woman is, I can't allow her to talk to the Tasha. The brunette, who has stripped off her heeled sandals, hurries up the narrow stairs on the side of the yacht, *as if she belongs*.

Trust a woman to come and fuck up my day. I might hate an unwilling virgin auction, but I can tell you who hates it more: other women. I'm half a minute behind the brunette and call my men off. They'll have to wait down here in case she decides to run and we need to contain her.

I rush to the side of the yacht, following in her footsteps up the narrow stairs. She's already disappeared onto the yacht's main deck. As I scale the stairs two at a time I listen, but there's too much other noise to make out words. I hear voices, though —Matteo's and this woman's musical tones as they introduce themselves, all friendly.

Until it's not.

"*Cara*," she says as I get my first visual of her on the deck. She's trying to step up to Tasha. "Are you held against your will? Have they hurt you?"

Fuck me twice over. This is the last thing we need.

Matteo has his hand on the brunette's shoulder, warning her not to approach Tasha. My brother looks exhausted.

"Gigi—" he starts as I rush onto the deck.

Gigi?

Fuck. *Gigi Trapani.* Don Trapani's daughter. Her dad is the owner of the yacht Matteo had exclusive use of for the job he had to do in Sicily. Don Trapani is one of the older Mafia king-pins in Italy. To think the old geyser can have such a beauty for a daughter. She can hardly be older than twenty-five. She also has an older brother and a younger sister, but that's the only information we've bothered to collect.

"Need some help there, Matteo?" We need to manage this situation. Redirect whatever is going on in Gigi's head. Silence her if necessary.

Fuck. This wasn't on my to-do list today.

Gigi turns to me, indignation flushing her cheeks.

"I don't care who the hell you are," she hisses, her words laced with a British accent, "but you're getting off my yacht. Right now."

Nice introduction. "I don't care who the hell you are, angel. I'm not going anywhere."

Gigi crosses the deck in quick strides and pushes me hard on the chest, making me freeze in surprise. I'm solid, and her palm connects with my pec as if it's a wall. It does nothing to me, but the heat of her hand spreads through the button-down I'm wearing.

"Leave!" she spits out.

Suddenly, that's the last thing I plan to do.

A woman only gets to slap me once. When she hits first, it's born out of fear that you'll get the first shot in and won't stop. I don't play such games. In fact, I hate them. This one has to calm the fuck down, and Matteo already has his hands full.

So I do the only thing I can to take charge of the situation. I fist Gigi's wrist, making her drop her sandals as I twist her into an armlock. She winces, and I hiss my own displeasure. I press my mouth to her ear, her thick hair against my lips, smelling of vanilla.

"Behave."

She struggles, her sweet ass pressing into my groin, and it's a split second before she does the next thing any woman does in this situation: scream. I cover her mouth with my hand and look at Matteo where he's clutching the railing, clearly as irritated as a storm cloud that needs to break but has to keep it together.

"Jesus Christ, Matteo." I sigh. "Can you stop collecting hoydenish shrews? It's bad for business."

"Fucking curve ball," he grunts. "Bring her inside so we can talk without an audience."

5

GIGI

Panic floods my veins, but indignation overpowers it. This stranger has me in an armlock, his massive, callused palm pressed over my mouth. His fingers clamp down on my jaw as if he's done this a thousand times.

And this on my stepdad's yacht.

Where the hell is the staff? I struggle, but it's no use—he's much taller than me, and by the feel of his hard chest and arm muscles where they're flush against me, he's physically able to toss me into the marina from here if he wants to.

He shifts, and the painful pinch in my shoulder eases, only for him to lace his fingers with mine. He wraps both our arms around my middle then lifts me up as if I weigh nothing, his other hand still covering my mouth. I kick out with muffled screams that are only trapped, and he presses his mouth to my ear.

"Be still, angel," he mutters as if I'm just a toy. "I'm not going to hurt you."

I know it's true. The way he carries me is with enough pressure to hold me in place but not to bruise or with force. And he's laughing. *Actually laughing.*

I fight him, because *him*. I spotted this man as I made my way along the marina to our mooring berth. Dressed in a tailored stone-colored suit, he was hard to miss. On the Riviera, people tend to dress more casually, even if it's in the most expensive couture out there. It's the way he carried himself I couldn't ignore.

As I strode up to our yacht, I honestly thought he was here to see a neighboring yacht up for sale. But then I spotted his bodyguards, the dead giveaway. *Mafia*.

Now I glance around, frantically trying to see if anybody is coming to my aid, but I only spot some of the waiters, wide-eyed and gaping. Useless.

"Leave us," Matteo says.

By the male authority in his tone, everything I say is going to be overridden. I'm just a woman. A *Mafia princess*. A pawn.

I grunt against my capturer's hand, wanting to bite. The frustration in me boils up. Ever since I've understood where I fall in the hierarchy of these crime rings, I've been avoiding getting sucked in. I've vowed to never bow to the unwritten rules the Mafia have for their female kin. But now, I'm here, and this girl—this *woman*, who is barely older than Carla—is clearly in trouble. Trouble I've now witnessed. This can't be happening to me. Surely, Don Trapani wouldn't let me step blindly into a Mafia mess.

I can't leave her. I can't even imagine—

"I'm going to let you go, angel." His voice is deep and masculine, sending chills of desire over my sensitive skin where his breath ghosts down my neck. "Try not to bite, okay?"

Bite? I see red. Not because he read my mind, but his words imply I'm a freaking dog and he is my owner.

No man will ever own me.

Least of all some Mafia motherfucker who should be on death row. Every cell in my body wants to go at him, but this is a precarious situation. If this were Carla... I need to put this woman first. Get her out of here. I know the ins and outs of the yacht, the marina, and I have friends in Cannes. I can help her escape.

I still, and he lets me go. His hand strokes over my stomach, his strong fingers untwining from mine as he clasps my hip, making sure I've found my footing before he lifts his palm from my mouth. He traces my jawline with a fingertip, almost in apology. His touch is so gentle and in contrast to every expectation that it deflates me.

"Get your filthy Mafia paws off me," I huff out, stepping away from his body, fully aware he's managed to turn me on in these few minutes of having me hugged to him, even more so with that final soft sweep of his fingertip. *A caress.* I curse my treacherous female body that's reacting to an overdose of male pheromones.

In two steps, I'm sitting next to the young woman and reach for her hand, my gaze homing in on her wrist where I thought I was seeing wrong. *Abrasions? On her wrists? God help us.* "*Cara*, what's your name?"

She only blinks at me before her eyes jump to my former capturer. My gaze follows hers, only to watch him reaching for his belt buckle.

"Can I gag this one?" he says. "It will give me endless pleasure."

Every last nerve shoots desire to my sex, and I curse under my breath. What is it with this man? I've never had the lunacy to react like this to anybody before, never mind in *this* situation, which reeks of human trafficking. If I don't watch out, I'm next.

"Nobody is getting gagged," Matteo says with a sigh. "Gigi, what goes on here is none of your business."

I'm stunned. The gall! "You're on my yacht. *She's* on my yacht. It *is* my business."

"Yep." He grinds his jaw. "*You* being on this yacht wasn't exactly the plan."

I love Papa to bits, but sometimes he does things that make zero sense to me. Why put me here if he knew there was human trafficking going on? I'm still trying to think when my capturer's eyes home in on those abrasions on the girl's wrists that also had me do a double take.

"There's some damage to the merch, Matteo," he says, his words slicing through the tension between us.

Merch? Like in merchandise?

"She did it to herself." Matteo stares him down.

"Oh, no, please, don't tell me you tried to cut your wrists!" I call out but realize they aren't self-harm scars but more those made by handcuffs.

She's been tied up. She also has an engagement ring and wedding band on her fingers, which shine with some of the biggest diamonds I've ever seen grace a woman's hand. I'm missing something here. She could be married to Matteo. She could be a Scalera.

"Are those Mom's rings?" The other man, whose name I still don't know, straightens and stares Matteo down. "What the actual fuck, bro?"

6

STEPHANO

I can't believe it. Mom's rings? I want to shake Matteo. My brother has crossed a line.

"Take them off. Never mind the fucking sacrilege. You can't wear them tonight."

I hold my hand out to Tasha. I made a sacred vow on Mom's rings, to her, quietly while we were alone, a few days after the fateful night that still haunts me. I can't stand seeing those rings. They only remind me of everything that's *in my blood.* About how broken Mom was, and how I was too young and dumb to realize it. For years, it haunted me—why did she never fight back? As if any of us ever fought him back. She was the first line of our defense, standing between him and us. Maybe she had fought back at some point, but by the time she died, she'd been glued and stitched back together too many times to hold strong through another birth. And then the Don had nobody holding him back.

"Tonight?" Gigi asks, her gaze jogging between us and ripping me out of my memories.

"None of your fucking business," I growl at her, annoyed at how those rings triggered me and how our family's dirty laundry is being aired for Gigi Trapani. She might think I have dirty Mafia paws, but she's Don Trapani's daughter and just as much Mafia as me, whether she likes it or not.

"Tonight's auction is cancelled," Matteo says.

"What?" Did I hear right? He can't be serious. Heat creeps up my neck. He could just as well have dropped a bomb. "Tonight's auction? Cancelled?"

My gaze sinks into his, and for the first time, I actually look at him. Look properly at his stance, at the way he protects Tasha subconsciously with his body by being a physical barrier between me and her.

Jesus Christ. *No.*

My gaze jumps between Tasha's and Matteo's and then locks with my brother's as we basically communicate without words. I don't know what happened in Sicily with the merch, but he's lost the plot. He *fell* for her. Matteo is a total goner. And that for the last woman on the planet he's allowed to have. I have no idea how far he's gone with her, but I'm ready to go at him.

"Oh my God! You're auctioning off your virginity!" Gigi's voice pitches in shock, bulldozing through my thoughts. "Is this for real? Are they forcing you? Is it your own choice?"

She's back in full force as she jumps up to push herself between Tasha and us men, as we are clearly the biggest threat in the room. Her fucking mouth on a run is more dangerous than anything here, and I wish I'd never removed my hand from those soft lips and cheeks.

"Don't do this," she begs now, her voice desperate.

Tasha stands, ignores Gigi, tugs Mom's rings off, and holds them out to Matteo.

"I've been promised a virgin auction," she says, her voice steady. "I want my virgin auction."

Fuck me. *I* don't want this auction. *Matteo* doesn't want this auction. But now, the *merch* wants to go ahead with it? My head spins.

"I have a right to clear my father's debt," Tasha says. "If this is the only way to do it, I'll go through with it."

"Please—" Gigi reaches out for her, but Tasha steps up to me, avoiding Matteo's gaze, which is growing more feral by the second.

"I'm ready to go if you are," Tasha says to me, softly, but certain.

I'm torn. I have no clue what to do. The only thing I know is we can't get deeper into shit with Gigi looking on, and I need time to figure out what to do. Tonight, our high-profile clients will clock in at seven, with expectations. I have time, but I'm not on home ground. This is France, not Boston. I've prepped everything with the focus on handing Tasha over to the winning bidder tonight. But Matteo—

"Tasha," he begs. "You don't know what you're getting into."

She leans into me, and I put my hand on her lower back, hoping she understands my gesture is only there for support. If this were a normal virgin auction, and she pulled out by herself at the last minute, I would roll with it. It's in our contract. Except she doesn't have one of those. This is a twist neither Matteo nor I anticipated.

Matteo's jaw ticks as I touch her. He's further along than even he knows. There's only one way to deal with this situation: get Tasha away from Gigi Trapani before things get out of hand. Matteo will have to make a decision before tonight's bidding ends or I'll make it for him. Seeing what I've seen now, I already know what I'm going to do.

"What the lady wants, the lady gets." I have significant costs to recover from this whole expedition, and the least he can do is contribute if he wants to have her for himself. "Stop fucking around, Matteo. The clock is ticking, and she needs to get ready.

If you're so eager to have her, you can place a fucking bid like the rest of them."

"God, you're a bunch of creeps! She isn't property!" Gigi yells now as she pulls on Tasha's arm.

Fuck. For a full blessed minute, Gigi has been quiet. Yep, not only do I have dirty Mafia paws, but now I'm also a creep. Nice. This is what I live for.

"Can you all stop talking as if I'm not in the room?" Tasha says in a raised voice as she shrugs Gigi off. "It's okay. Stephano will take care of me."

That I will. Until my brother comes to the party and commits to what he wants. I hope he makes up his mind before nine o'clock tonight.

I put pressure on Tasha's lower back, and she takes the first step. Gigi stands and attempts again to stop her.

"You. Sit. Stay," I bark at her.

The last thing I need is Gigi trailing along, meddling and messing up my schedule. This evening was planned with precision. I'll go through the motions until Matteo does what he needs to do.

To my surprise, Gigi falls back in her seat and does exactly what I told her to do.

I'm so tempted to say *good girl* but bite my tongue, more to hide my smirk than to stop the words from popping out. She's not my girl, good or anything. Damn shame, because I'd love to take her in hand and teach her a lesson or two.

7

GIGI

"Was that your brother?" I ask as Stephano disappears down the stairs, his hand resting on the woman's shoulder, possessive, protective, caring.

At the visual, my body pulses with need. That's the type of hold I love on *me*, rare as they are. Few men in my experience know how to demonstrate this in just one simple touch. And now, with my luck, it's this Mafia asshole who knows just how to tug at every sexual nerve in my being.

I force my thoughts away from the man and his hands and the fact that I want them all over me, and glance back at Matteo. I doubt Don Trapani knows what's happening on our yacht. This is no security company executive enjoying a complimentary cruise to seal the deal. What's happening here makes me want to vomit.

"Matteo?" I press him, but he doesn't respond. "Matteo!"

"Yes!" he grunts, exasperated. "Stephano Scalera. My younger brother and in charge of tonight's auction."

He's standing there, shaking in shock and fury. I bet nobody has ever vetoed his instructions like this, least of all a woman. I know better than to mess with a guy in such a state. I soft-foot it to the sliding doors and catch the eye of one of our crew. He comes up to me, hesitant. Useless.

"Tell the captain to get going. We're taking a sunset cruise. And secure the cabins," I say under my breath. "Tell the rest of the staff that nobody—and by *that* I mean *nobody*—takes orders from anybody but me. I'm the only Trapani on this yacht, and I'll dictate where we go next."

The waiter nods. His gaze flicks to Matteo. I hope my guest is still rooted to the same spot.

"Go," I hiss, and he rushes off.

I close the sliding door and lock it as a delay strategy. When I turn to face Matteo, his fisted hands are pumping by his sides as he fights to contain himself. I lean back against the sliding door, trying my best to swallow my fear. Matteo is tall, built, and clearly in the mood to punch something. Inwardly, I already flinch. It's been almost two decades since a man last laid a hand on me, but old habits die hard.

Why the hell didn't I run when I could have? It's not too late, but when the yacht's engines turn on, he blinks at me. I press closer to the door, blocking his way. Inside, I'm cowering, shaking like a leaf, but I won't allow him to step a foot onto the deck and make his escape. I will decide how this ends.

Matteo doesn't move or step in my direction, but his eyes narrow at me. "What the hell have you just done?"

I bite my lip, not quite ready to give my plan away here. I need a couple more minutes. Just long enough to get us out of the marina. Luckily, our yacht is moored close to the harbor mouth, and it wouldn't take much except a ton of fuel to get out to sea. Initially, it's so slow, you won't notice the movement unless you fixate on a spot to compare your location to.

"Would you like a drink?" I ask, but I don't move to the bar, protecting the door.

"Gigi Trapani," he says as he takes a step in my direction. "What have you ordered your staff to do?"

I shrug. "Sunset cruise?"

I'm thinking on my feet here, but the easiest way to get a fair exchange for that poor woman will be to make a hostage swap. I'm not buying into her wanting her virgin auction. She's done the dumb and desperate thing, thinking she can wipe out her dad's debts by selling herself. Clearly, she isn't from a Mafia family. If this were Carla, I would have gone in her place. I would've forced them to take me instead. I'd do anything to stop this auction from happening, and this is the only way I can save her. I'm kidnapping Matteo and intend to swap him for this woman Stephano is now holding hostage.

With effort, I inhale softly and force a slow exhale out, trying to relax my shoulders. The yacht is moving farther and farther away from the marina.

"Fuck!" Matteo screams, frustration thick in his tone. He spins on his heel as he drags his fingers through his hair. He circles the room, muttering incoherently under his breath. At last, as if all hope is gone, he slumps down onto the sofa and buries his face in his hands.

For a full five minutes, it's quiet as I guard the door and he just sits there. I glance through the window, watching as we finally slip into the waterway.

A knock on the glass door behind my back makes me jump. I turn around and stare wide-eyed at a massive man I've never seen before. Shit. I didn't think this far. This guy has bodyguard stamped all over him, his thick fingers curled in a fist that looks as if it can break my neck by pinching it between his thumb and forefinger. His pale skin is accentuated by his bald head, his cheeks almost grey in the shade. He cocks a brow at me as he knocks again, and I step away, fearing him even though there's bullet-proof glass between us.

"That's Burley, my bodyguard," Matteo says behind me. "Best you let him in before he breaks the door down."

"Wouldn't that be a nice way to thank Don Trapani for

lending you his family yacht," I sass him. I can't show my fear, but I also know when I'm outnumbered. Between Matteo and Burley, I'm a matchstick. I unlock the door, and Burley slides it open, stepping into the room with a limp.

"Boss. What the hell? We're almost out to sea again?" he huffs in a British accent. "I thought we were staying put for the night."

Matteo grunts. "Ask her what's going on. Stephano just took Tasha—"

"You let her go then? Motherfucker." Burley limps along, and I notice the bandage around his biceps and the way he presses a hand to his butt cheek.

Bullet wounds.

"She wanted to go!" Matteo shoots up, hands pulling at his hair. "What the actual fuck, Burley? Why would she do that if she wanted to cut my throat two weeks ago?"

That girl wanted to cut his throat? I like her already.

Burley stares at Matteo for a full minute before he slowly shakes his head. "Damn, you're thick sometimes. She's doing this to test you, you idiot!"

"What?" Matteo's eyes widen. Then he swallows impulsively, as if this knowledge is a pill he is taking without water. "Fuck. You've got to be kidding me."

"She likes to push your buttons, boss, just saying. You've met your match."

My gaze jumps between the two men. "What's going on?"

"This is none of your business," Matteo hisses. "And who the fuck invited you here in the first place?"

I quietly blow a fuse.

"Don Trapani, my Papa and owner of this yacht, asked me to come *welcome* you to Cannes, totally oblivious of the human trafficking going on here," I bite out, holding my finger up to let them know they better not interrupt me now.

Don Trapani is a powerful man. I don't know anything

about the Scaleras, but the fact I haven't been gagged and tied up at gunpoint yet speaks volumes. This is a delicate diplomatic situation with scope for negotiations between two equally powerful parties.

"Now that I've seen what I've seen, I know too much, don't I? Maybe your business is none of my business, but once you've decided it's *my yacht, my business,* let me know." I level Matteo in my most cutting tone, straight from Swiss finishing school. "I'm not dealing with petty little Mafia mantrums today. I've had enough of those to last me a lifetime."

"Mantrums?" Burley blurts out, eyes wide.

"You heard right. Mantrums." I volley my gaze between the two men. "Just like a tantrum, but the male version."

I shake my hair over my shoulders, open the sliding door, and walk off, leaving Matteo to verbally spar with his bodyguard. I'm not waiting around for them to realize they aren't going anywhere except the open Mediterranean. I'd rather take a nice long bath in my cabin to wash off this incessant heat.

I can read between the lines. At some point, Matteo will realize he hasn't got a minute to lose to shut down that auction, to make the exchange—himself for the woman. With this yacht going at top speed, he better make sure he has enough time to turn back to prevent the worst from happening.

I take a detour to the bar where I grab a chilled bottle of champagne, head up to the bridge to make sure the captain understood my instructions, and then go down to my cabin. That innocent woman was wearing my clothes, so Matteo and his Mafia paws have been digging in my closet, too. Disgusting.

But as I sink into a warm bubble bath, the last thing I think about is Matteo rummaging through my closet. All I can think of is his brother's hands. Stephano's touch, the warmth of his hard chest as he held me tight, and the promise of every desire fulfilled when he whispered to me to *behave*, as if he'd let me come only if I did exactly as he commanded me to.

That couldn't have been our last interaction. I know my style, and I know my type. Sexy as sin and completely in charge. He's already managed to turn me on and gets bonus points for being from the States with sub-zero chances of me ever running into him again. He is the perfect man to meet all my needs tonight.

An hour later, a knock sounds on my door. Matteo took his sweet time, didn't he? Dressed in a robe with my wet hair twisted in a towel, I get up from my bed where I've been reading a book I'd downloaded on my phone. Being without internet sucks, but I'll take one for the team. I had to do something to get my mind off Stephano Scalera and his hands on me.

I open the cabin door. Matteo stands there, looking as if he's aged a year in the short time we've been out at sea. Poor guy, getting seasick on this yacht that has zero rolling or pitching. But no, that isn't his problem.

"Gigi, I—" he breaks off. "We need to head back to Cannes."

"Oh. Why?"

"For fuck's sake, woman," he mutters, so soft it's barely audible. "I need to stop this virgin auction from happening."

I lean against the door jamb and fold my arms over my chest. "And why's that?"

"Because Tasha Armstrong—" He swallows hard, but there's more to it than realizing he said too much. "I need her."

How lame. "For what do you *need* her? You don't seem to want for anything."

"This is so fucked up." He closes his eyes, drops his head back, and curls his hands into fists. "I'm in love with her," he growls.

Oh.

"And if any other man so much as looks at her, or touches her, never mind fucks her, I will leave a trail of bodies behind."

Oh, hell. He isn't faking it. He is as sincere as a man can get.

Matteo opens his eyes and leans into my space. "And you know what? *You'll* be to blame for the carnage."

"Oh, dear. We can't have that now, can we?"

As much as I'd like to wipe the Mafia off the face of the earth, I need to keep my cool here. If he is really in love with her, Matteo will move heaven and earth to get to Tasha in time. Those rings on her finger should have spelled it out for me, but how was I to know? That said, I know better than to take his word for it. I stroll back into my cabin and check the time on my phone where I tossed it to the bed. "It's almost six. What time does this disgusting auction kick off?"

"At nine tonight."

"And where?" I ask, expecting some dungeon in the Cannes underworld.

"The St. Chalamet's presidential suite."

The *St. Chalamet?* Posh. I can get onboard with that. Seems Stephano likes to do things in style.

"You should have spoken up sooner. It'll take time to head back." Plus, I have to get dressed for a private party at the St. Chalamet's presidential suite. I'd love to see how this goes down...and I'd love to see Stephano again. Even if only to vex him by gate-crashing his auction.

Matteo steps inside my cabin, and his menacing presence makes me want to shrink, but I pull tall and face him.

"Make it happen," he hisses.

"A couple of things," I say, not giving him an inch. "Promise me this Tasha Armstrong will be safe with you, and that you'll never hurt her."

"What the fuck do you think I am? Of course she's safe with me! Fuck it. Do you take me for some kind of monster?"

"Well—"

"I don't have time for this," he bites out.

"Fine. We'll see how she reacts when she sees you."

I don't *know* him. But he seems distraught enough that his love declaration could be real. Men in love—Mafia men in particular—can get feral when it comes to their women. If he says he'll protect her, it will be with his life.

"What do you mean by *we'll see*?" he asks.

"I'm coming with you. To make sure you're doing what you're telling me you're going to do." *Amongst other things...*

"Fuck no." He shakes his head. "Stephano will have a fit."

I'd like to see Stephano have a fit.

"I suppose I'll have to watch you have a fit instead, then. I won't tell the captain to hurry back to Cannes unless you allow me to come with you."

And on cue, his face flushes red, his mouth pulling into a stern line. I bet he's counting to ten in his head.

"Fine. Have it your way, but if Stephano tosses you out, don't come cry at my door."

The idea of Stephano's arms around me as he tries to toss me out tugs at my core, where the need he has stirred in me hasn't abated. God, I wish I could think of anything else, but I already know it's futile. Stephano isn't the type I *just forget*. He's the type that makes me beg for more.

"Great. If I even get a whiff of something dodgier than this shit going down at the St. Chalamet, I'll call Don Trapani's men to come finish you all off."

At this, Matteo rolls his eyes. "There's nothing dodgy going on, Gigi."

"As if selling an unwilling virgin at some hideous auction isn't dodgy enough." *And then your bodyguard is riddled with bullet wounds which he didn't give himself.* I have so many questions...

"We both heard her: she wanted it."

"Apparently a strategic move on her part, not yours." Tasha Armstrong is a gutsy girl.

"Whatever. That's just semantics now." He sighs. "What else? Are you done now? We need to get going."

"One last thing: you owe me. You owe the Trapanis. And we never forget a debt."

He nods. "No need to remind me. Now I'll walk you to the bridge so you can give the captain your instructions in person since someone killed the fucking WiFi and I can't even make a call."

"I have my own priorities," I say, smiling sweetly at him while ushering him out of the cabin. "I need to get ready for tonight. I love the thrill of an auction-gone-wrong. Don't you?"

I close the door in his face, relishing the fact that, without internet, Matteo is going to sweat and panic a little longer.

8

STEPHANO

I'm going to kill my brother. Fuck knows. It's five minutes to nine, the presidential suite is buzzing, bidding is about to start, and there's still no sign of him. It's been five fucking hours since I walked Tasha off that yacht. I expected Matteo four hours and fifty-nine minutes ago.

Fuck it. This is all fucked up. I'm having a reaction on Matteo's behalf, and he hasn't even bothered to phone me. I sent him a message, but no response. Probably because it didn't deliver. The fucker let his phone battery die.

I have our virgin by the elbow, giving her an encouraging squeeze. This was the plan, but I can't go through with it. Once bidding has stopped, I'll put in the highest bid and save Tasha Armstrong from the Don's final retribution. This isn't my war. I can't tell her my ultimate solution because I have a full house waiting on the other side of the glass doors, and those men... they like the girls nervous. Virginal. I have no choice but to let her do the rounds like a show pony.

It freaks me out, but somehow, everything is more personal tonight. Fuck Matteo. He's literally killing me. This afternoon I thought something had happened between him and this woman, but his absence is making me doubt everything I saw in his face and demeanor.

I guide Tasha through the glass door and make her wave at the Don on the laptop I've set up for the live stream. *Never again.* I'm pulling her in the direction of the living area when footsteps fall behind me.

I close my eyes when I recognize my brother's gait. Thank fuck.

"Party's over. Bidding's closed." Matteo's voice sounds firm and clear.

Tasha jerks against my hold, but I don't let go because another voice rings in the foyer, accompanied by clicking heels on the porcelain tiles.

"Oh my God!"

Oh my God indeed. What the hell is Gigi Trapani doing here?

I let go of Tasha's elbow and spin around to face them.

"I'll take over from here," Matteo says as Tasha rushes over to him.

I want to fist Matteo by the shirt and crap him out for taking his goddamn time, while at the same time wanting to bear-hug him. But my gaze magnetizes to Gigi Trapani where she's strolling up to me, a model on the catwalk, in a red dress that makes my pulse skip a beat. My cock stirs in my tux's pants. *Fuck.*

"What took you so long?" Tasha asks, already wrapped in Matteo's tight embrace.

Yes, I'd like to know that, too.

"Gigi." Matteo huffs. "That one doesn't sit and stay. She killed the WiFi and ordered the captain to sail out to sea, practically kidnapping me to do a hostage exchange for you, kitten. Then she forced me to bring her along to make sure you don't come to any harm. She's got guts, that I'll give her."

Gigi has a tease of a smile toying on her lips at Matteo's last words. I would laugh if I wasn't this annoyed. Kudos to her for standing up and kidnapping Matteo—what a joke—but this is the last thing I need. A woman like her walking into this auction as if she owns the place. She's not my girl, but lessons are going to be learned, some of them the hard way. I push my fists into my pants pockets, rocking on my heels as she comes to stand right in front of me.

We stare at each other, and I take in her beautiful face, eyes wide-set and an almond brown, lips full and cheeky red, and a very Italian Roman nose that gives her an air of haughtiness without trying. Diamonds dangle from her ears, and her long red dress plunges in a deep V-neck, accentuating a natural rack that would make strippers cry. I should know. I've seen so many boob jobs, I can spot one from a mile. And if you can't spot them, you can feel them. Size doesn't matter. I like them natural. I slide my gaze down her body, giving her the full inspection she obviously craves.

Fuck. My cock reacts with each inch as my gaze travels lower. This woman—

She's made an effort, and it's a pity because I'm going to throw her out. In one minute flat. I need to throw her out for my own freaking sanity.

"Where's the live stream?" Matteo asks, but I don't look in his direction, merely pointing to where the laptop is on a console table.

In my peripheral, I see my brother casually flip the bird at the screen, his personal salute to the Don, then he bends down and throws Tasha over his shoulder.

I bet on the other side of the world the Don is blowing his last few fuses. It doesn't matter. What's he actually going to do? Come whip Matteo into shape? He's bedridden and no longer a match for his sons. Matteo has overruled his instructions about Armstrong's daughter, and even if the Don demands one of our brothers to fix this mess, none of us will turn on Matteo.

The Don's ship has sailed, and Matteo knows this. For a split second, I see the don Matteo is shaping up to be and it gives me hope for all our fucked-up little souls.

"Let's get out of here before shit hits the fan," he says as he heads to the front door.

"Where're you going?" I ask as I finally break eye contact with Gigi. Tomorrow, we're getting the hell out of here, and it won't be soon enough.

"You'll figure it out," he calls back.

A riddle. Exactly what I need to top this roadkill auction.

"Thanks for the fuck-up, brother." Time for the consolation prizes to roll in, but I need to deal with Gigi first. "And for leaving me to deal with this."

"I'll make it up to you."

With that empty promise, Matteo strides out of the suite.

I walk over to the laptop and close it. The Don has had his entertainment. He doesn't need to see how I deal with Gigi Trapani next.

9

GIGI

I feel his gaze on me as I move deeper into the suite. The clap of a laptop being slapped closed sounds in the foyer, and I try not to flinch. I hate how I startle so easily.

Stephano Scalera is pissed off, and I don't blame him. But he's met his match tonight.

In the lounge, several tuxedoed men are waiting, their eyes drinking me in. One man is puffing at a cigar, and its sweet smoke ribbons through the air. Whiskey and wine glasses are filled, and a waiter holds out a tray of amuse-bouches to a duo in conversation. They wave him away to look at me.

This dress is a man magnet. A deep cherry red signaling confidence, with a V-neck plunging way below my breasts. The long, fluid skirts caress my legs, and with each step I take, one of them peeks through the high slits aligned with my thighs. It's sexual in every possible feminine way.

My gaze jumps from one man to the next until I do a double-take. Jean-Michel Baudin. Who would have thought? I feel Stephano's body as he comes to stand right behind me, so close but without touching me.

"You need to leave," he whispers, and the words ghost over my neck. "Unless you want to be taken for a prostitute—"

"No man here is going to think I'm a prostitute."

"They might not think you're one, angel, but they'll treat you like one."

He comes to stand next to me. He doesn't touch me, and all I wish is for him to put his hand on the small of my back and lead me away, out of this suite to somewhere else.

"Leave," he says under his breath. "Or I'll get a bodyguard to help you along."

I glance up at him. Even with my heels, he must be a foot taller than me. "You mean you won't throw me out yourself?"

"Not touching you with my filthy Mafia paws, angel."

I hit a nerve earlier today, it seems.

"How disappointing." I pull in a deep breath. "I'm not going anywhere. I see one of my clients, and not acknowledging him would be the ultimate *faux pas*."

I swoop away, head held high, shoulders pulled back, not even sparing Stephano a glance to see how much I just infuriated him.

"Jean-Michel! How nice to see you," I say in French.

Jean-Michel Baudin, a billionaire hedge fund owner from Paris, smirks at me as he stands. "Gigi Trapani. I feel caught with my hand in the cookie jar."

I wave his comment off. He might be married, but who am I to judge where he puts his dick. What a man does with his money isn't my business either, as long as he spends some of it with me.

He stands and kisses me on both cheeks. "You need to tell me what you're doing here and what just happened. Stay for a drink."

"Thank you. I think I will." I take a seat next to him on the half-circle sofa as he indicates to the waiter to bring some champagne. Several ice buckets filled with high-end bottles are on display, and I might have a glass to settle my nerves. I cross my legs, arrange my skirts, and lean back with my arm on the backrest, facing Jean-Michel. As I get comfortable, I'm overly conscious of Stephano where he's leaning against the wide foyer's door jamb, studying me.

The heat of his gaze is almost consuming, but it's one of annoyance and not lust. And yet, it turns me on because he only has eyes for me. Not that there are any other women in the room, but—

"Stephano looks irate." Jean-Michel smirks. "You, my dear, have stepped on toes."

"So many today. All for a good cause."

"And was that scene in aid of your good cause? I assume our little virgin has been claimed by the American who stalked in and carried her out like a caveman?"

I chuckle as I take the offered glass of champagne from the waiter. "A most intriguing beginning to the night, I'm sure. Apparently, he's in love."

"Good for her. Stephano knows how to pick his crowd," Jean-Michel says as his gaze travels the room. "None of the bullies are here tonight, because if they were, I can promise you there would have been a fist fight over our little virgin after that scene."

Bunch of creeps. And thank God Tasha practically threw herself into Matteo's arms. If she'd frozen in fear, I don't know what I would have done. It's not the first time my own bodyguard would have been handy, but by the looks of the two bulky men Stephano talks to now, I might have needed four to ward them off. Blood would have been everywhere.

When Stephano looks up and meets my gaze, I stare back. Let him do his worst. Men like Jean-Michel might have particular tastes, but at the end of the day, I'm a Trapani, plus Jean-Michel won't let anybody here touch me. Least of all one of those fat-fisted bodyguards. I am not for sale, and nobody is going to doubt that. As for Stephano, he has too much composure to let this evening turn into a brawl.

I've done some crazy, reckless things today, meddling with the Mafia, with the Scaleras, but it was the right thing to do, and nobody can convince me otherwise. I face Jean-Michel again and lead the conversation to art and the recent purchase I made for him at Christie's in London.

Stephano is strolling from one man to the next, sometimes addressing them in the groups they're sitting in. There's laughter and some man-slaps on the shoulder, and with growing admiration, I watch him work the room. With Tasha's exit, there won't be any auction or a winning bid, and if Jean-Michel came from Paris for this auction, who knows where the rest of the men are from. I should follow in Stephano's footsteps and do the rounds. There could be some handy connections and big spenders here.

When he finally makes his way to where I'm seated, he shakes Jean-Michel's hand in greeting.

"Small world, Baudin," he says with a nod in my direction.

"Indeed," Jean-Michel says. "How do you know each other?"

"A family connection," he cuts in before I can say anything. "Tonight took a turn in an unexpected direction. I'm afraid the man who took our virgin made her an offer she couldn't refuse."

I frown. Stephano doesn't want them to know the man in question is his brother.

Jean-Michel cocks his brow. "Indeed. It is what it is."

"Our evening will proceed as usual. Take your pick and help yourself to one of our party packs. They don't disappoint, as you know."

For the first time, I notice the stack of glossy white gift boxes on a side console, each tied with an elaborate bow in white silk. Oh, my. He does go the extra mile. I'd love to see what's in one of those.

And then, as if on cue, the suite's door opens, and through the foyer, a line-up of beautiful women walks in. My heart skips a beat. The women are young and dressed somewhat provocatively. My dress is essentially the same, but the haute couture and price tag saves it from being slutty.

"As you'll see, Baudin, your regular is here, as well. Enjoy your evening."

Stephano gives me a last glance, but it's dismissive. I watch as he strides away, deeper into the suite in the direction of the bedrooms.

"This is rather...interesting," I say as the women close in on the men, clearly with one goal in mind.

"What did you expect, *ma chérie*? That we'd go home empty-handed? Not with a Scalera-arranged virgin auction."

One blonde homes in on us, and my breath catches. *His regular.*

How the hell did Stephano manage that? To have this level of intel on someone—

"You'll have to excuse me, Gigi," Jean-Michel says as he stands, his hand on my shoulder with a soft brush. "It's been a pleasure, but as you can see, we're well taken care of. I wish you the same."

I'm still flailing for words when he turns to kiss the woman, his hand on her ass, squeezing her to him. She shoots me a small, victorious smile, as if I'm one of them and she won the prize.

I sit, clinging to my half-empty glass of champagne, and watch as the bidders pair up with one, sometimes two women, or leaving in groups for their own rooms in the St. Chalamet. At some point, the waiter comes to top up my glass, and I let him.

He wishes me the same.

If Jean-Michel knew my usual modus operandi, he'd wish harder. Much, much harder.

Soon, the lounge is empty. One bodyguard does a last check before bidding me goodnight and exiting through the front door. Then it's all quiet. I'm all alone. In the St. Chalamet presidential suite, and several of those party packs are left unclaimed.

Stephano must still be here, because I never saw him leave, and I had my eye on the front door the whole evening. My pulse, which has been running sprints between marathons today, shoots out of the starting blocks again.

I kick off my heels. Rushing all the way from Monte Carlo earlier to meet with the Scaleras killed my feet. I pad over to the console table and tug at the ribbon on one of the boxes. I lift the lid and brush the golden tissue paper away.

Wow...

I'm still peering into the box, digesting its contents, when the tingle of someone else's presence eases down my spine. The peculiar feeling you get when you know you're being watched.

I turn, only to see Stephano standing mere meters away from me, hands shoved in his pants pockets, stripped of his tux jacket, his white shirt partly unbuttoned to reveal a smooth, tanned chest, the sleeves rolled up to his elbows. His arms are corded with muscles, and there's a hint of a tattoo on his inner forearm.

"Like what you're seeing in there, angel?" he asks softly as his gaze takes me in.

"It's extra, and a nice...special touch?"

He quirks his brow with a smirk as he comes closer. "Tell me, did this evening turn you on? The idea of it? That box's content?"

"No." But it's a lie. Everything tonight has been fine-tuned to turn me on, the idea of him most of all.

"Then why are you still here?" he asks.

"I—" I break off, not knowing how to answer him.

"I told you to leave, angel, and yet, here you are, last woman standing, as if you're waiting."

I shrug, heat spreading between my thighs at the way he's looking at me, intense, almost predatory. "It was a fascinating evening. And auctions are part of my day-to-day."

"Is that so?"

He's so close and even taller now that I've shed my heels. As I look up at him, I feel the heat radiating off his body. "Art. Art auctions."

"Hmm. In my experience, when a woman is still at a party long after the rest of the guests have left, she's only staying for one thing."

He's crowding me now, and I back away, edging along the console table until my butt and back hit the wall. *Cornered.*

"That's rather presumptuous of you, isn't it?" I retort, a blush flooding my face.

"But I'm right."

He leans closer, pressing one hand to the wall above my head. My breath catches. His other hand is still in his pocket, and all I want is for him to touch me.

"You're a bit of a challenge, aren't you?" he says as he lowers to my ear.

The rush of his warm breath over my skin sends sparks of desire all the way to my sex.

"The question really is, angel, if I can make you come without touching you with my *filthy Mafia paws.*"

10

STEPHANO

Gigi's breath hitches, and I ease back to watch the rise and fall of her breasts as she digests my words and their implication. Her eyes are dazed with arousal, and I'm burning to make her come apart. To have such a hold on her that her mind succumbs to me and lets her body soar.

"What do you think, Gigi?" I slide my lips along her hairline to the shell of her ear, then trace a thin line along its edge with my tongue. "I'll touch you with my mouth only, even if you beg for more."

And beg, she will. I'll find satisfaction in not giving in to her, not giving her what she really craves. Cock. And lots of it.

"I'd like to see you try," she says, her voice breathy.

I continue my journey to the spot south of her ear and press a lingering kiss there, opening my lips and sucking a bit. Her breathing becomes strained, and I smile against the sensitive skin. As if I would fail.

She raises a hand to touch me, but I step out of reach, knowing full well she'd see the painful swell of my rock-hard cock battling my pants.

"Tit for tat, angel. You don't get to touch me either. Accept that you'll be burning to within minutes."

And I can't wait to feel her break this very rule. Feel that hot palm of hers cupping my sack, her fingers circling my girth and finding they can't quite close around it.

"Fine." She laughs. "You're so fucking arrogant."

"And you're such a fucking pain in my ass." And the reason why I'm going to teach her this lesson. Looking down at me as if she's better than me. A Mafia don's daughter. Either way, one thing I know to be true: between the legs of every condescending rich woman, there's a pussy that doesn't get enough attention.

I step away and stare into the party pack she opened. It's a good selection. The handcuffs are tempting, so is the whip because this one can do with some discipline, and since I can't use my hands, it's a good alternative. As I take it out, she clears her throat.

"No whip."

I meet her gaze. "No?"

"Nothing that leaves marks or...or bruises."

Fuck. She might as well have dunked me in an Arctic ice bath. Those words only mean one thing: she's been there, done that, and didn't like it one bit. And none of it was probably for sexual pleasure in the first place.

It's not what I had in mind, but I drop the whip back into the box without saying anything. I pick out some condoms, lube, the chocolate body paint, stuff them in my pockets, and then pluck a single white rose from the arrangement on the table.

I brush the soft petals along the length of her arm. "More to your liking?"

Goose bumps swarm to the surface of her skin, and she leans her head back against the wall, closing her eyes. "Yes."

The way she leans back opens her neck and the elegant line from her chin down to her chest and the valley between her breasts. This dress was made for this, exposing skin and hinting at the pleasures hidden by the many folds of the skirt hugging her curves.

I caress her with the rose, tracing a line down her neck, and by the time I'm between her breasts, her nipples have pebbled hard, straining against the fabric. My cock is ready to break her, but I know how to contain myself, to control every last need and emotion pulsing through my veins.

I inch closer and bend to follow the rose's path, licking and pressing open kisses against her neck, lower, tasting her and inhaling the flower bouquet captured in her perfume. Her arms hang limp by her sides, but she flexes her fingers, and I find purchase on the wall again to keep from digging into the dark tresses falling over her shoulders. I caress my lips over the swell of her breast.

"Help me out here, angel," I murmur, and she reaches up to slip off the dress's shoulder, revealing the most perfect pert and begging nipple; an island in a sea of creamy skin I want to get stranded on.

I groan my pleasure and lick it once, rolling my tongue over it, and her body quivers.

"Stephano," she whispers.

She's going to beg, all right.

I straighten, and our gazes latch. "Yes?"

She pushes from the wall and takes the head of the rose between her fingers. I don't let go of the stem, and she leads me with it to the circular sofa. Delicate heeled sandals are discarded on the rug, and the plush cushions are indented where guests sat earlier. She pushes the cushions to the sides, making a nest. And when she settles in it, decadent with her dress half slipped off and exposing her breast, she arranges her skirts and spreads her legs.

I tower over her, my cock pulsing with need at this sudden show of confidence, but I don't even adjust it where it's testing my pants' limits.

"Come now, Mr. Scalera," she says as she slowly rides her skirts up her legs. "Ruin me for other men."

It's a challenge. It's a tease. It's a test of my control. No man can resist such an invitation.

It's a one-night stand we can both indulge in. And I need it. Fuck knows it's been too long.

We won't be seeing each other again. We're from different continents, and the idea of ruining her for other men, for her to always remember this night as punishment for her condescension earlier, is so tempting.

But for that, I'd need to plunder her perfect body with my cock. Relentlessly. Take her the whole night long and make her come until she's so spent, she'll beg me to hold her and let her sleep. Only to wake her with my cock warming in her sweet pussy first thing in the morning.

I watch as she slowly raises her skirts, the fabric gliding over her silky-smooth legs. My breathing stalls as she finally reaches her sex, perfectly wrapped in...*nothing*...bare and open and wet.

So fucking wet. An open invitation if there ever was one. Gigi Trapani came over to this virgin auction with a plan.

I should leave her like this, strip her confidence to the bone. Walk out and go jerk off in the next room reserved for our winning bidder. But my mouth is dry with the need to taste her, to make her succumb to me in the ultimate way a man controls a woman—through her mind. I want to leave her at her most magnificent peak, because the most beautiful, transient thing a man can create is the blush of spent pleasure on a woman's cheeks.

So instead of walking away, I empty my pockets of the lube and other items and kneel onto the sofa. I find purchase by putting both my hands on the sofa's backrest, careful not to touch her face in the process. I press a string of open-mouthed kisses to her neck and she arches into me.

When she moans, I whisper in her ear. "To ruin you will be my pleasure, angel."

My absolute pleasure.

11

GIGI

Stephano hovers over me, but our bodies aren't touching. The only point where we connect is where his lips are trailing a seductive path down my chest. He seems to have no difficulty holding this position, and all I want is to push my hips up and meet his cock where it's making a very impressive dick print on his tux's pants.

He's homing in on my exposed nipple, and he licks and sucks it tenderly. My clit pulses with need, and I press back into the sofa as I slip off my dress's other shoulder. He grunts his approval and pays attention to my other breast, both my nipples aching with the longing to have fingers on them. Tugging, massaging, sliding his fingertips around them until I come.

I bet he's the type of guy who could do this to a woman. He is so sure of himself, and there's no bigger turn on. I want to rake my fingers through his thick hair, but I hold back, fisting the cushions instead. If he carries on like this—

"Stephano," I murmur, needing more.

I spread my legs wider, only wanting to have some pressure

there. Ever since this afternoon, he's had me aroused like this, since he touched me with that tender brush along my jaw.

"Angel?" He looks up, and as if he sees the need in my eyes, he lowers his hips, his cock pressing against my sex. He rocks into me then, sliding his cock up and down my slit. I'm so wet, the soft fabric of his pants glides, and the pressure is perfect. "You're so fucking needy. I bet you're going to come like this."

"Yes." And I don't want it to be over. I want it to be only the beginning. I know at some point, he'll cave. He is, after all, just a man. I want him to cave in and caress me, so badly.

He doesn't stop riding me, and when he licks and sucks and bites my one nipple again, I reach for his head and bury my fingers in his hair. Instead of reprimanding me or pulling away as I feared he would, he doesn't stop. His hips don't stop. His mouth doesn't stop.

And the orgasm that rises from me crashes out of nowhere. I moan, my breathing strained, my body pulsing, but not done. More. I always want more.

He pulls away and heat flushes my cheeks, but it's not only from my orgasm. I hate how he could do this to me with such ease. He smirks down at me, and for a second, I want to kick at him, at the satisfied smirk on his lips.

"You've proven your point." Making me come by touching me with nothing but his lips and the sweet pressure of his dick. "You can fuck off now," I say as I try to close my legs.

But he's faster. He presses a knee to my thigh as he leans in again.

"Such a dirty mouth for a woman who claims to be above everybody else."

"You've got such a chip on your shoulder, don't you?"

"Maybe. But this is my hotel room, angel. *You* came for *this,* and I say you stay." He emphasizes with pressure on my leg, and I'm forced open again to where I was, numb with desire, on the verge of begging. "I'm not done with you."

I bite my lip and drag in a ragged breath. He's like a mind reader. I swallow as he stands, but I stay splayed open, sunk into the soft cushions with my legs weak. I watch as he reaches for a bottle of chilled champagne on the coffee table, and ice water drips from it as he pulls it from the bucket. He stands closer and lets the drops fall on my sex as he strips off the foil cover.

I quiver under the drops, every part of my sex feeling like it's on fire as cold meets heat. "I don't want champagne," I whisper, feeling the need to defy him in everything.

"It's not for drinking, angel. Not yet."

Oh, God.

He twists and takes off the muselet, and when the cork doesn't pop, puts the bottle to the side. "Now where were we?"

I blink. He's trailing his gaze over my body, and I can just imagine what he sees. All my imperfections in this mess of a woman, red dress all over the white sofa cushions, legs spread in desperate invitation. I want to clam up again, scared he'll see into me, see my darkest fears laid bare, but instead, he sinks to the floor, on his knees, and presses a tender kiss to my ankle.

"For a pain in the ass, you're fucking beautiful, Gigi Trapani," he murmurs as he makes his way to the fold of my knee. "So fucking beautiful."

His words do something to me. I don't know what, but my heart feels like it turns in my chest. I'm not traditionally pretty. Eyes set too wide apart, nose too hooked, lips too full for the rest of my face. No perfect proportions like I studied in art.

I close my eyes, turn my face into the cushion, and grab the backrest above my head to avoid reaching out for him again. I can't let him see how desperate I am. For this. For those words from a man like *him*.

He doesn't rush. No, Stephano Scalera is taking his time to work his way up my inner thigh, to my sex, where my clit is already begging for his tongue. He bites and nips, and my hips jerk of their own volition, wanting what only he can give.

When he breathes over my sex, the heat tingles and my pussy contracts. And then, he licks my slit, slow and intentional, sliding his tongue around my clit. I sink into a cloud of sensation as he eats me out as if I'm his last meal. Already, my need to orgasm rises from deep in my core. He doesn't stop, but between the sounds he makes that only arouse me more, I hear the tearing of a wrapper.

I open my eyes and blink against the soft light. When I glance down at him, he hasn't got his cock in hand, putting on the condom to fuck me into bliss.

As if he feels my gaze on him, he looks up and quirks his brow at me. He's rolling the condom down the champagne bottle's neck.

"I'll be gentle," he murmurs. "Unless you want it hard."

Oh my God. He isn't going to fuck me like I want him to. He's going to keep to his resolve to make me come with his lips alone. For a cock, this is what I'm getting.

"Trust me, angel," he says as he puts the condom-covered corked head by my entrance. "I'll make it good."

I have no reason not to trust him, as he's never stepped out of line. He even tossed the whip back into the gift box without asking questions. The pressure is there, the nudge telling me to let him in.

I open wider, acquiescing, and he slides the bottle's neck inside me. It's hard and cold, but smooth, and the widening neck hits the spot. Where my orgasm was put on hold, it now seems to roar back with each thrust he times so well.

When Stephano balances over me, his free hand perched next to my face, he gazes at me with each thrust, reading my face. I stare back into his eyes, feeling like I'm drowning in him, in what he's doing to me.

"Almost there, angel," he whispers, then he dips his head, and his lips are on my breast again, his tongue riding my nipple as he ups the pace.

I break apart in seconds. I come, and as if he knows it, he holds the bottle still.

"Tighten your pussy for me," he commands, and I obey, feeling each ripple of my orgasm as the cork finally pops. My pussy's grip and the condom seem to stop the cork from going anywhere, holding it in place like a fist, but the whole sensation is too intense because I'm squirting.

God, no. Maybe. I don't know. All I know is cold champagne foam pulses out of me. Stephano extracts the bottle and rips off the condom, letting the champagne froth and pour over my sex. The cold liquid is a rush of tingles spreading over my sensitive skin as bubbles pop and my body quivers.

He watches me for what feels like a very long minute, then raises the bottle to his lips. He takes a sip and lifts it in a toast with a naughty, wicked grin. "Welcome to the Stephano Scalera version of a golden shower."

He takes another sip, and holy hell, I don't know what he just did to me, besides making me come twice in a row, but I might be ruined for other men. He's caught me off guard, going so far off the usual track that I feel disoriented.

I struggle up, sated and lazy with the rush of two orgasms. His eyes are still on me, studying me intently as I close my legs and hitch the dress's shoulders back into place.

"You're okay?" he asks when I'm decent.

"Yes. I—" I don't know what to say. I've never been fucked like this before. But I know what's expected from me and how to reciprocate. I reach out for him, for his cock where it still bulges in his pants.

"No." He picks up a champagne flute, pours what's left in the bottle into the glass, and holds it out to me. "Here."

I take the glass from him, but this isn't what I want. The night is still young, and I bet if I can make him succumb to me like I succumbed to him, he'll touch me. "I still don't want any champagne."

"No?"

No. I want *him. All of him.*

"You like ordering people around, don't you, angel? In that condescending tone like a real princess, but you're needy like a —" He breaks off, studying me.

"A whore?" I say, the vile word piercing the silence. I'm needy and like to fuck like whore? That's what he wanted to say, isn't it? With me like this, coming here in this dress, no underwear, wanton and so freaking needy... I can't blame him for thinking the worst of me.

He stares down at me from his height, the look in his eyes gradually changing as his jaw ticks. He might have asked whether I was fine and handed me something to drink, but now, he's going to be cruel. Aren't all men, whether with words or with their fists?

"You like to put words in people's mouths, too, don't you?" He sneers as he steps back. "Stop thinking you're above everybody else, angel, especially if you don't know them from a bar of soap."

Unwanted tears push up the back of my throat. Neither my actions nor my words are in sync tonight, but my mind seems to have lost all sense of direction as soon as I saw him in his tux, his brow cocked in a challenge. And now this. I'm stunned that he can affect me this much.

He doesn't say anything more, but I won't have it. I fling the champagne at him, glass and all. Stephano is fast though, and he catches it in midair, the liquid splattering. He puts the glass back on the table, slowly, in control, not even making it clink.

He shoots me a last glance. "You're a big girl. See yourself out."

I'm livid. How dare he? I scoot to the edge of the seat and reach for the champagne bottle, but he's walking away, already at the foyer.

"You might think I'm a whore," I spit at him, "but you're no gentleman either. You can't disguise how sleazy your virgin auction is by putting it in a five-star hotel's presidential suite and wrapping it in pretty bows. You're just a fucking pimp."

I stand and fling the bottle at his back. He doesn't even know it's coming his way. My aim is terrible, and it hits a door jamb and shatters to the floor.

Stephano turns and gives the broken glass a disinterested stare. "Work on your aim, angel. For next time."

"As if."

He walks out, and the front door clicks closed. It's so quiet, I can hear my pounding heart. I stare at the door in shock. No one has ever provoked me to the point of flinging things at them.

Next time? Over my dead body.

My chest heaves with my outburst; my eyes sting with tears. Beyond his hurtful, hideous words, that was the best sex I've ever had. It wasn't even proper sex. He didn't touch me. He didn't want to. He didn't cave in as I thought he would.

Stephano didn't want me. I laid there, open and offered, and he snubbed me.

There were prostitutes in this suite mere hours ago, and he could have had his pick. He didn't want a prostitute either.

He mastered me...but he's been more a master of himself, not caving into his evident need as any other man would have. He was in control, completely, from the start this afternoon. *Behave*, he'd whispered to me, as if it was the easiest thing in the world. And the last thing I did was throw a bottle at him, totally out of control. There were glimpses of him losing his temper with Matteo, but even those were measured and contained.

He craved control in every moment more than craving sex. He has no Achille's Heel.

And that just means he's probably the most dangerous man I've ever met.

12

STEPHANO

I knock on the suite's door, freshly irritated. It took some time to track down Matteo and Tasha's room, especially since he isn't answering his phone. Must have been a busy night. Fucker.

When he opens the door in a hotel robe, the bedhead isn't the only thing giving it away. He looks more relaxed than I've seen him in ages. Plus, there's that whiff of sex and sleep.

Needless to say, this riles me up more. Especially since I'm still tense from last night's aborted session with Gigi. No amount of jerking off has managed to make me feel sated. What the fuck's up with that?

"Good morning to you, too," Matteo says as I stomp past him, dragging a cabin bag with clothes for Tasha behind me.

"Next time, let me know where you're slumming it so I don't need to demean myself by begging St. Chalamet to share your room number. You took the phone off the hook and switched your cell phone off. Come on, Matty."

"Yeah. Fine. Sorry, Fanny." He yawns and stretches languidly. "Didn't want to be disturbed, you know."

"Fuck off." I study his face as I park the cabin bag by the wall. He still looks tired, but it isn't the exhaustion of a man who successfully planned and completed an assassination mission in Sicily.

"Have breakfast." He waves towards the suite's lounge and dining area. "You're throwing a hangry tantrum."

More like a lack-of-sex tantrum, but I don't know if that even exists if it's self-inflicted. I put Tasha's aftercare package on the round dining table. A continental breakfast spread takes up most of the surface, but there's coffee, and I can do with another cup. Matteo has clearly started eating, but there's no sign of Tasha.

"Where's she?"

"Showering."

I revel in a smug drop of satisfaction that he isn't in the shower with her. I pull my phone out of my jacket pocket to show him a screenshot. "Just so you know, your little adventure in Sicily has hit the web."

Matteo sits down by the table and plucks a croissant from the bread basket.

"It has?" He eyes the screen but doesn't really pay attention.

"Yeah. What the fuck, bro? Did you have to go burn down the whole fucking estate? We weren't planning to start a war. This was supposed to be a quick in-and-out operation. Only Randazzo's head. Quietly. No trace. Now the whole fucking 'Ndrangheta, Cosa Nostra, and every other Mafia ring who has a finger in the pie are losing their shit."

"I didn't burn the place down. That was the mole's work. It's not our territory, Steph. It's not our war. Those guys were poised to blow each other up since the beginning of time. It was bound to happen sooner or later."

"This isn't a joke, Matteo. This can come back and bite all of us in the ass, and more."

"Yeah." He brushes a hand down his face. "Had to be done, though. They'll sort themselves out. It isn't our turf."

"You hope so, especially—"

Tasha pads into the room, hesitant and shy, wearing a fluffy white hotel robe, just like Matteo's. A full blush blooms over her cheeks, and I look away to spare her. That's the look of a woman thoroughly fucked. Gigi had the same glow when I left her last night.

Gigi. I push the image of her away, but it's been popping up in my mind's eye the whole morning. Annoying as fuck. Even when she's not in my presence, she finds her way into my head—

Fuck.

Matteo holds out his hand for Tasha and pulls her onto his lap. I want to gag with jealousy as he presses his nose into her neck and inhales deeply. They look like an ad for honeymooners. I don't know how he managed this or if he even understands what this means. He's gone and kicked the house of cards that's the European Mafia and fallen in love at the same time. Never mind the fact they'll come for us, they'll also come for our women.

This is the reason I've always kept women at arm's length. With Tatiana, who meant more to me than what she should have, it's only been proven again that I couldn't protect a normal woman like I'd wanted to, never mind a Mafia wife. This is one of the reasons I've sworn off marriage, and even if I meet someone who makes me look at her like Matteo looks at Tasha, I'll have the self-control to push her away.

"You smell divine,' Matteo says, ripping me out of my dark thoughts.

Gigi smelled divine, too. And she tasted so fucking good. I wanted to lick and drink another bottle of champagne off her pussy.

I push the white gift box with an elaborate pink bow in Tasha's direction.

"Your aftercare package. A suitcase with clothes for you." I point to the door where I parked the cabin bag. "I'll leave you to it," I say as I stand. "We meet in thirty minutes. The plane takes off in two hours."

I'll skip my cup of coffee, because I'm not going to hang around and watch them make out. We have an eight-hour flight ahead of us, in a private jet. I'm going to be caged with these two, and they won't be able to keep their hands off each other. I stalk to the door, but Tasha's voice makes me pause.

"What happened to Gigi?" she asks as she moves to her own seat.

"Gigi?" I deadpan.

"Yes. Gigi Trapani?" Matteo repeats. "The *one and only* Gigi Trapani."

The one and only.

He won't forget her soon. She kidnapped him, after all. Neither will I. She never thought about herself for one second during her rescue mission. She only had the intention to protect and save a stranger. She ticked me off by being so disdainful, fitting the perfect image of just another conceited, spoiled Mafia princess with a bloated self-esteem, but what she did for Tasha was selfless.

Last night, Gigi came for one thing but stayed for another. She didn't have a bodyguard, and I have no clue about her day to day. For all I know, she's one of those that broke the mold and got away. I have no place messing with someone like her.

Instead of getting to know her, I chose to punish-fuck her, then ground my heel down on her, insinuating that those last words of hers were my own. *Whore.* And all this, after she showed me how vulnerable she really is. That moment when her eyes revealed what she felt as I rolled my gaze over her perfect body gave everything away.

I could have corrected her, could have told her that wasn't what I'd been thinking at all, but no. I'd kept quiet, being a total fucking dick just because she pressed the one button that's been eating at me my entire life. Sounds about right. No wonder I can't seem to box up the memories of her.

"Nothing." I grunt. "See you in thirty."

I woke up telling myself absolutely nothing happened between me and Gigi Trapani. If our last words haunt me for the rest of my life, I only have myself to blame.

13

GIGI

It's not often I get summoned, but this was a summons. Don Trapani's message was stark and clear: I'm needed on Lake Como this weekend.

When I tried to wriggle out of it, I got a message from Carla. It's been a month since I've seen her in Monte Carlo, and she's halfway through her summer vacation. Her rather desperate message swayed me. I glance down to my phone and read it again: *I know you're busy, but I need to see you. Please come stay a couple of days. I miss you.*

I miss her more, but this type of request has become so few and far between, I can't help wondering what's going on. We might be close, but like any young adult, Carla has a life beyond what she chooses to share with me. If she's in trouble, could she just brush some broad strokes to give me a basic idea? I glance down at the rest of our message chain, trying to read between the lines, but there's nothing giving me pause.

With Carla and Don Trapani coming at me from both sides, I can't say no. Besides, going to Papa's vacation home on Lake Como is always fun, and it holds some of the most treasured childhood memories of me and Carla before Mom died.

I look at the ETA to our destination. Half an hour to the villa. I have no clue whether Vincenzo is going to be there. At the thought of my stepbrother, my stomach turns, and I shoot up a prayer he won't be there to ruin my short visit.

For the past month, a rare rumor has been spreading that a major Mafia kingpin had been killed in Sicily. When the name Randazzo popped up, I had to take the afternoon off to digest. You don't grow up in Sicily, never mind the Mafia, without knowing the name Randazzo. And if it doesn't fill you with cold stark fear and dread, it's because you're already dead.

Nobody has confirmed the rumor, and beyond asking Don Trapani directly if he knew something, which he denied, I've let it slide. And yet, for the past two weeks, Papa's words to me on Carla's eighteenth birthday, the premonition that monsters are rising, have haunted me, and now it feels as if I could be walking into a trap. But it's family, and it's home, and surely, Don Trapani—*Papa*—will look out for me. And if he doesn't, I'll do so myself.

The driver takes the road winding down the valley, and far off, lights flicker on the scalloped edge of the dark water mass. Lake Como rests quietly in the summer's evening. The sky is a slate blue, the sun long gone, but its presence lingering at this time of year. It's late to arrive on a Friday night, but it's intentional. A quick in and out. I'll be gone by Sunday morning because of work.

As the driver pulls up to the house, I notice only the outside entry lights are on. There seems to be nobody at home. It's not *that* late. I thank the driver, remind him of my Sunday morning flight back to London, and grab my bag. I've mastered the art of traveling light and can get away with this tote for the weekend.

I walk up the stairs, and as I reach the door, it swings open.

"Gigi. My dear sister." Vincenzo stands there, as if he was waiting for me.

I curse under my breath. There's a reason I've been avoiding

Vincenzo. As he hugs me close, his hands slide three inches lower than the accepted familial distance to my ass.

I push him away.

"I wasn't sure you'd be here." Even if the signs were there, I couldn't ignore the call of duty. "Where's Papa? And Carla?"

"We're in the library."

Strange. It's so pleasant on the terrace, the peak of the summer, and perfectly balmy outside. Vincenzo has his hand on my elbow, guiding me as if I don't know where to go. I spot a bodyguard in my peripheral—Carla's bodyguard. There will be others, of course, but Don Trapani has always liked the discreet look.

When our gazes connect, he blinks at me. I try to recall his name. We were only introduced once. Every other time I saw Carla, he was always on the periphery, not cramping her style. I'd glanced through his resume, but that was it. Vito... Vittorio Rossi. Not your usual bodyguard profile. He speaks five languages and is ex-navy. He's big for an Italian; the size that doesn't like to be squashed into a submarine.

I nod at him and try to shrug Vincenzo's hold loose.

"I know my way to the library. Where's Carla?" I ask again, showing my nerves.

"She's in the library. As I said." Vincenzo pinches my elbow, holding tight. "We have guests, *cara*, and I need you to play along."

His tone is soft, but fear sparks down my spine.

Why did I come? Honestly, my sixth sense has been on high alert for weeks now, but I know why I came. I came for Carla. I came to fetch my sister. To take her to London for the rest of the summer. For longer if needed. There's a storm brewing, and I don't want either of us to be caught in it.

The corridor's lights are dimmed, and this is a restored period villa, but I can't recall it being so dark in here. As we pass one room after the other, I notice the shutters are closed, not even allowing in the moonlight.

"Vincenzo...Cenzo—" I sound uncertain and hate how I revert to his childhood nickname in this begging tone, with a little crack in my voice giving me away.

"It's all good, Gigi. It's just a negotiation. One you could have avoided ten years ago if you'd just married me."

Not this. I escaped then. What's awaiting me now? I bite my lip and let him literally drag me to the closed double doors of the library. My legs are jelly, begging for the surge of adrenaline that will allow me to sprint away, but I must go in there. I must see Carla.

Vincenzo opens the door, and the little glow from the few standing lamps inside makes it hard to take in the room with one glance. Don Trapani's desk. The endless library shelves with their priceless Italian collection. The fireplace. The aged leather sofas. The dark corners where I used to play hide-and-seek with Carla when she was a toddler.

Figures etch out in the dark, and a constrained sob startles me.

"Carla?" I cry out as I home in on her.

I want to rush over to her, but Vincenzo slides his grip down and tightens his hold on my wrist.

My sister's sitting on the sofa, hugging her legs to her chest, in skimpy shorts and a T-shirt as if she came right off a boat cruise on the lake. I look to the man who sits at the desk and do a double take. It isn't Don Trapani residing over his domain. I've never seen him before, and the way he's looking at me makes me ice over in dread.

"Gigi Trapani," he says. "We're so glad you joined us."

I want to scream, but I know it's futile. We're far enough from the next estate and surrounded by forest. Exclusivity comes at a price, and this is one of them.

"Gigi."

I glance to my left. Papa's voice is strained, and he doesn't stand from where he's sitting in a wingback.

"Papa? What's going on? Who...?"

Can he even stand? They could have tortured him. I have no clue how deep I've stumbled into the quicksand here.

"*Cara*..." Don Trapani starts again. "I'd like you to meet Franco Fiore. Our new Don. He's replacing Emilio Randazzo."

So Randazzo is really dead. God help us all. Randazzo didn't have children as far as I know, not even out of wedlock. A shrewd decision, until shit hits the fan. Which it obviously did.

Franco Fiore stands and comes around the desk, and Vincenzo keeps me in place, a warning in his death grip on my wrist. As if on cue, someone switches more lights on, and it pours over Franco's face. He isn't old as I expected, not even close to fifty, but more Vincenzo's age. He's in a tailored suit but has shed the tie. His black shirt is unbuttoned, showing off a body tattoo that reaches his chin. He's clean-shaven, his mouth pulled in a deceptive smile, and when his gaze hooks mine, I quiver.

He raises a hand, and the first thing I notice, hypnotized, is the bruising, the scars and scabs on his knuckles. The ring that still has blood crusted in the fine edge between the diamond and its gold setting. A tattoo of a snake coils around his forefinger, its head where there should be a nail, but he has none. *God.*

I swallow, my pulse hammering in my temples. He leans in and brushes his knuckles down my cheek, and each scab scratches like sandpaper. I force myself not to flinch.

"The younger one's prettier. At eighteen maybe still a virgin." He forks my chin with his fingers and turns my face this way and that, inspecting me. "Although, some experience is useful in the marriage bed. I'd hate to be bored."

I want to spit in his face but know better.

"And why would anybody be marrying you?" I ask point

blank, shaking my head to make him let go of me. I can't afford to appear weak. Not here, not now.

Franco smirks as he lowers his hand. "I'll let Vincenzo answer that."

Vincenzo clears his throat and shoves me gently in the direction of the sofa. I keep my composure as I sink down next to Carla, but she leans into me and claws at my hand. I squeeze back. It's warm in here, but she's shivering, petrified.

"Emilio Randazzo was killed a month ago on his estate near Catania," Vincenzo says. "We're still trying to figure out who killed him, but as you can imagine, without an heir apparent, there's been...unrest."

And more deaths than I can probably imagine. Maybe forcing myself out of the Mafia grapevine has been a stupid move. Not being informed...why didn't Don Trapani say anything? Surely, he knew exactly what was going on. He didn't warn me we were being ambushed. Carla shouldn't be here. She's still a child. Except she isn't.

"The fact that Randazzo was murdered is moot," Vincenzo says. "Franco has been planning to take over his operations for some time. Randazzo was old, too laid back, and things were getting out of hand."

I don't even want to know what he means by that.

"You know how this works, Gigi," he carries on when I say nothing, but only stare blindly at him.

Yes, I know. I glance at Don Trapani for help, but he's closed his eyes, sagging into himself. "Enlighten me?"

Vincenzo has the decency to rest his gaze for a second on Carla's distraught face. "Franco wants a wife. And we, as the Trapanis, need to strengthen our alliance with the new Don. I've already pledged my alliance. In fact, I took my *omertà* in April."

"Good for you," I say. "Your alliance doesn't need me. It also doesn't need an eighteen-year-old student who's about to go to university. We have nothing to give to your organization."

"Gigi," Don Trapani starts, and I eagerly meet his gaze.

He pauses for a moment. The weight attached to his silence presses on my chest like a boulder. Here it comes. What would happen if I don't comply.

"We're trying to do this with as little bloodshed as possible. With a marriage, we're signaling peace. Things can go on as normal, as they were."

'Normal' for all those under extortion. Everyday people caught in a turf war between Franco and whoever else wants to claim a stake in the sex and drug trafficking on this side of the planet now that Emilio Randazzo is dead.

I swallow down my fear and cling to Carla's hand for support. "I'm not for sale. Neither is Carla."

Franco steps closer to me and frowns. If he touches me again, I swear I'll bite him.

"I'm surprised you think you have a say, angel. The deal's been made. I just didn't know I had such a difficult choice to make."

14

GIGI

Angel. The last man who called me that didn't spike my blood with fear. No, he shook me up in a cocktail of lust I couldn't swallow down fast enough.

I'm not your fucking angel! I want to hiss at Franco, but it won't play in my favor. "Please don't call me angel," I whisper instead, demure and obedient.

"Hmmm," Franco hums. "Been called that by someone else, have you?"

"It was a long time ago," I lie.

The memories of my one night with Stephano Scalera come out of my mind's filing system daily, multiple times, still as fresh as if it happened last night.

"Good," he says, seeming to lose interest already.

I need to keep my cool here. I had years to prepare for this. Carla had none. I'll play this game, gain points and time so I can get her out of here.

"I'll make it easy for you, Franco. Leave my sister out of it. She's too young for marriage, and she's going to need molding to meet the criteria for a *mafioso* wife. When she is ready and the time is right, you can use her to strengthen your position and make a worthy alliance with someone else. I'm sure there'll be ample opportunities."

I don't want to say the next words, but I have to.

"Take me." I swallow and make sure I look him in the eye. "Take me. I'm ready, and I promise to be a good wife."

Please, I beg you, just take me and leave Carla alone.

With those damaged hands, I know what I'm up against. A man who uses his fists. On everything. Indiscriminately. A marriage will never come to pass, but I'm not subjecting Carla to a minute more of this tortuous situation. "In fact, I think it's time she leaves the room so we can talk about the details."

Franco rocks on his heels where he's standing within arm's reach, those fists stuffed into his pockets. He's measuring me up. Maybe I've sounded too eager, but I don't look away. I stare back as if in a dare.

He's handsome if you look beyond the broken nose that healed slightly askew and thick over the bridge. His dark eyes are small, and it makes him look a bit piggish, but he's tall and looks fit. Fighting fit. And probably not a day older than forty-five. Later in life to take a wife unless he's already had one and she's dead.

I clench my hands, hiding them in the folds of my dress. So much to look forward to.

Franco drops his gaze to my cleavage, perfectly cupped in this summer dress. *Men*. Not for the first time in my life do I thank the Lord for giving me a decent pair of tits. If this is all it's going to take to sway him, I can work with the rest.

After another minute of inspection, as he probably assesses how well I'm going to fuck and breed, he inhales and sighs with resignation.

"Let the girl go to her room," he says. "My future wife talks common sense, which makes for a refreshing change." He glances around the room. "Vincenzo, see to your father. You," he says as he nods towards another man I don't know. "Get it going so we can wrap up here."

"Go," I whisper to Carla. "I'll see you later."

"You're going to be okay?" she whispers back, her voice pitched, silent tears streaming down her face. "Gigi?"

"Sure, stay calm. This is how it is, *cara*. I've always known this is where I was going. Why do you think I've been waiting to settle with someone?" I can't afford to have her more riled up. It's lie upon lie now. "I'm going to be fine."

She's bug-eyed at the bullshit I just spewed, but I squeeze her hand in warning one last time. She nods and then shakes her head but stands and rushes out. Vincenzo is helping Papa out of his seat, and I bite down on my lip, a cry wanting to tear out of my chest. He's limping. I want to rush over, but he raises a hand to stop me. What did they do to him...and Vincenzo? He didn't stop anything from happening.

Once they're gone, Franco turns to me. "A drink, to celebrate? This seems to come as a surprise."

"I'm fine." But inside, I'm cowering.

"Have one in any case, *amorina*. You might need it."

"I think I'll call it a night." I stand, putting some action behind my words. "I've come all the way from London, and it's late."

"But we're not done. We hardly know each other."

And I plan to keep it this way.

Franco takes the whiskey another man holds out to him. I give him a quick once-over. A three-in-one bodyguard, torture device, and executioner. Dressed all in black, he gives all those vibes just by standing there, glaring at me under hooded lids.

"Some things are best left for after the wedding, don't you think?" I tease, keeping my tone light.

I won't be raped tonight. Over my dead body. Already, my gaze has homed in on the poker sticks by the fireplace as potential weapons.

"Maybe, but some things I'd like to sort out before we get married."

"Such as?"

I sweep my gaze around the room. Four men are on standby to protect Franco, all clones of each other, camouflaged in the corners of the library with their all-black attire.

"We'll talk about it." He takes my hand and leads me to the sofa. His touch is warm and scratchy against my cold fingers. He waits for me to sit, then circles the ice in his glass while he towers over me. He's intimidating, and I can't help but recall the way Stephano looked at me that night as he stood over me just like this. There was nothing sinister in his look, not like Franco, who stares at me like he's about to dissect a frog for fun. "I am going to rebuild Randazzo's empire, only this time, it will be stronger. He was a remarkable man, but he left his legacy in shambles, ready for the taking. Think about it, *amorina*, you'll be the wife of the most revered and powerful Don in the whole of Europe."

I swallow and watch how his gaze dips to my throat. If only I can stop giving my fear away. "I'm used to all that."

"Maybe." Franco sighs. "From what I understand, you've been allowed to run wild. What with your own business, your constant travels and art auctions."

His words are a noose around my neck, tightening.

"I won't allow you—surely, you must understand the danger, *amorina*—to continue in this way." He still hasn't sat down, but cups my face, and I force myself not to flinch. "You'll be home, with our children, like a good wife. I might take on Randazzo's operations as my own, but I won't allow my hard work to go to anybody but my sons."

And by 'take', he means war. The signs are all there: the man in front of me is a maniac. So calm as he sips his whiskey.

He nods at one of the men who stands behind me, and I freeze as a hand clasps over my mouth and a fist burrows in my hair to hold my head in place. The other two men are on me, each one gripping an arm as Franco steps in between my flailing legs.

"Calm down, Gigi," he croons softly. "This can take hours, or minutes. Depends totally on how much fuss you make."

15

GIGI

"Randazzo liked to tattoo his girls," Franco says as another man, this one carrying a medical case, comes forward. "But people can remove tattoos. I prefer something permanent."

Something permanent?

I thrash around, kicking and trying to break free. I slip on the leather sofa, but strong hands hold my arms, and the fist in my hair jerks and pulls me up to sit. Pain shoots around my skull, and I gasp against the hand reeking of old cigarettes.

"Gag her." Franco glares down at me, his mouth pulled into a cruel smirk. "Hold still, *amorina*, or my hand might slip."

I close my eyes, not wanting to see what comes next. The grip on my mouth loosens, and I scream on instinct. It's hardly a wail before a fist punches me in the gut, followed by another hitting my ribcage.

I double over in agony. The grips on my arms don't slacken, and my shoulders strain painfully. Winded, I drop back on the sofa but can't breathe. Pain radiates with every attempt to move.

When the hand slips from my mouth, I only manage desperate pulls of air that don't seem to reach my lungs. A leather belt scratches the sides of my open lips as it forces my mouth open and tightens.

Weight comes down on my mound, pressing on my sex through the fabric of this frivolous summer dress. I glance up through my tears at Franco. He has dropped his knee to my crotch, pinning me down.

"Sorry, *amorina*, but you had that coming. Work with us now, so we can all go to bed."

He's not sorry at all. And I've seen his hands. I know how this goes. If I'm pulp, I can't help Carla. *If I ever see her again.*

I go limp like a rag doll, quivering uncontrollably. This could have been my baby sister. Somehow, the thought calms me. It's me, not Carla. She left with Vincenzo and Papa. Her bodyguard waited for her. He will protect her. I'm doing this so she doesn't have to. My body stills, even if it's only superficial.

Franco senses my capitulation, because he lifts his weight off me, and his goons loosen their grip.

"Tie her up in any case. I don't need her jerking around."

I don't know what's coming, but it's going to hurt. Instead of looking, I close my eyes and feel how they manipulate my body. Arms tied above my head, attached to something keeping me immobile. I force myself to breathe through my nose, deep breaths that are supposed to be calming, but my heart is a battering ram in my chest, my blood stormwater through my veins. Somewhere, something flips open, the lid of the medical case, the clang of metal against metal. The callused hand on my knees, opening me up, tells me only one thing. Franco is going to go *there*.

He glides his hand up my inner thigh, and when a thumb strokes over my sex, I want to curl away from his touch, but I can't, held in place by restraints circling my ankles.

"We'll keep this for later," he says softly as he rides his thumb up and down my slit. "You have no piercings now, but we'll go slowly, one at a time. What we're doing tonight is more important, and it needs more time to heal."

His hand slips higher then, tugging the band of my panties lower, exposing my sex.

"Very pretty," he mutters, but he doesn't pull them farther down to bare me completely.

I shudder when the medicinal alcohol's scent floats past my nose, the cold wipe swiping close to my loin, just above my mound. There's pressure then, a pen drawing.

"I'm really good at this," Franco says, pride in his voice. "But it hurts, so hold still."

As if I have a choice. Now someone is holding me down on my stomach, too. I have no idea what he's doing, but the first slice into my flesh makes me want to jolt up. The goons who're pinning me down knew this was coming, because they intensify the pressure on every part of my body.

Tears flow freely now, and Franco, without missing a beat, says, "Should've had that drink, hmm?"

I don't know how long it takes, only that the warm trickle of blood sliding down my groin and to my sex puddles in my panties where Franco's pulled them down.

What feels like hours later, there's a dab of something cold, a wipe over my mutilated skin.

"We'll look at this tomorrow to see how it heals," Franco says as he stands.

I blink up at him. At his hands, in blue surgical gloves, stained with my blood. He drops the scalpel into a metal bowl with a clang, and as if on cue, a goon hands him another whiskey.

There will be no tomorrow for me and this man. I will never see him again. This is a vow I make to myself, and I'd rather die than break it. Somehow, I came ready for this—a part of me knew and has been waiting for years. *Monsters are rising...*

He takes a sip of his drink then looks down at his handiwork. "I get better all the time. It's a pity I didn't keep count of the number of cunts from the beginning."

Chuckles run through the room. The other men have been remarkably quiet, probably in deference. Franco Fiore is a sadistic maniac, and I'm supposed to get married to him.

We'll leave tonight and disappear forever.

He pulls off his surgical gloves, one by one, and drops them in the bowl with the scalpel. He picks up his whiskey glass again, but it has my blood on the sides where he held it before. He brings the glass to his lips and licks the blood off with his tongue. When he slides and rolls it along the edge, bile rises to my throat.

With a wink, he looks down at me. "I like the taste of you already, *amorina*."

I turn my face away from his madman's gaze as my stomach churns.

"Put the tracker in her arm, and bandage my work so it heals properly," he says, and someone grunts.

That wasn't it? In panic, I glance around. With my arms tied as they are, I can't see much more than the ceiling and another man, the one who looked like an executioner, stepping in, his face upside down from where I'm lying.

He runs a finger down one inner arm, and then down the other. "What hand do you use to write?"

I flex my fingers of my right hand, and he nods.

I watch on in horror as he pulls on surgical gloves and wipes my left arm down with alcohol.

"This is quick." He disappears out of view, but when he comes back, he has an ear-piercing gun in one hand and a scalpel in the other.

Except it isn't an ear-piercing gun. It's a tool I've never seen before.

"Just a small cut," he says as he slices into me.

I grimace as I brace myself. In comparison, there's much less pain than what I had down there. He angles the tool, but instead of pulling the trigger, he shoves a lever. I can feel the thing forced under my skin, and now, I'm going to vomit. My body convulses, primed for this since that first cut. I can't sit up, I can't lean forward, but it surges up my throat.

"Fuck," the executioner hisses. "Don't choke on your own fucking sick."

The tension in my arms and legs is gone, and I'm forced up as I spew vomit that just gets blocked by the belt gagging me. It has nowhere to go, and my eyes tear as I choke. I'm being roughhoused as the belt gets ripped from my face, and hard slaps on my back make the floodgates open. Sitting up has brought my skirts down, and my vomit catches in the bowl between my legs formed by the fabric. I heave, blinking at the blood seeping from my arm.

"Ah, fuck." Franco groans from where he took a seat in a wingback. "You had to? Things were going so well, so clean."

I shiver as my body still convulses, but I watch him from under my lashes, my vision blurry with tears.

"What the fuck did you expect," I snarl when I'm eventually done.

He stands and drops his thick-bottomed whiskey glass onto a side table, and the clang echoes through the room.

"I expect my wife to stomach more than that. Best you work on it, *amorina*." He waves at the executioner. "Finish her up and take her to her room. Guard her at all times."

I follow every step as Franco leaves the library and blink in the direction of the grandfather clock. Time stood still for me, but it's already past one in the morning.

"I must cover this," the executioner says, and he takes my arm to wipe at the blood still running from my latest incision. A flat, pill-shaped object is nestled under my skin. He cuts some

Steri-strips and closes me up, but I can already see it's a botched job. This cut needs stitches.

Vomit stench is rife, and the executioner is affected like any other human being, looking a bit green. He steps away from me as soon as he's done. The other men in the room avoid the circle of stench. To think vomit is going to be my saving grace.

"I'll deal with it." I gather my skirts, toe on my ballet flats, and pick up my tote where it I dropped it by the sofa earlier. As I stand, I keep the vomit neatly contained in my skirt. "You can wait outside my room. It's on the villa's third floor."

It sounds as if there's nowhere for me to go from there, except there is. I'm one step ahead of the game here. There's no chance in hell these men have been at this house before. They can have no clue about the layout and the hidden passages.

The question really is if I can maintain my advantage.

16

GIGI

We've reached the third floor where several bedrooms are lined up along the corridor. I hiked those stairs as if everything hinged on me getting to the top floor, ignoring the echoes of pain from my arm to my lower belly. With the adrenalin and endorphins numbing me, it's easier than I thought it would be. I glance down the grand staircase with its wooden balustrade circling down all the way to the cellars of this mansion that's over two hundred and fifty years old. But it's not the only staircase in the house.

"This is me," I say as we reach my closed bedroom door. I glance to where another guard is standing sentry at the top of the stairs. Good.

The executioner leans past me, holding his breath, and swings the door open. As I scoot past him, I stumble, which isn't new. I'm a klutz that way, but for the first time, it's planned. I might even lean a bit in. The vomit flops and splatters in thick smears over his jacket and pants, then runs down to his shoes.

"Fuck," he hisses. "You bitch."

"Sorry." I bite my lip, seeing every emotion playing over his face. If I weren't Franco's fiancée, he would have slapped me so hard I would've gone flying. "There's a bathroom at the end of the corridor you can use."

He huffs. Looks one way then the other, peers into the room that has a king-size four-poster bed and sitting area, the walls decorated with elaborate floral wallpaper. "I'll be here in five."

"Sure. Please...just some privacy for the shower. It's en suite here."

He doesn't nod, only makes eye contact with the other guard, and lets me go in alone. I don't bother to lock the door and strip as I walk to the closet, dropping the soiled dress to the floor. I have no time.

I run my fingers through the hangers of old clothes I've left behind through the years. I grab some soft wide-legged pants and a T-shirt, get dressed, empty my tote onto the bed, and head to the bathroom, cellphone in hand as I hock my empty tote across my chest. There's a stash of sanitary products in the vanity's drawer, and I stuff a napkin between my skin and my panties to cover the bleeding from whatever Franco did on my lower belly.

Someone still has to bandage it properly, but I'm not sticking around for that. I can't look at it. I don't want to look at it. I'm still on an adrenaline high from the library, and I need to tap into it for a while. I can't crash now.

In the bathroom, I turn the shower's faucet on and let it run. Instead of getting in, I open the hidden door behind the towel railing. White towels hide it at first glance, and it helps how the tiles line up to fool the eye. I crouch in, and before I close the door, I make sure the towels hang neatly.

With my cellphone's flashlight on, I crawl along the dark tunnel that's part of the antique metal roof structure. I gather the odd spiderweb and kick dust clouds up, but I can see where I'm heading. This was my favorite summertime game with Carla—coming over at night to read stories long after bedtime. We haven't done this in more than a decade. Once I reach the other side and the entry to her bathroom, I knock softly five times.

Nothing.

I kill my flashlight. As I exit the hideout into Carla's bathroom, everything is dark. I feel my way along the wall and pad onto the soft bedroom carpet.

My eyes grow accustomed to the dark, and the moonlight falling through the bedroom windows helps. I glance around. Carla sits frozen on her bed, eyes wide. *Waiting.*

I put my forefinger to my lips, and she nods. She points to the wall where Vito Rossi blends into the shadows, guarding my sister like an angel. Or the devil in disguise.

He could be Vincenzo's man.

Vincenzo who just allowed what happened to me in the library. He took his *omertà*...there's no way he isn't in the loop with what Franco does to *his girls.*

God help us.

Why is Vito in her room and not outside? My whole plan crumbles to pieces, and I want to curl up and die. But Carla clambers out of bed, fully dressed, phone in hand. She read the situation in the library like a book. Code red. She types fast and shows me the message. *He's with us.*

Vito steps closer, and my gaze jogs between the two. I'm on a knife's edge. Trust my sister—easy. Trust a man I don't know except from a piece of paper—not so easy.

We don't have time, and I make a split-second decision I might regret for the rest of my life...which won't be long if this goes wrong. I signal to Carla, and she nods. We know where we're going next. This might have been a game a long time ago, but every game is some form of reality, past, present, or future.

We need to be quick. Carla makes to embrace me, but I shake my head and pull her to the bathroom. One thing my body can't deal with now is pressure. Against my ribs, my shredded arm, my stomach where Franco punched me, and lower, where the pain of a million paper cuts burns like acid.

I light up the drawer to quietly search through the collection of brushes, hairpins, and other accessories. I grab a few things, lay them on the vanity, and hand the phone to her with the light switched on.

This is going to be gross and freak her out, but I don't care. I indicate she should hold the light up, and I lift my arm. The Steri-strip is drenched in blood and peels off easily. I bite down on my bottom lip and flinch at the wound. Then I take a deep breath as I dig the tweezers underneath my skin. The pain is hideous and I want to cry out, but I bite down harder on my lip.

Carla's hand quivers, making the light vibrate. Vito steps in, shaking his head as he takes my hand. And I let him. I let him take the tweezers and dig out the implant while I clench the vanity with my fist, strangling my cries with pure will. Carla's hand is on my shoulder, breaths shuddering as she tries to control herself. I don't care. It's done.

Vito drops the tiny device in the sink, and we all stare at it as my blood stains the white porcelain. The device disappears down the dark hole. More blood runs down my arm, and I press the wound closed. Carla reaches in the drawer for a facecloth, and Vito tugs his shirt from his pants, then tears at it, making a long strip of linen. He nods at me and wraps the make-shift bandage around my arm, catching the facecloth in the process.

It's good enough. It needs to last just a few hours.

We're good to go, I signal. Vito's big, but we need him. And he's proven himself halfway. I hope he doesn't mind crawl space.

I light the way to another hidden door in Carla's bedroom. All the fake ceilings aren't connected, but this one gives access to the secret staircase leading to a tunnel away from the house and opens close to the street below. Far enough from eyes that will try to find us inside the house first.

As we clamber in, I beg and pray we'll be quiet enough and that this plan, which I hatched ages ago, will be foolproof. Vito is the only variable I hadn't bargained on, and until we've ditched him, I won't feel in control.

The stretch we need to traverse in the ceiling isn't far, but when I reach the trapdoor connecting with the secret staircase, we collectively hold our breaths. We listen. All is quiet. I lift the door and shine the light. Nobody.

I lower myself, biting down on the pain as I slide on my stomach until my feet touch the stone stairs. I guide my way lower with my hand on the wall, crouching in the narrow space as I hold the light for them. The others follow, and soon, we're a bundle of humans sneaking down the stairs, trying to make as little noise as possible.

I hardly breathe, my whole body locked in do-or-die. I don't breathe easier when we reach the tunnel, which is also connected to the cellar. From that side, its entrance is hidden by empty wine barrels. The old wooden door is locked, but a copy of the key is buried where I left it ages ago. It gets stuck, and after a few tries, Vito squeezes in and takes over. He isn't weak from shock and manages to unlock the rusty door, and with a shoulder, opens our final stretch.

Now that we're no longer directly under the house, we rush, still not talking, the flashlight whipping left and right as I jog, head bent low, to the exit. It's about a hundred meters from the house, hidden by a fountain in the lower garden and overgrown with shrubs. A few meters below, the road winds along. Tourists often park their cars here when space gets tight in summer. I lean against the wall to catch my breath, no longer caring that I'm a nest of spiderwebs, plant debris, and dirt.

"What next?" Carla whispers.

"I steal a car," Vito whispers back. "You drive to the nearest airport and get the hell out of here. Nowhere in Europe is safe. Franco planned this takeover for years. Randazzo's death only made it easier for him to implement." He leans into my ear. "You can't go to London, or any other hideouts linked to the Trapanis. He'll have men stationed there as soon as he finds out you're gone. We have minutes. Who knows how much Don Trapani revealed."

I close my eyes. Papa. Tonight might have been the last time I ever saw him alive.

"What if Franco kills him?" I ask, fear breaking my voice. "Because we're gone? We need to go back, I—"

"No, you get out while you can. Both of you. I'll go back for Don Trapani."

For what it's worth. My heart bleeds, but this man...he's unexpected.

"Do you have anywhere else you can go where Franco's network doesn't reach?" he urges me on. "Australia? South America?"

I can't think. "No?"

"Think, Gigi. You have a world full of contacts." His hand is on my shoulder, stressing how this will be all for nothing if we can't disappear. "It won't be forever. Just until this tectonic shift has settled."

"Maybe."

Make it happen, cara. *Go meet them. Charm them. Make new friends. Friends from America. And you know why. We might need them.*

Don Trapani's words ring back in my head like alarm bells. *Monsters are rising...* No wonder he was so adamant I go meet the Scaleras. He knew this day was coming, but I bet he got the timing wrong. Nobody else knows about our connection with the Scaleras, Franco Fiore least of all.

"Yes. There's—"

"Don't tell me where you're going. You've cash?"

"Fifty thousand euros in my handbag's lining." Plus some more in an account I've opened ages ago that's not even in my real name.

"Good. Passports?" Vito is working through his mental checklist.

"Yes, fake ones, for both of us." My business may all be above board, but I have contacts. Fake passports were the first thing I've secured after that talk with Papa on Carla's birthday. I've always had one, but I made sure Carla had one too.

He smiles. "Never underestimate a Mafia princess. Take the cash and ditch the bag and clothes as soon as you can do so safely. Get everything new. We don't know where they planted what. And you both leave your phones here. It's a risk you can't take."

Carla inhales sharply in protest, but I grab her wrist in warning. "We have no choice."

We blink at each other in the dark, and then Vito crouches and squeezes through the narrow gap between the stone and the fountain wall, working the overgrown foliage to the side. As he disappears into the night, all I can think is how I owe him, big time.

I told Matteo the Scaleras owe me—they owe *us*. The Trapanis never forget a debt, and I'm going to call in this one.

17

STEPHANO

It's midnight, and the DJ is about to break the roof. The club is pounding with people dancing, and the light show accompanying the music makes everything more frenzied.

I can feel the vibrations under my feet where I'm standing at a railing on the second floor giving an eagle-eye view over the dance floor. The office is behind me, a quieter place to pass the hours I spend here. But midnight is always a highlight, and I have to come and feel the vibes for myself.

When I was younger, I thought clubbing would never get old, but time stands still for nobody. It's not as if I'm old, but at twenty-nine, I've seen and lived through more shit than any man should. Lately, I've come to realize this type of life might have an expiry date for me. It's time I put succession plans in place.

The dancers in the cages along the wall and suspended over the dance floor are part of the theatrics. Some of them work as strippers at our other clubs; some of them are just fucking good at what they do and don't need to shed clothing in the process. Ever since Tatiana, I've vowed to never get involved with one of them again. I shouldn't get involved with any woman, least of all one that makes me think long-term... Scalera boys don't get to love and fuck me if I have to learn that lesson again. The *Il Consiglio* life doesn't gel with things normal people do.

My phone buzzes in my pocket, and I pull it out. *Matteo.* Weird. Since we got back from Cannes and he married Tasha, late night calls are not a thing at all. I'm still digesting the whole turn of events in Cannes, but I've forgiven him for putting me through all that hell for this outcome. To see Matteo this happy only made me realize how fucking sad and lonely life has become. I don't know how he's going to balance life with a wife he loves and life as the Don. All I know is we will all protect Tasha, with our lives if needed.

I let the phone ring, not in the mood to talk to him. Eventually, the call dies, but he calls again. This time, I walk back into the quieter office, past the security team monitoring the cameras in the club, to my back office.

"What's up?" I hope this isn't some dirty business that needs wrapping up. I'm not exactly in the mood.

"We have a problem."

Here we go. "Yeah?"

"I need you to pick someone up at the airport."

"Okay..." I say, rolling my eyes. "Doesn't sound like a problem to me. We have drivers for that, no?"

"It's a bit more complicated. Gigi Trapani is arriving at Logan at ten in the morning."

Gigi Trapani. The one woman I'd planned to never see again. The one woman who keeps on slipping into my thoughts uninvited. Into my bed at night where I fist my cock with frustrated longing. The one and only woman I've ever hate-fucked in my life. Not that I actually fucked her, but I did kind of hate on her.

That night eats at me, and I know why. I never treat women

this way, and nothing she did warranted such a level of dick-ishness.

Filthy Mafia paws. Creep. You're just a fucking pimp.

I sigh, trying to suppress the memory. "And this is now my problem?"

"Yep." Matteo makes it clear with this one word that I'm not getting out of it. It's the Don talking, not the brother. "Thing is, she doesn't have a phone with her. You've met her and know what she looks like. So, conclusion: you need to pick her up."

"And then? What's she even doing here?"

Matteo is quiet for a full ten seconds, and already I'm pacing the office.

"She's calling in a favor," he finally says.

For fuck's sake. There it is. I knew our trip to Europe was going to haunt us. There's no such thing as a free lunch. "You're the one who used their yacht. Hell, you spent more time with her than I did when she *kidnapped* you."

This isn't exactly true, but—

"I have a meeting in the morning," he says, ignoring my segue. "She's with her younger sister, Carla, so—"

"What level of favor are we talking here, Matteo?"

There's a lot of *I scratch your back, you scratch mine* in the crime circles we function in, but before I commit to something, I'd like to know what I'm getting into.

"We didn't have time to discuss the details."

Well, shit. This could be anything. From a private tour of Boston to burning a body. "So, I pick them up and drop them off at your place?"

"Probably, yes."

"Still don't understand why a driver with a name board can't do it. I train at ten."

"I've a feeling they don't want their names plastered all over the place."

I drop my head back with a groan. No phones. No names. *Mafia princesses on the run.* "I'll pick them up. But when I drop them off, I'm done."

"That's fine. Tasha will be at home."

We ring off, and I pocket my phone. For a moment, I stand idle, wrapping my head around seeing Gigi again, four weeks after I made her come with a bottle of champagne.

A lady who fucks like a whore. As if I'd ever call a woman that.

Mafia paws. Creep. Pimp.

Of all the things she called me, the first one hit the hardest.

I know why her words still eat at me, why they made me spin slowly out of control until I tossed the vilest thing back at her, knowing how it would hurt.

Ever since I nearly beat a kid to death at fourteen, I've been keeping my *filthy Mafia paws* in check. I was expelled from school for what I did. It was kept under wraps, but I spent time in a juvenile facility for two years for anger management. None of that helps when *it's in your blood.*

If it weren't for Alex, my older brother who died in the shootout twelve years ago, I probably wouldn't be here today.

He's only half your blood, Stephano, but it doesn't mean you're like him. Be the better man and learn how to control it. Otherwise, he'll have control over you forever, and that's the last thing any of us want.

As if Alex knew he was going to die young, he had the most wisdom of us all. He knew how to work the Don, warding the man off when he could. Between him and Matteo, they made a barrier between us and the man who fucked with my head. Turns out the damage was already done, though.

Now Don Scalera is dead. He died just after we came back from Cannes. I never saw him again, but he haunts me, just like he did when he was alive. You can fight all your demons, but when it's in your blood, in your veins, it's so much part of you, you *are* the demon. You'd die without it, and you die with it.

I beat him out of my system every day. An exhausted man isn't keen to use his fists. Now I'm going to miss my training session tomorrow, because as karma has it, the one woman I've treated like a piece of shit is coming to town.

18

GIGI

As we touch down at Boston's Logan airport, my anxiety spikes again. We've managed to escape Lake Como and Italy, but ever since we've been on the run, I'm like a rabbit with a fox biting at my tail.

While we were in the air, there was a moment of relief. Nobody seems to have followed us onto the plane. The probability was almost zero, but we *will* be hunted down. All I can hope is Matteo is the solution that can work for now, or at least until the storm has blown over. Franco Fiore will take a wife from another Mafia family—surely, the Trapanis aren't the only ones bowing to the new order.

I don't know what happened to Don Trapani after we escaped. At some point, Carla's bodyguard will let us know. As Vito saw us off at the airport, he promised to send news via email.

Carla has been unnaturally quiet, probably shocked about the turn of events. What she doesn't know is how before my biological dad got killed by the Cosa Nostra, this was my life. The thing is, the higher up your parents are in the Mafia, the more distanced you become from it. In the highest echelons, you're almost untouchable. *Almost*. My mom's marriage to Don Trapani might have catapulted us to the highest inner circle of the Cosa Nostra, but I'll never forget my childhood.

I shift in my chair. The seatbelt rubs uncomfortably against my lower belly where I'm swollen and raw. I still haven't looked at what Franco did to me. I can't bear it. I didn't change the sanitary napkin I so hastily shoved between my skin and the front part of my panties. Not even while Vito was with us when we bought new clothes at the airport. We ditched everything we were wearing right there, even my tote. Carla's eyes bulged when I ripped through the tote's lining and transferred the stack of euros to my new purse.

"You've been walking around with this amount of cash?" she asked. "Just like that?"

"I always walk around with this amount of cash." I didn't want to spook her, but the reality of our situation was slowly sinking in.

"Who are we meeting at the airport?" she asks now as she looks out the window. The airplane is taxiing to its parking bay.

"Matteo Scalera. I met him last month in Cannes. He owes us."

He owes me.

As for his brother Stephano... I reckon he might cross my path. Hopefully not. But here I am, *alive*. When he tossed back how I need to work on my aim *for next time* that night in Cannes, I'd wanted to call back *over my dead body*. It doesn't sound so farfetched now, which just gives me the chills.

I still think of that night. Of me and him. It runs in my mind like a reel. The presidential suite, Stephano in his tux, him leaning over me and seducing me with his words, then with his lips. At these memories, my body heats up with desire catching flame. Every single annoying time. And I hate myself for it.

I wipe at my brow. I'm hot. And in pain. The painkillers I took have worn off, and my arm pulses where they cut me and I dug around with unsterilized tweezers. Where Franco hit me, my body aches every time I move. He bruised or cracked a rib or two. I've been sitting too long in an economy-class seat, and I'm stiff from all the crawling and contorting I did in the roof and tunnel as we escaped the house in Lake Como.

"Are you okay, Gigi?" Carla asks as she reaches for my hand where I'm gripping the armrest.

"I'm just tired." I hardly slept. My adrenaline still spikes out of nowhere, and I'm in too much pain. The reality I've always dreaded is on us, and I won't sleep properly until we're safe.

Carla presses the back of her hand against my cheek. "You're boiling."

"It's exhaustion." We've been on the run for a whole day now, having to change flights twice. I didn't sleep on Friday night either.

"No. Please, tell me. What did they do to you? Franco... And his men?"

When Franco marked me, the thing that kept me going was how it was happening to me and not to Carla. Now, I've had time to digest how he touched me, how he did everything to me while his men—*his dirty, fucking men*—looked on. How he told them what he was going to do to me once we were wed. Piercings. One by one. As he caressed my sex while all of them watched. I bet he'll let them fuck me, too. One by one.

I'll never be Franco's trophy wife. I'd be his slave for whatever duty he sees fit. His reward to hand out to men who'd want to have me as a prize.

"Nothing to worry about, Carla," I say, but I shudder inside. "The worst was the implant, and we left that behind."

The airplane has come to a stop. The other passengers get up to gather their cabin bags. We have nothing but two purses between us, the clothes we're wearing, and what's left of fifty thousand euros after paying for these flights.

"How long are we staying for?"

"Probably no longer than a month."

But it's a lie. *As long as it takes.* I heave up, and pain shoots through me. I wince, and Carla's hand is on my back.

"Can you walk?"

"Yes." I made it this far. I just need to get into Matteo's car.

He must be here. I don't know what we're going to do if he isn't. I've memorized his phone number just in case. That last desperate phone call, made from Vito's phone using a burner SIM card, was dreadful. I forced myself to be cool and calm, authoritative, demanding. Calling in this favor. We didn't have time to discuss the full extent of this disaster, but Matteo isn't stupid. He'll know what it means to have us landing on his doorstep. I made him promise he wouldn't let Don Trapani know where we are. Not yet. Not until this storm has passed.

We make our way out of the plane with the throng of other passengers. Once we're in the terminal corridor, I step to the side. I can't walk fast, not with my ribcage feeling like it's gaping open and my jeans taking a bite out of my groin with every step. Carla slows down and has me by the elbow.

"Come on, it's not far now."

What a lie. It feels like miles. We go through passport control, basically lying our way into the country with the false documents I have on hand, telling them we're here for two weeks as tourists to see Boston and then New York. I'm going to change or not show up for our return flights, depending on how soon I know what's happening next.

Nothing flags on the border control officer's side, not from what I can see in any event, and I deflate, feeling even weaker as we make our way through baggage claim.

I stumble as we walk out into the arrivals lounge, and Carla grips me tighter.

"God, Gigi, come on, stay with me."

"I'm okay," I whisper, but I lean into her.

I scan the arrivals lounge for the only person I want to see.

I've met him only once, but Matteo's face, going through every emotion when I kidnapped him on the yacht that day, is a solid memory. I won't miss him.

The airport is busy, and I'm scanning the area for Matteo when my gaze snags on Stephano Scalera. I snatch in a breath. The one man I vowed to never see again if I could help it.

He's coming towards us, and his eyes lock with mine. He is just as I remember him. Tall, dark hair, broad shoulders only accentuated by his suit's perfect fit. My heart skips a beat. My ribcage protests. I sag a bit on my feet.

"Gigi?" Stephano is right here, his gaze filled with concern.

"Where's Matteo?" I manage, but I'm seeing black spots. I might faint.

"He sent me to fetch you." He steps even closer.

"My sister needs a doctor," Carla tells him, and before I can straighten properly, I've lost my grip on Carla.

But Stephano has me, and I lean into him as my head sways.

"Hey," he murmurs. "I've got you."

His arm snakes around my waist for support. I wince as I press into his chest to keep upright, but honestly, I want to collapse in his embrace. In these Mafia paws that hold me tenderly and don't punch with the least provocation like my dad's did. Or like Franco's did. I swore to never get hitched to a man like that, and for now, I seem to have escaped such a fate.

"Where're you hurting, angel?" Stephano asks softly.

Tears are flowing now. For Carla's sake, I've contained them, but his tone, his touch, so caring and tender as he holds me steady, is too much.

"She won't say," Carla tells him when I say nothing. "Ever since Friday night— I don't know what happened in the library, but he hurt her." She chokes. "He hurt her real bad."

A shudder runs through Stephano's body, and for a second, he just rubs my back.

"Okay. I'll take care of you. Lean against me, angel," he says in my ear. "That's right. As if we're having a hug like we haven't seen each other for years. I'm going to call the car to come around to the pickup and go. I'm sorry, but I think you need to walk out of here. I'd carry you, but I don't want to draw any attention."

"No," I whisper. "No attention. I'll manage. We made it, and Carla is safe."

I'm wrapped in his arms, his hold firm and solid around my back. I inhale the fresh scent of his laundered shirt, my one hand resting against his pecs, the other settling on his hip under his jacket. I can't smell very nice at all, but through his shirt, I can smell him. His male scent that seems to pair perfectly with every feminine need my body has. He is so solid and warm, and for the first time, I'm able to let go. This giant wall of responsibility I've been scaling seems to shrink against this wall of a man. He is here now. He's in control, and he'll keep us safe. I can hand the reins over to him.

Within seconds, he's on the phone, giving orders.

"Come on," he says once he's rung off. "It isn't far. You don't have luggage?"

"No," Carla says.

"It was a 'come as you are' moment," I mutter.

Nobody laughs at my little joke.

19

STEPHANO

I did a double take. At a first glance, I hardly recognized Gigi. This isn't the glamorous woman who strode down the Cannes marina with a skip in her step, or the siren who walked into Tasha's auction as if she owned the place, in the red dress I still want to rip off her. This isn't the woman who stayed and seduced me by just being there. Fuck. I might have kept my hands to myself that night, but now I have them on her, and it's like holding a cracked china doll.

Fragile. On the verge of breaking. I can feel it in the way she breathes, haltingly, how she quietly winces as she shifts, probably thinking I can't pick up on these little signals.

The only thing that's the same from the day in Cannes is that she's keeping a girl safe. In Cannes, she was hellbent on saving Tasha from the auction, but this time, it's clear it's only her sister's safety she's concerned about. Carla looks unscathed. I bet Gigi stepped in and took all the blows. Maybe we have more in common than either of us will ever admit to each other.

All I know is, the fucker who's done this to her is going to have his reckoning.

We've made it to the exit, and I spot my SUV with the tinted windows driving up to us. "Come on, this is us." I have my arm around her back, supporting her by her waist.

Tony, my bodyguard, who's been trailing a few steps behind us, opens the back door, and I help Gigi in. Carla rounds the car and gets in on the other side.

With a suppressed grimace, Gigi shifts to the middle seat to make space for me. As soon as I'm seated next to her, I strap her in. I'm careful not to touch her, but even the seatbelt makes her suck in a breath.

"You're going to tell me everything," I say. "Get me the medical kit in the back for some pain meds," I tell Tony, and he opens the trunk to pull out the emergency kit we always have on hand. He gets into the front passenger seat, and I nod at the driver to go. Tony passes me the pill box, and I hold out bottled water for Gigi. "Take two of these."

"I need a shower," she groans. "Will they knock me out?"

"Maybe, but you need to rest." I shake out two pills. "If you have broken ribs, the shower can wait. You'll feel better once you've slept on a bed."

"It's more than broken ribs." Carla leans forward to meet my gaze. "She won't say."

"Carla—" Gigi breaks off as she takes the pills. She doesn't look me in the eye. "If I fall asleep, look after my sister, please."

"I promise to take care of you both, and you know she's safe with me." I wasn't on my best behavior that day in Cannes, and I have no excuse for my last words to her, but surely, after that afternoon and night, she knows I'll never hurt a woman. Not that I've tested this theory, but—I can't go there. Not now. I watch how she swallows the two pills and take the water from her. "The drive isn't far."

"Where're we going?" Carla asks.

"My brother Matteo's apartment. It's basically a high-rise Alcatraz without the island."

"Sounds perfect," Gigi says, her eyes closed.

Her head bobs, and then it settles on my shoulder. She didn't need meds to knock her out; she needed the green light stating it's finally safe to fall asleep as someone else holds the fort. Whatever happened to her, it's totally drained her.

We drive out of the airport and take the tunnel to the other side of the harbor. It's quiet in the car as Carla stares out of the window. When we get to the high-rise apartment building *Il Consiglio* owns, the security team rolls the gate open for us, and we drive into Matteo's private underground garage. The driver parks close to the elevator. I manage to cradle Gigi in my arms, trying to be as gentle as possible. She moans but doesn't wake up.

Tony gets us into the elevator. Carla is fidgety now, probably because she doesn't know us at all, and with Gigi passed out, her mind could be in a tailspin. She also looks ridiculously young.

"How old are you?" I ask.

"Eighteen."

"You're going to tell me what happened, and you're not going to skip one single detail."

She bites her lip. "I'll tell you what I know."

"Good."

Soon, the elevator doors open to the penthouse foyer, which hosts three doors. A central double door leads to Matteo's apartment, a single to his bodyguard's apartment, and the third leads to a room we keep for *special* guests. There haven't been any of those lately, and when Matteo kidnapped Tasha, he opted to use the safe room inside his apartment as she didn't fit the profile of people we usually park there.

We've hardly stepped out of the elevator when the door to Matteo's place opens.

"You're here!" Tasha's eyes widen when she sees me carrying a body. "Oh, God, is that Gigi?"

"Yes." I meet her gaze, and our eyes communicate silently as she lets us in. This woman dressed in jeans and an oversized *Milano, Ti Amo* sweater and sneakers is a world apart from the elegant goddess we both met on Don Trapani's yacht.

"Is she okay?"

"I don't know. We might need to take her for X-rays. I gave her some meds for the pain."

"Okay, sure, this way."

I nod to Tony; he knows the drill. He'll hang out with the security team until I need him.

Tasha leads the way to the second floor, and I carry Gigi to the first guest bedroom. Carla is trailing behind, taking in the sumptuous, über-luxurious and ultramodern apartment. I lay Gigi down gently on her back, and Tasha removes her shoes. There are dark circles under Gigi's eyes, and her thick hair is gathered in a knot that's falling apart.

Carla stands in the door, looking teary-eyed at her sister.

"It was Franco Fiore. He was there Friday night, choosing his bride. One of us." She swallows, her voice shaky. "Gigi convinced him to let me go. I didn't know what happened until she came through the secret connecting tunnel in our rooms. She dug some sort of tracking device out of her arm. Vito helped her with a pair of tweezers."

She convulses, and Tasha has her by the arm, rushing her to the bathroom.

I'm fuming as I reach for Gigi's sweater and lift it up. "Fuck."

The sound of retching comes from the adjacent bathroom, and I just shake my head. I hear the women talk, but I can't take anything in, only staring blindly with building rage at Gigi's abdomen.

Tasha walks back, and her gaze drops to where I'm holding the sweater up. She hisses in a breath.

A bruise the size of a fist has spread as if it's opening its fingers underneath her breast. I lift the sweater higher, looking to see if there's more, but can't see much more than her bra.

"There could be internal bleeding," I say.

"Yes." Tasha indicates I should lift Gigi so she can take off her sweater.

As Tasha is helping Gigi's arms out of the sleeves, the movement wakes her, and she blinks drowsily and confused, panic flitting through her eyes.

"Hey," I say as I cup her cheek. "It's okay. We're just checking where it's hurting, angel."

She looks up at Tasha. "You're here...and you look so well."

"I am," Tasha says with a soft smile. "Happily married to Matteo."

"I was so worried that day."

A look passes between the women. These two already have a bond nothing is going to break.

Gigi helps us peel her sweater off. I glance down her back before I ease her down to lie again. The bruising seems to be only on one side. "He punched me twice. And there's this cut." She shifts her arm where a make-shift bandage is dark red with caked-up blood.

"That doesn't look good." I meet Tasha's gaze.

"I'll clean the wound to see how serious it is," Tasha says.

We're holding our breaths as she rolls the bandage off and the facecloth pressed against Gigi's arm falls away. There's an inch-long cut in her upper arm, red, inflamed, and bruised.

"I'm okay, really, I am." Gigi tries to reassure us, but I sense she's brushing over it. "The pain meds are helping. It's my side...my ribs. There's nothing more serious than that and this little cut."

Tasha shoots me a glance, and I can see she gets the same feeling. That's not all of it. A toilet flushes, and a faucet runs. Carla comes to stand in the bathroom door, pale with an undertone of green.

"I'll ask Rosalia to come look after you, Carla. She's our housekeeper and lives next door," Tasha says as she holds out her hand for the younger woman. "We have another spare room, and you can have a shower and rest there while we take care of Gigi. Come with me. I'll also sort out the necessary to deal with her wound."

Gigi looks at her sister and nods. "I'm good, *cara*. Everything is going to be fine. I'll just be here. We're safe now."

"Okay," Carla says, hovering. "I'm... Call when you need me?" She hesitantly takes Tasha's hand.

"I will. Go get some rest. It's been too crazy." Gigi nods again, but she bites her lip as Tasha heads to the door with Carla in tow.

There's something she isn't telling me. Something she doesn't want her sister to hear. Or see. My gut twists. It's no secret what some crime rings do to their women. Whether wives or prostitutes or slaves. Tattoos, piercings, mutilations. Anything goes if you dig deep enough.

We say nothing until they've filed out of the room. Tasha closes the door, giving us privacy.

"Where else, Gigi? Show me. Now."

My tone is more clipped than I intended. I'm ready to rip her jeans off her body and inspect that sweet pussy that's been haunting me for weeks to see what punishment is in store for the man who did this to her.

She hesitates, her bottom lip quivering.

"Tell me. Or show me."

She meets my searching gaze, quiet tears escaping the corners of her eyes. "I haven't looked. I'm too scared."

Those tears kill me. Gigi Trapani scared? She kidnapped Matteo and barged in on a Mafia virgin auction! Where's the sassy woman who threw a champagne bottle at me in fury? I'd do anything to lure her out again.

"I've got you, angel."

"Okay." Her hand rests on her hip and points lower as she whispers. "Here. And I don't want to know. And Carla...Carla must never know."

I say nothing as she collapses her hand to the side, inviting me in. I unbutton and ease off her jeans. I'm so careful, so gentle, my fingers barely make a whisper of touch on her belly, but still, her skin sparks goose bumps.

As soon as I have the zip down, I see she's shoved something in the front of her underwear. "Lift your hips."

She does, and I have the jeans down in a gentle pull and toss them to the side. I scan her beautiful bare legs for markings, but there're only bruises on her knees and shins.

I glance higher to her sex and the splotches of caked blood on her panties where it seeped from the napkin stuck to her underwear.

"Fuck." I run my finger along the panties' edge and gently lift, my gaze on her face. It doesn't budge, and now, she's gone even paler.

"It was supposed to be bandaged but that never happened. Now it feels glued." She covers her face with her hands. "Every time I had to go to the bathroom, it would rip and bleed, so I started pulling the crotch away instead when I needed to go."

"Okay." That sounds so fucking painful. "I don't want to hurt you."

"Just do it already."

"Then open up for me, angel, so I can come in from both sides." I have my hand on her thigh, and with a little nudge, she lifts her leg up so I can hook the panty line deeper down by her sex.

She's dragging in haggard breaths with each scab that rips where the napkin has coagulated with blood to her skin. I'm gentle, careful, but she visibly flinches.

"You good?" I glance up at her. "Almost there."

"Yes." When my fingers have disconnected the last spot, the

whole thing shifts. She exhales a huff and opens her eyes for the first time. "Just take it all off."

I ease the panties off her legs, and she lies naked in front of me with only her breasts covered. Those bits of fabric aren't doing nothing much. Her nipples have pebbled, etched out in the thin cotton of her bra. *Fuck.*

"What did he do?" she asks, her voice quivering.

I'm staring at her mound, at the sweet tip of her pussy where blood has gravitated to and dried.

"Stephano! What do you see?"

"A death sentence, angel. That's what I see."

20

STEPHANO

My fingers tremble as rage floods every part of me. If the fucker who'd done this to her were in this room right now, he'd be dead in fucking minutes. I burn to caress the lines on her skin with my fingertips, to by some magic erase them with tenderness and care, but these are here to stay. This woman will never be unmarked again.

I tug the end of the comforter over her body, knowing with boiling fury that nothing I can do is going to take those marks away.

Worst of all is, this could be only the surface-level physical evidence of how he's hurt her. There are layers here, and I need to understand the full extent of what happened to her so I can help her. For Gigi's sake, I don't want to go there, but I have to. She's so fragile, and everything leading to this moment must remind her vividly of what happened on Friday night, but I can't walk out of here without having a complete tally of this man's crimes.

I reach for her hand where her fingers clench and rub at each other, tense. At my touch, she grips me tight, and I soothe my thumb over her knuckles until she stills. Her fingers are cold and trembling now, and I push down my own anger as I look into her eyes.

"Be honest with me, Gigi," I start, bracing myself to dig down into the deepest layer of her hurt. "Did he rape you before he did this to you?"

She swallows hard, trying to keep her emotions in check. "No, but—"

She stalls, biting down so hard on her bottom lip, I flinch. I wish she wouldn't feel this need to save face in front of me.

"But?" I urge her gently when she still hesitates. It's now or never. We might never have a moment like this again.

"He had his men there, and they all looked on as he—as he —" She chokes on her words and lets go of my hand to push her fist to her mouth. As sobs tear through her, she curls into a ball and onto her side, the ultimate protective position.

Fucking asshole. Another psychopath on the loose. Basically, torturing and degrading her—*his future wife*—in front of his men. They would never treat her with respect. Sounds like a situation I've been in. Sounds like a man I knew. The Don. Beating up his wife—*my mother*—in front of me.

I stroke her hair and gather the soft wisps at her temple to open her face. "You're going to be okay, angel."

It's a weak platitude, and I don't feel her physical pain, but inside me, there's a blind rage for the emotional damage that's been done.

Her skin is swollen, red, and inflamed. Thin strips of the top layer were sliced away, revealing the raw flesh underneath. Scarification. Cruel if unwanted. I bet he didn't even numb the skin. Now, it's oozing puss and needs antibiotics. It will heal but will leave a nasty scar.

Gigi will wear his mark until she dies. And I will kill the man who did this to her. I fist my hands and make the silent vow as my heart crashes around in my chest.

"What is it?" she whispers now, desperate.

Even with all the swelling, I could see what the fucker cut out on her skin. Two capital F's: the letters spoon each other, but don't touch, the lower F filling the blank spot under the upper F.

"It's his insignia. A double F for Franco Fiore. He did this to you on Friday night?"

"How do you know?"

I take her sweater and put it within reach. "Carla told us some of what happened. How he came over to choose a wife."

To think a man would do this to the woman he plans to honor, treasure, and protect.

It's in your blood.

I'd hack my ears off if it would mean I'd never hear those words again. In his voice from that night. The tone stating it was a foregone conclusion I'm like him. The voice is in my head, and I will live with it until the day I die.

"Yes. A wife, and Carla's at least half his age. I made him chose me."

"I bet you did."

She sits up with a soft moan and swings her feet to the floor. She pulls her sweater on but sways slightly, and I grip her shoulder to steady her.

I peer into her eyes. "Why were you being forced into marriage with him?"

She looks up at me. "Because Randazzo got killed, and the aftershocks are hitting the old order. Franco is taking over, and Vincenzo—my stepbrother—has to get our family into Franco's good graces. For all I know, they killed my stepdad." She shakes her head. "Not that it matters to you. You won't even know who Randazzo was."

My hand slips from her shoulder as cold, sharp stabs slice me up inside. The reason she got mutilated like this is *us. Il Consiglio*. And fucking Don Scalera—my own fucking blood—who is dead now, but whose reach still stretches beyond the grave. Don Scalera is responsible for this woman's shredded skin, and I want to fucking murder him. I never got the chance. I still suspect Matteo did all of us that favor. If only *Dad* could rise from the dead so I can kill him again, I'd make sure he felt every inch of what Franco has done to Gigi.

"Come," I say, forcing myself to be calm and in control of every last emotion. I can go rip loose at the gym later. "I'll help you to the bathroom and then go see if Tasha can lend you some clothes."

"Thank you."

I have her by the hand and guide her there. "Are you feeling faint?"

"No, just exhausted. The meds are helping a lot." Her voice breaks on the last words, and then a violent sob tears from her chest. "I'm so glad we made it."

Acting on instinct, I wrap her in my arms. I hold her close, cupping her head to my chest. "Let it out, angel, let it all out."

I won't let anybody hurt you ever again.

And that's the truth. Gigi might have insulted me and hit the one raw nerve that always triggers me, and I have reciprocated, but the vow I made to my mother is the one I actively live by.

I don't know how long we stand like this, but I let her cry. Eventually, a knock sounds on the bedroom door, and she quiets in my arms. I'm so tempted to press a kiss to her head, but instead, I let go as she shifts.

"Gigi? Stephano?" Tasha calls.

"I don't want her to see—to know—"

"Nobody's going to know, angel. Just you and me." I squeeze her shoulder. "You'll be fine by yourself?"

"Yes."

"I'll be back with something for you to wear." I leave her there and close the door, feeling crap about her having to wash herself without help, but she needs privacy, and I need to intercept Tasha.

Our gazes lock across the room. Tasha has a stack of clothes in her hands and a medical kit. "Rosalia is with Carla. I think she's in shock."

"I can imagine. Gigi's taking a shower."

"I've brought her some clean clothes. T-shirts and shorts, a dress if she feels like it, some PJs," she says as she puts the pile down on the bed. "She'll manage by herself?"

"Yes. You've called the doctor?"

"She needs meds for that wound. Doc will be here in the next hour."

"Good. When's Matteo back from his meeting?"

"Late this afternoon."

The faucet turns on in the bathroom, and I wish I had the right to walk back in there and help her.

This can't wait. I told Matteo *Il Consiglio* overstepped the boundary when his contact blew up Randazzo's compound, and now, we have proof of the consequences. But that's not what triggered this mess. Murdering Randazzo triggered it.

"I'll check in on her later, but for now, I'll be in Matteo's office."

I need to start digging. If Matteo could walk into Randazzo's compound and kill him, I don't see why I can't do the same with Franco Fiore. Only one problem: I have no intel on this guy, but I know how to dig.

Half an hour later, I've come up with nothing, and I'm frustrated as fuck. The guy is so deep underground, I'll have to rope Benedict in to get any information.

21

GIGI

I step in under the tepid water and shudder. I don't want it warmer, not with my raw skin. Bile rises in me as the water runs down my body and finds the grooves of those lines as if they're aqueducts. I inch a finger closer and feel the cut with the tip. I jerk away, too grossed out.

If I don't think about it, if I don't look at it, if the pain subsides which it will, this scar won't exist anywhere except in my memory. There, it will fade like all bad memories. I sag against the shower's cold marble wall and sob. With every heave of my chest, my ribcage protests.

A death sentence.

Stephano is like a flipped coin, and I don't know which side I'm dealing with. This isn't the cold and calculated man from Cannes who refused to touch me and stuck to his word. This is a man who had me from the moment I collapsed against his chest at the airport, holding me gently, carrying me, touching me with such care as if I would break. Telling me Franco Fiore signed his own death warrant on my skin.

Same coin, same man, and my body's same treacherous reaction. Why is it that most men are walking red flags, and then there's this one man who only needs to touch me, to tell me to behave, and to promise to murder my fiancé, who makes me want to curl up in his lap and beg him to—to—

God knows I've been fighting the memories of us in Cannes, but now that I've seen a different side of him, I'll never be able to shed them.

Stephano Scalera is a dangerous man, and not because he is Mafia, but because he's drilling a little hole in the walls of my rock-cold heart. I have vowed to never be involved with a man in the Mafia, never mind marrying one, and have steered clear of any serious relationships, because I don't trust men. They are all coins, and when most of them flip, it's to a side you don't want to know or experience.

I wash my hair and body, ridding myself of travel grime and spots of caked blood where I care to reach for it. Eventually, I feel as clean as I ever will, what with this degrading mark on my skin that will never wash off. At least Franco didn't rape me or claim me in any way beyond this.

I step out of the shower and towel off, then walk out to the bedroom to find Tasha's stack of clothes. I opt for a big T-shirt and go bare underneath. Voices sound from outside the door, followed by a knock.

"Yes?"

Tasha peers in. "It's the doctor. I'll leave you?"

"Yes, thank you."

A home visit... I don't want to know how much this is going to cost. I hope Matteo isn't the type to keep a tab.

To my surprise, it's an older Asian woman. She looks me over but doesn't smile. I bet she doesn't talk either. I sit on the bed as she pulls on surgical gloves. Without speaking, she deals with my arm, which has closed enough to no longer needs stitches. It's going to leave an ugly scar though. When I show her my cuts, she just shakes her head as she proceeds to clean them. I wince and curse under my breath, wishing she'd be gone already.

"Ribs?" she asks, and I lift my shirt higher. "Okay. I've seen a lot worse. He hit you twice?"

"Yes."

"Fucker." She starts to rummage in her doctor's bag, and I drop my shirt again. "I'm not going to cover the scarring, but I'll give you an injection to help fight the infection." She's pulling various items from her bag. "Use this ointment on your groin. And these pain pills and antibiotics. Finish the course. Call me if anything gets worse. Stand now. Butt cheek this side."

Obediently, I stand, glad she doesn't ask me to lie down on my stomach and hitch up my shirt. She's efficient, quick, and so to the point that it's over before I even know she's injected me.

As I drop the T-shirt, a knock sounds on the door, and she shakes her head. "It's never good when it gets busy here."

"Come in," I say, and Stephano swings the door open, holding a tray with food and water.

"Dr. Wong. Thank you for coming on such short notice."

She picks up her medicine bag, not sparing Stephano a glance. "Your guest needs rest. Make sure her infection doesn't get worse. Call me if it does."

"Yes, of course." He stands to the side as the small woman stalks out of the room. When he meets my gaze, there's a twinkle in his eye.

"She's scary," I say with a weak smile.

"Wait until she digs a bullet out of you. Zero sympathy." He places the tray on the bed as his gaze runs the length of my body. "Feeling better?"

"Yes. Thank you. Is Carla okay?"

"She's sleeping. Here's something to eat if you're hungry. Rosalia prepared some fruit and gnocchi."

I carefully sit down and take the bowl of gnocchi. From the

divine smell steaming from it, Rosalia can cook. And now, I want to cry again. Not because of everything that's happened, but because this is a bit like home. I didn't expect a warm welcome from the Scaleras, and Matteo hasn't even been here, but as for Stephano and Tasha, they've been nothing but kind and caring.

Stephano pulls the occasional chair closer and sits, leaning with his elbows on his thighs. "I promise I'll let you sleep, but before you do, tell me everything you know about Franco Fiore."

I've taken a bite and it's so good, but at his name, my stomach roils. I swallow, but the bite isn't going down with ease. I'm still tense, and this after getting here and the long shower.

"I don't know much. I met him for the first time on Friday night, and well… he's around forty, forty-five years old, could be older, could be younger. Body tattoo all the way up to his chin. On his hands…tattoos of snakes. I'm not sure if he's 'Ndrangheta. I doubt he's Cosa Nostra. I have no idea. I've been out of the loop for ages. It's as if he's crawled out from an underworld I didn't know existed."

Stephano nods. "And disappeared again."

"I wouldn't know about that."

"Do you think he'll come for you? Here?"

"I don't know. Why would he?" But I know exactly why Franco Fiore will hunt me down. Vincenzo sold me out in more ways than one. "Nobody knows where we are. That's why I contacted Matteo in the first place."

"Okay." He sighs, and I know exactly what that means. So many fucked up reasons why Franco will hunt me down—his wounded pride, for one. "We'll figure him out. I don't want you to worry about it, okay?"

I give an incredulous laugh. "You expect me not to worry that I have a mad man's target on my back?"

"No, because we always repay our debts. We'll be protecting you whatever it takes."

22

STEPHANO

It's late Sunday night. The usual *Il Consiglio* meeting is happening in Matteo's office, but we're short two brothers. Luca is overseeing a shipment that arrived late, and Dominic is in New York where he's been involved in some high-end security jobs. For the past thirty minutes, we've discussed Gigi and Carla's surprise arrival.

"The obvious solution is to marry her off to someone else, so she's no longer available to marry this Franco fucker." Benedict takes another swig of his whiskey. "Best plan, to be honest."

Matteo smirks. "And *you'd* sign up for that? I'm already married."

"I've never met this woman." Benedict points his glass in my direction. "Stephano is the obvious choice."

Matteo's gaze lands on me where I've frozen in my seat. Oh, boy. He's going to mess with me. I can just sense it.

"I've vowed to never get married," I say, hackles up, making sure I'm getting the first word in. "And you all know why. Plus, that only sorts out the one sister. What about Carla, the younger one?"

"We can get her into a university program here with a

student visa, so she won't have to leave," Matteo says, brushing Carla off. "Surely, this turf war won't last longer than the length of a bachelor's degree."

"Too many variables there," Benedict says with a smirk. "Not every student nails it the first time around."

I roll my eyes. Both Trapanis are still asleep, unaware we are deciding on their futures as if we own them, not owe them.

"Listen." I drag in a breath. They don't know the extent of this Franco fucker's sadistic cruelty, but there's one point I have to drive home. "Matteo killed Randazzo, and that triggered this whole fucking mess. He escaped Sicily on the Trapanis' yacht. I bet after Randazzo's estate got blown up, the airport wasn't exactly an option, so the only reason Matteo is here today, unscathed, are the Trapanis. We owe it to these girls to keep them safe, but marriage...that's taking it a bit too far."

"Why?" Benedict shrugs. "It's not as if you need to stay married. Divorce like any other couple once the danger has passed."

"Now-now," Matteo chirps. "Don't dish what you don't know. How else is she going to stay in this country legally? The last thing I want is Homeland Security sniffing around my ass."

"And marrying someone so they can stay in the US is a felony." I shift in my seat. So many reasons why this is a bad idea. As the Mafia, we're always walking a tightrope between the shadow world of crime and the real one where normal people exist. The police have their place, and although we can negotiate and straddle two worlds at the same time, we don't poke law enforcement for the fun of it.

"Did they travel on their normal passports or fake documents?" Benedict asks, ignoring my statement.

"They're fake passports."

We all turn towards the soft voice coming from the door. Fuck. Who knows how long she has been standing there. Did she hear about Randazzo?

"Gigi," I say as I stand. "Why're you up?"

She looks lost and forlorn in that oversized T-shirt and those sweatpants that are not letting her cuts breathe.

"I woke up and couldn't fall asleep again. It must be jet lag. I'm worried about Carla and got lost trying to find her room."

Sounds more like anxiety, what with those dark circles under her eyes. Maybe she needs to take pain meds. At the thought, I take a step towards her, wanting to wipe it all away. "Carla is down the corridor from your room. You must have taken a wrong turn."

"Welcome to Boston," Matteo says as he walks up to her. "Steph told us what happened."

She visibly flinches away as Matteo raises his hand—probably only to touch her shoulder in greeting—but my blood boils.

"Don't touch her. She's hurting." I take swift strides in their direction, ready to jerk him away from her.

"Sorry," she says softly as she inches towards me. "Being in a new place I don't know...I'm just rattled."

"It's okay, angel."

I wedge myself between her and Matteo. Benedict, as usual, hasn't even moved from his seat, but studies the whole scene like a spectator. Matteo steps away, and our eyes lock.

Yes, Matty, this woman is petrified and with reason.

"Hi," Benedict says, breaking the tense moment as he waves from his seat. "Benedict Scalera, the youngest."

"Hi." Gigi waves back, then folds her arms over her chest, protective, as her gaze jumps between us.

I get it, we're intimidating, especially when we're together—all of us built, tall, and tattooed. And there's only three of us here. We're also fiercely loyal and protective of each other, and we've taken the Trapani women under our wing. Nothing and nobody will dare touch them here.

"Come." I put my hand on the small of her back and guide

her to the sofa where I make sure she's comfortable. "We're trying to find a long-term solution," I say as I sit down next to her but giving her space. "I won't—I mean, *we won't*—send you back to Italy until things have settled in Europe."

Benedict cocks his brow at me, and I curse the Freudian slip as he leans forward in his seat. "You all met in Cannes, right?"

"Yes," Matteo says as he holds out an empty glass to Gigi, questioning if she'd like a drink. She nods, and he pours her a double whiskey and drops in a few ice cubes. "We met the night of the auction."

"And you left with Tasha." Benedict swings his whiskey glass in Matteo's direction, then swings it back to me. Ice rattles as he indicates to me and Gigi. "And you two—"

"Went our separate ways," I cut in, irritation grating.

Who knows what Matteo told the others, but I got razzed for weeks about how grumpy I was after that night in Cannes when Matteo left me with a mystery woman in red who promised to make my life hell. And then Tatiana died.

She overdosed as predicted, and everybody steered clear of me for days, letting me mourn the woman she once was, a very long time ago. After the assault, she was so fucking broken that the news of her death came as a relief to me. I can't watch a woman suffer like that, which makes this whole situation with Gigi even more intense. I've failed Tatiana. I've failed my mom. But fuck knows, I won't fail Gigi Trapani.

With Tatiana, I got in too deep, and for me, it will never be about love again. I've learned the hard way that Scalera boys don't get to love. We do, however, get to keep our vows.

I shift in my seat and inwardly groan as I watch Benedict put two and two together. That all-knowing brow cocks again.

"Sounds like unfinished business to me, Steph," he teases, a twitch to his lips. "I'm not needed here. I'll dig for you and see what I can find on Franco Fiore, but for the rest, I think you three can negotiate the next steps." He stands, puts his glass down on the coffee table, and shoots Gigi a smile. "We'll see each other around, *angel*."

My youngest brother is playing with fucking fire. "Watch your fucking tongue, Benny."

"Uh huh." Benedict chuckles as he walks to the office's door. "We all now know where yours has been, Fanny."

His sly laugh still echoes with his footsteps as he walks through the double-volume space of the adjacent living room. I glance at Gigi. Luckily, the whole interchange seems to have gone over her head.

Matteo's gaze volleys between the two of us. "Right," he says with an unnecessary twinkle in his eye. "Where were we?"

"Something about how we're going to stay here long term, and legally?" Gigi says. "I never intended for this to happen or to impose on you for longer than a few weeks."

"It's no imposition," he says. "We honor our debts. From what Stephano told us, there's no way you're going back to Italy until the dust has settled in Europe."

"He did? Tell you everything?" she asks then, her eyes on me.

There's trust in her gaze, but it seems to hover on a precipice.

"I drew a rough sketch of Friday night's events," I say, wanting to lean in and squeeze her hand to make her understand her secret is safe with me.

She swallows, clutching the glass of whiskey so hard, her fingertips are turning white. "Okay. What solutions did you come up with?"

"Carla is easy," Matteo says. "We have connections and can get her into any course she wants. Harvard, MIT, Emerson, whatever she wants to do, we'll make it happen."

"You can? Just like that?" Gigi's tone says it all. She doubts we have this level of influence in this city. "I honestly don't want a deal that's going to draw attention."

"We don't draw attention," I say. "It will all be above board."

She stares at me, incredulous. "Well. That's my sister sorted."

"As for you," Matteo says as he leans with his elbows on his knees, studying her closely. "Marriage is the easiest and quickest option to staying here long term."

"Marriage?" She chokes on the word. "To whom?"

I hate to admit the idea has grown on me since Benedict put it on the table. It's grown so much on me, there isn't an ounce of rebellion in me now.

"To me," I say with a smirk. *Because fucking karma.*

"Marriage? To *you*?" Gigi's eyes widen, and then she laughs, but it's filled with disdain.

Yep, there it is. The snobbish superiority that grated on me in Cannes. "Yep, to me, since Matteo's already taken."

"I've vowed to never marry into the Mafia," she spits out. "And I certainly didn't just jump ship from one crazy bunch of Italian crime lords to land in a bucket of American ones."

"Angel," I say, reaching for her hand. "We both know the Scaleras don't operate like the Franco Fiores of the world."

Her eyes flash with fury as she pulls her hand away, showing a glimpse of the woman I met in Cannes. There she is. My pulse skips a beat in relief. Thank God.

"It's the perfect solution," Matteo says as he stands. "Stephano has vowed to never get married. You've vowed to never get married to the Mafia, so getting a divorce down the line will be a breeze." He downs the last of his whiskey. "I'll leave you to discuss the details."

We both watch as he walks out of the office.

"I'm a good Catholic girl. We don't divorce," she mutters under her breath.

"Hmm. Good Catholic girls don't get fucked with champagne bottles either," I say as I take a sip of my whiskey.

"Fuck you," she hisses.

Oh, boy. That night still triggers her, too.

"To do so will be a pleasure, I'm sure."

She's got no reason to complain; she did, after all, get two orgasms out of it. Things would most probably not have come to this if I actually had fucked her.

"God." She turns to me, eyes wide. "How arrogant can one man be?"

"How conceited can one woman be?" I counter.

"I'm not getting married," she snapped at me. "Not to you, of all people."

I don't blame her for this reaction. Gigi Trapani stumbled into my life on that marina in Cannes and kicked my usual equilibrium out of sync. What she'd said to me that day pressed my buttons because I never hurt her, and this only prompted me to put her in her place.

But after today and seeing her this brutalized, never mind the burning need to protect her, I have this urge to show her I'm not like Franco Fiore. I want to marry her, not only to prove to myself I'm a better man than her fiancé, but as a test to myself, to show *me* who I am. To see whether it's really *in my blood*.

Images of the Don with Mom flash through my mind. Of the night I walked in on them when he was beating her up. How she called me later that week, her face untouched but her body broken, and extracted a promise from me. I made a vow to her on those wedding rings Tasha wore in Cannes. I will never do that to a woman again, even though the Don forced me to join in the *fun* because *it's in my blood*.

And then, I went and beat someone my own age, almost to death, proving him right. I've never tested the theory with a woman. The horror of being like him drives me to the gym every day, beating the shit out of myself before I can take it out on someone else.

Control. That's all I want.

The beauty of this potential fake marriage is in how it has

an end date. It'll be a test run. A taste of something I've promised to never have. I've proven I'm in total control of my mind and body when it comes to Gigi Trapani. And the best part of it is, as much as this woman tests my limits, she's also the type who won't take shit from any man.

She's my perfect solution.

"When you've calmed the fuck down," I say, so tempted to brush a strand of hair from her face in truce, "let us know what alternative solutions you've come up with." I keep my hands to myself as I stand and stare her down. "One thing I can tell you is that we keep our records clean. Irrespective of the debt between our families, no Scalera is going to harbor an illegal in his house for the fun of it. Eyes are on us all the time, and just like you, we don't like to draw attention."

She glares up at me and shakes her head. "This was never the plan."

"Plans change." I point towards the door in invitation. "I'll show you to Carla's room before I head out."

23

GIGI

The problem is I never had a plan beyond fleeing. Now what? I could kick myself for never thinking beyond coming here and being safe. I always thought London would be far enough, but the world has shrunk, and tentacles have stretched. I didn't foresee the magnitude of this mess in Europe, or Vincenzo's duplicity in handing us over without blinking to that psychopath.

I'm a fool. I got away from Franco, but he's the type who will come for me—*for us*. Not only because he's a sadist, but because I have something he needs. Desperately. It's been eating at me since Friday night, because I don't know what Franco Fiore knows. If Vincenzo spoke out of line, we are all in very real danger.

I heave out of the deep seat, trying not to wince, and follow Stephano out of Matteo's office. We ascend the stairs to the second floor, and for the first time, I take in the penthouse apartment with more than just panic. The double-volume living room has massive glass windows and doors that lead out to a big rooftop garden and balcony with breathtaking views.

From here, I can see the Boston skyline, whichever part it is, but the solid dark swatch can only be the ocean.

We're on the landing, and Stephano leads the way past my room.

"This is Carla's."

He knocks softly, waits, then opens the door and holds it. I scoot past him to step inside and spot my sister, fast asleep on her side with her back to me. Unscathed. Safe.

I'll do anything to keep her here, just like this.

But marriage? That never crossed my mind. It's such an easy, perfect solution. With a difficult, imperfect man. Surely, Stephano Scalera can't be my only option...but in this case, it's a choice between the devil you know and the devil you don't. I have no idea how long we'll last if we're out on the streets in Boston. How long it will take for Franco to track us down. Being a Scalera wife will come with top-tier security, and by the look of Matteo's apartment, it can't be all bad. There's money here, and in my experience, you can put up with a lot for an easy life of luxury.

I am such a fucking Mafia princess.

The truth hits me like a bullet to the heart, and I've never hated myself more than in this moment. It's in my freaking blood. I'm going to cave in and break my own vow at the first sign of real danger. I thought I was stronger than this, but I'm no match for Franco Fiore.

The question is whether Stephano or any other Scalera is a match for his level of psychotic. I know so little of Stephano and the rest of his brothers, so I can't say. My gaze drops to where he's holding the door, his strong fingers curled over the knob, his skin unmarked with nothing but the last letters of a tattoo peeking out under his rolled-up sleeve. I still feel his touch from this morning. He looked after me in such a gentle, caring way, telling me Franco Fiore wrote his own death warrant on my skin.

The cuts pulse right on cue. I've seen what Franco is capable of, and that was the tip of his iceberg. He promised to do more to me once we're married. I've also experienced Stephano Scalera's slow seduction and the control he had over himself. Now, he rests a hand on my lower back and nudges me out of the room, in the possessive way I've always loved. He closes the door with a soft click, but that hand doesn't move away. Even through my T-shirt, his touch makes my skin tingle with goose bumps as we move down the landing.

Screw my life. The only thing I can think of when I look at him is how he made me come, twice in a row. *Without even touching me.* Then insinuating I'm a whore and what we did was cheap, wanting only to degrade me.

I step away from his touch as we come to a stop at my bedroom door. "How many brothers do you have?"

He hitches a brow. "We're five. Used to be six."

I drop my gaze as I suck my lip. "I'm sorry."

"Yeah. You know what they say. Only the good die young."

I drag in a slow, deliberate breath, steeling myself.

"Any other takers?" I ask, putting my feelers out.

Stephano searches my face as my question slowly sinks in. His face splits into a smile, and then he laughs—*actually laughs*—deep from his belly. It transforms his face, making him look even hotter than before. Somewhat naughty, less serious, and more relaxed.

Why must he be so goddamn sexy, and why must my hormones go into overdrive around him?

"Ah, Gigi," he huffs as he catches his breath. "There's no chance in hell any of my brothers will step up and be the martyr here."

Heat spreads over my whole body in indignation. *Martyr?* That's taking it a bit too far. "Why is that?"

He shakes his head. "Because they know we met in Cannes and *something* happened, even though I told Matteo *nothing* happened. Matteo and Benedict both saw straight through us earlier tonight. Trust me, my other brothers will read between the lines soon enough and give you a very wide berth."

"Is that so? Why?"

He raises his hand—his *filthy Mafia paw*—and cups my cheek, his fingertips resting softly on my temple as he traces a line over my bottom lip with his thumb. "Because you're mine, angel, whether you like it or not."

His touch is like a drug. Ever since our first encounter, I've only wanted more, and then he denied me. God, what a pleasure it would be to have him begging for it, like my body is secretly begging for him now. I hurt everywhere, but I pulse with desire too, which is a dichotomy I never thought possible. I want to lean into his touch, but instead I step away at the exact moment he drops his hand.

"Sleep on it, angel," he says as he turns toward the staircase. "And give me your answer tomorrow."

"You haven't even asked me a question." I'm even more irritated he thinks I will seriously consider this dumb proposal.

"If you expect me to drop to one knee, don't hold your breath."

Ugh! I grunt inwardly. This guy is a total dick. "Just know I'll be the most horrible wife you'll ever have."

He laughs as he starts descending the stairs. "Then I'll be the best husband you'll ever have, just to piss on your pity party."

This has gone into such fictional territory now, I can't help myself. "What other terms do you have?"

Stephano slows down and turns to face me, as if we're Romeo and Juliet and this is the balcony scene. Instead of breaking into a soliloquy about my beauty and his undying love for me, he retraces his steps and comes to stand flush with me.

I inch back to get away from his dominance, his body radiating heat and power. My back connects with my room's closed door. He comes even closer then, leaning with his arm against the doorjamb and trapping me with his body.

Oh, God. We've been here before. That night in Cannes. Him in total control of himself and the situation, me a wanton mess. I inhale his scent as my eyes run over the stubble on his jaw, up to his ear and a knife scar below his lobe. I've never noticed it before, but half an inch deeper and it could have been deadly. We don't touch, but my breath has caught, and when our gazes connect, the look in his eyes sends shivers of desire down my spine.

"Of all the shit they could lock me up for, marriage fraud won't be one of them. So this will be a real marriage," he says, his tone soft but serious. "You'll move in with me, I'll look after you as I would look after the wife I vowed to never have, and you will let me take care of things, no questions asked."

I close my eyes for a second, dipping into the dream of letting go and having this man take care of everything, Franco Fiore included.

Allowing him to look after a wife he vowed to never have. That could involve so many things...

It's too easy. It's too dangerous. I know what Stephano Scalera is capable of, and it's a whole new level of danger I've never anticipated.

I can't let him have control over me like this. Already, this situation is veering towards being a repeat of Cannes, but this time, so much more is at stake.

He's already proven how easily he can make my body succumb to him, but getting more intimate with him, going all the way, will connect me with him on an emotional level I can't afford. No, not with this man. There is something about him that will make me latch onto him, a needy mess of a woman who'd always want more, need more, give more, until there was no return.

I'm so used to keeping my distance, knowing where to draw

the line to protect myself when it comes to men. I'd be an idiot to think having sex with Stephano would be a one-off. The way that night in Cannes has been occupying my mind, my fantasies, only gives a hint of what going all the way with him would do to me. Once will never be enough and I won't be able to distance myself from him. I'd fall hopelessly in love.

Falling in love is the last thing I can afford, least of all with a man in the Mafia. I can't break every vow I've ever made to myself by falling irretrievably in love with Stephano Scalera.

Thank God a marriage to him will be temporary, but for my sake, it will also have to be as short as possible. And as much as I want him to succumb to me, to lose control for once, I can't afford for it to happen.

When I look at him again, his eyes are so close, I can see how the lighter milk chocolate brown on the inside of his iris melts into the darker outside rim.

"And a divorce at the end of it, no questions asked?" I murmur, trying to steel myself against his charm which he turns on like a faucet, but being weak in the knees at him standing this close to me again.

"Yes. You'll go back to Italy, and our lives will go on as if the marriage never happened." His gaze caresses my face, as if he's memorizing each part of my bone structure like a sculptor would. "What are your terms, angel?"

"My terms?" Except for making his life hell? Which would probably grow old quickly once routine sets in. "We'll never consummate the marriage." Being a good Catholic girl, I need a solid reason for divorce. *As if.* He doesn't need to know what his physical presence does to me. "We'll never have sex. *Ever.*"

There. I've said it. He can have everything except *me.*

Stephano pushes away from the wall, a smirk on his face. "That's your only stipulation?"

"Yes. No kissing either. No nothing." That should cover all bases.

"Right. No kissing, no sex *ever*, angel, because you definitely don't want me to fuck you. Noted."

Stephano is out of my personal space and down the stairs so quickly, I feel like catching a breath. And throwing something at him. He is such an arrogant ass. He doesn't look back, not once as he jogs down the stairs or when he crosses the open-concept living area to the foyer that leads to the front door.

If only I could have a smidgen of the control he seems to have over himself and over everything he does, I'd be at peace around him. But I don't. My body's reaction to him belies every emotion I'm trying to suppress when it comes to Stephano.

God. I love to hate him, because all I can do is stare after him as he walks away, sagging against the door with the sinking feeling that I've just denied myself the thing I secretly want the most.

24

GIGI

I struggled to fall asleep last night. Our options are limited. I can't come up with any other solutions, and panicking doesn't help. It rises in me every time I think back of Friday night, because I have no clue what happened to Don Trapani. Whether he is dead or alive.

We're cut off from the rest of the world. I desperately need to shop for some basics, and even this seems like a mountain to climb now we're stranded. Tasha lent me some clothes, and the adjacent bathroom is kitted with everything I need, but this isn't sustainable either. Stephano's promise he'll *look after the wife* he vowed to never have and *take care of things* is very tempting, but I'm not sure what he'll table under *look after the wife* and *take care of things.*

After showering, I deal with my cuts while trying not to look at them or gag, and dress again in some borrowed clothes. As I open the door to the landing, voices echo from downstairs. This apartment is weirdly soundproof—I wasn't even aware other people were awake. By the stark sunlight falling through the windows, it's past midday already.

I glance over the glass railing to the big room below. Carla sits at the dining table with Tasha, Matteo, and Stephano. Several boxes, empty plates, and some food platters clutter up the twelve-seater. Two chairs are covered with clothes, and a pile of boutique totes and shoe boxes are discarded to the side.

As if she senses me, Carla looks up with a smile. "Hey, Gigi."

Tears I have no control over well in me. She looks so much better. Rested, relaxed...*happy*? It's the last thing I ever expected. Carla is a lot of things, but happy isn't exactly one of them. Parts of her are still a teenager, whereas she thinks she's a full-grown adult.

The rest of the group turn their eyes up to me, but I'm only drawn to Stephano's which seem to inspect every inch of me in slow motion. Heat blazes a trail where his gaze makes a journey over my body, and I pull away from the glass railing to descend the stairs.

"I overslept," I say in excuse. It's so late, they've already had lunch.

"It's a good thing," Tasha says as she comes up to me. "Have something to eat."

"You look better for it." Matteo pushes a plate laden with salad and roast chicken in my direction.

"Thank you." I sink into the chair Stephano holds for me. He hasn't said a single word, but when I meet his intense gaze, his brow is quirked in question. *Dammit.* "What's all of this?" I ask as he settles back in his seat next to mine.

"Stephano brought us laptops and cellphones," Carla says, not hiding her enthusiasm. "And some clothes. Gigi, you need to settle with him."

"Of course." I eye the brand-new laptops and latest-edition phones, making a rough calculation in my head. At this rate, my fifty thousand euros isn't going to last very long. I have more funds, but they're trickier to get hold of. And there's my business I don't know how I'm going to keep afloat from here.

"It isn't necessary," Stephano says. "The electronics are standard company issue, and the clothes...well, it's only to tide you over until you have the energy to shop for yourselves."

"Heavens," Carla says on a sigh. "I'd love to go shop in New York."

I want to reach over the table and shake her. "This isn't exactly a holiday, Carla. And please tell me you haven't gone and randomly messaged your friends and told them where you are?"

"No! God, do you take me for such an idiot?"

Heat flushes my face, and I drop my gaze. Having a tiff with my sister in front of the Scaleras isn't how I wanted to start my day.

"I've told her to be careful and wait," Tasha says. "Don't worry, we've got this."

Tasha and Carla look at each other, and my sister's lips twitches with a smile. Who knows what happened this morning while I was asleep? These two seem to be thick as thieves already, and as much as I hoped to close the gap between Carla and me, I just cracked it open wider again.

"We've also looked at courses for her to take, given what she wanted to do in Italy. It would be easy to get her into something here. There are so many universities and options in Boston," Tasha says. "And I have time to take her around. My own classes only start in September."

Hell, Tasha's young, but I didn't realize she's still a student. My face must give my shock away because she chuckles.

"I'm doing medicine," she says in explanation. "And it takes forever."

"Steph," Matteo says as he stands. "I'll leave you to sort out what else they need. I've got to get to work."

I stand, too. "Thank you for everything, Matteo."

"Thank Stephano." Matteo smirks. "He's two steps ahead of everybody here."

He leans down and kisses Tasha on the forehead, but she

pulls him in for a lingering one on the mouth. It's somehow so intimate, I look away only to meet Stephano's gaze where he's staring at me.

I sink back in my seat, wishing I was anywhere else.

"Thank you, Stephano." I hope that was official enough. "Let me know how much I owe you. We're a lot of things, but we're not leeches."

"No, you're not." Tasha leans over and touches my arm. "I know what you would have done for me, so it's a pleasure to help you out. I was thinking of driving Carla around this afternoon to show her a few places, if you don't mind? We waited to see if you want to come with us?"

My gaze jogs between the two women. I can only imagine what would happen if I said no to Carla right now. "I'm not up for it, and we have a lot to discuss—"

"I know, Gigi, but later, okay?" Carla takes her laptop and phone and bundles the stack of clothes into her arms. "I'd be sorted for university here, and it would be great to do a gap year in Boston, don't you think?"

A year? She thinks we're going to be here for a full year? I can't leave my clients hanging or take my fingers off the pulse of the art scene in Europe for so long. I might as well close shop. "Yes, a gap year would be fun, but—"

"You should know. You did three years in London."

I refrain from rolling my eyes. It's always tit for tat with her. "We'll talk about university later. As for this afternoon, you can only go if it's safe."

For this, I glance in Stephano's direction.

"Of course it's safe," Tasha says as she stands. "I have Burley with me and a driver. We can have an extra security detail if you think it's needed?" She looks at Stephano for confirmation, and he nods. "See? It's going to be fine."

"Yay!" Carla hands Tasha some clothes to help carry, and together, they take the stairs, deep in cahoots. "Thank you,

Steph, I love everything you and Tasha got for me," Carla calls down as if in an afterthought as they reach her room. "I'm going to try on some of these and wear them now."

"Any time, Carla," he calls back.

Steph? Just like that, my little sister is on a nickname basis with him. Her bedroom door clicks closed, and then it's almost eerily quiet as only the two of us are left.

Stephano turns to me, and there's a wry smile on his lips. "Giving you hell, isn't she?"

I poke at my salad. "I've never felt our ten-year age gap more than now, to be honest. She's spoilt and reckless."

"She's just young, and you've protected her, with your life by the sounds of it."

I blink, wishing he could make me angry instead of poking at my emotions that have been so close to the surface since Friday night. "She doesn't understand. She's grown up with so many layers of protection, she can't fathom the danger—" I break off. I'm trembling, the lettuce leaf on my fork shaking as if there's a breeze. "And even now, doesn't she worry about Papa? I don't know what happened to Don Trapani—"

"We've had news," he interrupts. "We should have told you first thing. Don Trapani is fine."

I drop my cutlery to my plate and turn to him, desperate. "How do you know?"

"Matteo has a contact on that side who has an inside track on what's happening. He used to work for this Randazzo, so Matteo reached out last night and had a message from him this morning."

My heart pounds, lodged in my throat. They know someone who used to work for Randazzo. "What's his name?"

"I don't know, but I trust Matteo. He just calls him the mole."

I search his eyes, trying to find the lie in his words, but there's none. "And where's my stepdad now?"

"He's in Lake Como, under house arrest as Franco's waiting to see if you contact him. Franco has no clue where you are, but the search is on."

My stomach twists, and bile rises in my throat. I shiver and then it overwhelms me. I'm trembling uncontrollably.

"Hey," Stephano says as he leans closer. His hand cups my neck, and he pushes my jaw with his thumb, forcing me to look at him. "Gigi. You need to be honest with me here. If there's more to Franco Fiore's urge to marry you than business connections, I need to know. Now."

Gentle. Always so freaking gentle. And warm. I swallow, at a crossroads with this man.

"I can't help you if you're not honest with me, angel."

"I know."

I lean into his touch, and he circles my neck, pulling me closer. This has been pressing on my chest for ten heavy years, but to finally share this secret with a man I barely know...it's pure madness. Evidently though, the secret about the Trapani family finances is out already, thanks to Vincenzo. At least, the Scaleras have no business in Italy, and by the looks of it, don't need the money.

"I'm pretty lucky to be alive," I whisper. "Franco offered to marry me, but what he really wants are my hands and my eyes."

"What?" Stephano's eyes grow dark, and he drops his head even closer to mine. "Why?"

"Ten years ago, when my mom died, most of Don Trapani's unrecorded assets were put in my name, with the understanding that when Carla turns eighteen, we'll split it again, as she was underage. I'd hope it slipped everybody's minds, but clearly, it hasn't. Vincenzo must have told Franco about the funds. I'm the only one who can unlock secret vaults the Trapanis have in the Swiss banking system without jumping through some serious hoops. With my fingerprints and retina scans."

Stephano's expression says it all. Shock and disbelief. "Why would anybody do that?"

"Don Trapani saw this day coming. Vincenzo isn't a good man, and he wants it all for himself. I bet he's in bed with Franco Fiore in more than just a metaphorical sense. This was always the Don's way of keeping me alive."

"And to protect you from your own brother?"

He drops his hand away, and I miss the reassuring touch.

"He isn't my brother. For ten years, it's worked. I never needed a bodyguard, and Vincenzo left me alone. Those vaults are probably the best-guarded secret in Europe, but I'll be pretty dead once they have what they want."

"Which is?"

"Blood diamonds and physical gold. Hundreds of millions of euros of both." I'm in such a chokehold, my breathing is strained. "One of the pillars of the Trapani fortune." And one I've vowed to never touch. "Once laundered, it's all the money they'll ever need to expand their operations and whatever criminal shit they're involved in now. Franco doesn't want me. The marriage will be a mere by-product. What he wants is the money."

We just stare at each other, knowing the truth. In our world, there are no pre-nuptial contracts, no law that binds us like the general populous. In my case, Franco Fiore would torture me until I caved in and took him to the vaults to raid as much as he could.

"And he'd hack off my hands if it were only the fingerprints he needed." I shudder as I choke up. I've had enough of Franco's torture to last me a lifetime.

Stephano's arm is around me, and he pulls me close. I collapse against his chest as sobs rip through me.

"Carla knows all of this?"

"No." I sound strangled. "She turned eighteen three months ago, and I've been too busy to go do the necessary. Don Trapani didn't push me either to get it done. In fact, I forgot about it, on and off, you know?"

Now I understand why Don Trapani let it slide, too. If half the amount were in Carla's name, she would be as much a target as me. Thank God none of it is in her name. Don Trapani made sure his own daughter is safe. I don't want to think he's serving me up to Franco Fiore as a sacrificial lamb, because that isn't his nature. None of us saw this coming, and who knows how Vincenzo manipulated his own father?

"We've protected her to the last," I say. "And I won't stop."

He holds me as his hand strokes my arm. "There's only one way this ends. You know that, right?"

I nod. I've always known. Married or not, the end game for Franco Fiore and me has always been like writing on the wall.

Until death do us part.

25

STEPHANO

It's a witch hunt. And they're going to track her down, use her, and then burn her at the stake. She's so fragile in my arms, and now she's trusted me with her truth, it's as if she's punched a hole straight through my defenses, opening my heart for an invasion.

There's been something about this woman from our first meeting in Cannes. I've vowed to never let someone in, that Tatiana was the last, but Gigi...she's different. She's from my world and in so much trouble, it's going to take the whole squad of Scaleras to get her out of this mess alive.

Upstairs, Carla's bedroom door opens, and Tasha walks out with Carla right behind her.

Gigi pulls out of my arms and wipes at her face as she glances up at her sister, who is oblivious to the level of danger here.

"Oh," Gigi breathes. "She always looks so pretty. Just like our mom always did."

The love in her eyes as she looks at her sister feels like an echo of my own for my brothers. I get it. Here is someone who would die to keep her sister safe.

The two women head down the stairs.

"Tasha needs this as much as Carla," I say softly. "After everything that happened in Sicily and Cannes, and with Matteo, she's disconnected from her usual friend group. This is good, for both of them."

Gigi nods, composing herself.

"You look beautiful," she says as Carla comes up to the table.

"Tasha sorted me out this morning." Carla smiles and gives a twirl, making the white summer dress flare up. "To think the boutique's owner delivered everything within an hour after we spoke to her. And all the sizes are just right."

"We'll see you later," Tasha says as she hooks her purse over her shoulder. "I have my phone should you need us."

"Have fun," Gigi calls as they walk off.

I lean back, in awe. Carla didn't even pick up the fact that her sister is distraught. The front door clicks closed, and the women are gone.

"What now?" Gigi asks after a moment of silence between us.

"From where you're sitting now, I bet you don't think we can extract you out of this situation. But trust me, we can."

"But how? I can't run forever. I'd rather hand over the money to Franco on a platter, but I don't want to support what they are doing in Europe. I hate the roots of our fortune, and I know the type of crime rings Franco's type runs. Underage...all-age sex trafficking—" She breaks off, her fingers working her T-shirt's thin fabric as she purses her lips, trying to curb her tears.

"For which you've been brutally marked," I complete her sentence. "We both know Franco will push you into that as soon as he has what he wants."

If he doesn't kill her.

She sucks her bottom lip and closes her eyes, trying to control her emotions.

"And the drugs," she whispers. "Human trafficking that includes everything from the whole to parts. Slavery."

"Angel. Franco Fiore is a dead man. We just have to figure out how. And for that, I need my brothers. Please trust me."

"But why? Putting yourself in danger like this for someone you don't know—"

"I know you better than a lot of people I spend time with."

She cups her hands to her face to hide a blush as she leans her elbows on the table.

"Hey," I say as I reach for her fingers to peel her hands from her face, wanting her to look at me.

She lowers her hands and stares at me through tears.

"At least if we get married, you know I'm not after your money, because we discussed it yesterday before I knew about this situation."

A chuckle bubbles up, and she gives me a woebegone smile. "I vowed to never marry into the Mafia."

"I'd like to think there's more to me than being in the Mafia," I say with a lopsided grin. "And it won't be forever."

She shakes her head. "I don't get why you'd do it. You've got nothing to gain out of this if you're not in it for the money." She searches my gaze, her eyes like shovels digging straight to my soul.

I don't look away, tempting as it is, but let her see what she can. "I made a vow, to my mom, that I will protect women, any woman, and all women, irrespective of circumstances. This is what it takes, and I'll do it, for her and for the sacred vow I made."

And for revenge. When it comes to Franco's level of brutality, which echoes the Don's, revenge is infinite.

"You'll break one vow to honor another?"

"Yes. The one about never marrying is one I made to myself. The one I made to my mom supersedes all others." I reach for her hands where she's fidgeting with her napkin now, her lunch pushed to the side. She hardly had two bites. I wouldn't be able to eat either if I were her. "The first step to secure your safety is to give you my name. Nobody fucks with what belongs to me."

"Here maybe, but Franco is in Italy."

"And you're not going back there. Not until this has been settled."

"So, you're going to go there? Don't be crazy. It isn't your territory."

No, it isn't. But I'll have something Franco wants, and by the sounds of it, he wants it desperately. If we can get him to come here, we'll be ready for him.

"We have time to make our plans." To set a trap. Already, an idea is taking shape, but I'll need my brothers' help to fine-tune it. As a team, we never fail. "Come see what the boutique dropped off for you."

I want to distract her and de-escalate the tension in her body, so I round the table to where Carla and Tasha draped her clothes over a dining chair.

She stands, eyeing the two dresses I hold up by their hangers. "That's this season's Dior."

"It is?" I turn to look at the label. "Yes."

"Stephano," she groans. "I can't afford dresses with those price tags right now."

I shrug. "I can. Plus, we might be American, but we're Italian. I won't have my wife walk around in anything less than couture perfection."

I love how she's comfortable in the soft T-shirt Tasha dug out from who knows where, but I burn to see her in a beautiful dress again. Somehow, that will reassure me she's still the same confident woman I met in Cannes, and that Franco didn't break her.

Gigi scoffs and rolls her eyes. "As if. You haven't even asked me yet."

"Don't hold your breath, angel," I tease. "Here." I reach out for a tote the other women didn't unpack as I made sure the delivery came directly to me. "Tasha and Gigi helped picked out most of your things, but this, I got for you."

She takes the pale pink tote from me and peeks inside. Then she puts it down on the table and pulls the first item from the bag. "What is...*oh*."

The blush is back, and I drink it in. This woman is all lady, but wanton in all the ways that make me so fucking hard. And I can't wait to rip this off her, or even better, work my way up to her naked butt and bend her over, her hair falling loose over her shoulders, then fuck her like she needs to be fucked.

"It's so old school...and delicate." She holds up the full-length white cotton nightgown as her fingers trace the lace on the bust. "And soft. And wide."

"And perfect to let things heal."

"God." With a sigh, she lowers it to the side and feels for the other things I got her. "Why?" she asks as she lifts silk and satin from the bag, not looking at the individual items but fisting them and holding them out to me.

Granted, I've gone overboard as I got carried away in the lingerie section. I aimed more for comfort than anything else, but I know she'll look sexy in everything I got her.

"Because when I told you I'll take care of things, angel, I wasn't fucking around."

26

STEPHANO

"This is your guy," Benedict says as the projector throws an image on the screen of a man with his side to the camera. His face is turned toward the lens, but it's clear he was unaware someone was taking this photo.

"Matches the image the mole sent through," Matteo says.

At least we still have that contact in Italy, and Matteo strengthened the connection when he was there earlier this summer. Franco Fiore's neck tattoo is just as Gigi described it.

"He likes his tattoos," Benedict says as he slides to the next image. "And apparently, snakes are his favorite."

The one photo is a close-up of Franco as he smokes a cigarette. His hands are tattooed with snakes, slithering over his fingers as if they're branches. What an idiot. To make yourself so easily identifiable.

We're in a boardroom at our security company's head offices, technically Dominic's domain, but all five of us are here to strategize. Gigi and Carla have been in Boston for five days now. Dominic and I have been working on their security detail, putting new things in place for Gigi's imminent arrival at my apartment. We've been in each other's company a lot, but there's always someone else around, so we haven't spoken about marriage again, but it will happen.

"There isn't a lot on him, as expected. Let's just say, he isn't the type you want to meet alone in the dark." We've been waiting for Benedict to scour his sources for proper intel on Franco and to dig around on the dark web. "He's a known sadist and has grown a bit wild since he got clean. As a teen, he used to work in some cocaine packaging plant. Got a bit hooked. Italian parents, both dead, ex 'Ndrangheta. When they died, he was forced to go live with an uncle in Calabria. Said uncle was a Randazzo henchman. And the rest is history, as they say."

"Just your typical Mafia bedtime story then," Dominic says with a grimace.

"He has a weakness. Once a user, always a user," Luca says.

"Maybe," I say. "He looks like the type who loves power more than cocaine."

Franco got off drugs and kept off them. That's control, mind over matter, and an iron will. Good. I know the type. Like me, he must do something to keep himself in check. Something that feeds the hole in his soul. I shudder as I imagine that snaked hand wielding a scalpel, Franco relaxing into the high of cutting into skin and smelling blood. Observing his victim's pain and feeding off it like a parasite.

My fingers twitch, my thighs tense with the need to squeeze all the air out of his lungs. I exhale slowly.

"What's the plan?" Matteo asks. "We obviously need to get him here. We don't stand a chance on his home ground."

"No. And I don't see why he'd come here," Benedict says. "Gigi is charming, but—"

"She's also worth almost a billion euros," I cut in. It's time to put all the cards on the table here.

"What?" Matteo says.

Every man in this room looks at me with wide eyes.

"Trapani's illicit diamonds and gold locked up in Switzerland. Only she has direct access to it without a shitload of checks and balances. It was a family secret. Obviously no longer."

"How do you even clean a billion euros?" Dominic groans. "It's a money laundering nightmare."

"All I know is Franco has a plan, and her stepbrother, Vincenzo Trapani, has sold her out." I bet it's because she refused to marry him. I can see that happening. I'd love to meet the fucker in person.

"That's brutal. Imagine selling out your sisters," Luca says as he leans on the table. "So, we have something Franco wants. He'll have to come here to get it."

"Exactly. He won't be able to fly over a massive security detail and will want men for hire on this side." I nod in Benedict's direction. "You are an unknown entity, to be honest. You literally live underground, so it would make sense for you to head this fake operation."

"Geez, thanks, Fanny," Benedict says.

"You're welcome, Benny." I suppress a smirk as he rolls his eyes.

"Let's hear your plan then, Steph," Matteo says as he leans back in his chair.

This is how we made Randazzo's assassination happen. This time, we're going to invite the fucker in, just like Randazzo had invited Matteo into his sanctuary. Despite being the Don, Matteo defers to me here, and I appreciate the respect and trust.

This idea has been brewing for the past few days, but I need my brothers' input to see how we can catch Franco Fiore and reel him in.

"Benedict will set up a security company on the dark web that runs on the east coast, men for hire with solid track records, reputations, references, the whole shebang."

Benedict cocks a brow as Dominic wipes at his jaw.

"And then?" Dominic asks.

"Then we make sure it's Benedict's men Franco hires when he comes to town."

"And he basically walks into a trap, and we get to finish him off," Matteo concludes.

"Yep." *I'll* finish Franco off. Gigi will be my wife. I've seen what he's done to her, so I'll kill him with my bare hands if that's what it takes. "There can be some bait and switch—"

"Bait and switch?" Luca laughs. "We're not twelve anymore, Steph. Plus, there're more things that differentiate us now."

"To us, yes, but I bet both Gigi and Carla still don't know us apart when we're dressed the same."

"Too many variables there," Dominic says. "But if we put our minds to it, we can probably control most of them."

"Franco might not bring many of his own men, but he might also hire in Europe and fly in some back-up we won't be aware of."

"I'll expect nothing less. Benedict, you're going to have to put your whole team on this one to make sure we're ahead where we can be."

"Sure thing."

I glance around the table. I've laid out the basic plan—now we'll brainstorm until we've come up with the foolproof one. "Before Franco even knows he's going to need a local team, we need to bait him with Gigi and Carla's presence here. We need to control the knowledge of their whereabouts to such a point where their location is only revealed once we're ready."

"You're actually going to use those two women to lure Franco over to Boston?" Dominic's tone makes it clear he doesn't like it at all.

"How else?" I say, not happy with it either. "Gigi is what Franco wants. He'll come for her."

"And why won't he send a hired hand to do it for him?" Matteo asks. "Would be easier, and cleaner."

"Because he doesn't want her dead," I say, the mere idea like a punch in the gut. "Franco needs Gigi alive." We all know how this works. How things go wrong. It's a risk, but I've thought long and hard about it, and I don't see any other way around it. "Whatever happens, neither Gigi nor Carla can know our game plan."

"Really, Steph." Dominic groans. "There must be another way."

"They could stay hidden forever, or we can do this and get it over with. How long do you need to set things up, Benedict?" I ask, wanting to dig into details and not into the way everything can go wrong.

Benedict rakes his hands through his hair. "I could have this up and running in two weeks, for sure. I already have a few trusted guys in mind to help us set this up."

Yep, that's Benedict: an octopus, camouflaged, but with tentacles reaching far into the underbelly of our world.

"Good." Gigi will hate me when she realizes how I plan to use her. This can't go wrong because she could die. Carla could die. I won't be able to live with myself if that happens. "Gigi and Carla can't know, because when this goes down, they might give the game away. This will only work if they're ignorant of our plans until Franco's dead."

It's going to feel like betrayal, but the end justifies the means.

27

GIGI

"Is this really what you want?" Carla's gaze meets mine in the mirror. "I know it's temporary and fake to boot, but it seems a bit extreme—"

"Yes," I cut her off. "And please, for God's sake, never mention it's fake to anybody. The last thing we need is gossip reaching the wrong ears."

She's standing behind me, having just closed the last in the row of buttons at the back of my dress. Our gazes meet in the mirror, and her silent promise comes with a soft nod.

I've racked my brain for every other solution, but this one is by far the best. If this leaks and we're caught committing marriage fraud, Stephano will go to prison. I'll only be deported, so given the risks he's facing, he's doing me a massive favor.

It's a bit late in the day to start questioning if this is the right move. The past two weeks have been a haze. The one thing standing out is this: Stephano does take care of things, and he doesn't mess around.

We're getting married in half an hour in Matteo's apartment. Technically in the rooftop garden overlooking the Boston skyline at an intimate family-only affair but done properly if just for show. It might be a marriage of convenience for me, and a fake one for Stephano, but to the outside world it must seem real.

"Okay." Carla steps away and reaches for my bouquet. "You look stunning, for what it's worth."

I want to cry. I dreamed of this day as many girls do. I'm not sure why, since Mom's marriage to my biological father was anything but moonlight and roses. The dress is spot on—not the massive meringue I envisioned as a girl, but a strapless fitted silk gown without any embellishment. My bouquet of orchids is eye-catching, filled with color. I needed something to brighten up the day. Not that I feel like a lamb led to slaughter as I would have with Franco, but I always thought if I got this far, it would be for love, with a man I know and whom I'd tested a thousand times over.

In a way, it is. My love for my sister is why I'm doing this, and although Stephano isn't indifferent to me—we have chemistry if nothing else—part of me wants the whole dream, and not just snatches in the fog.

I step back to give us a once-over in the mirror. What I wouldn't give to have Mom here, to see us like this. To see Carla for the woman she's becoming. This sudden move to the US has rattled her, and the past few days seemed more intense as reality set in. She's complained of not feeling great and struggling to adjust to the food, with bouts of diarrhea. I get it; it's been stressful, and she's lost some weight. She hasn't asked to see a doctor, so I've let it slide. If she's still having issues next week, I'll insist she sees someone.

"I wish Papa could be here." Carla is dressed in a gown similar to mine, but in a light pink that suits her perfectly.

"I know," I say as I turn to her. "I'm glad he's safe."

So far, the only message we dared send him was via Matteo's contact, and all we know is he's received it in secret.

Don Trapani knows we're safe, but doesn't know where we are, and it needs to stay that way.

Stephano enrolled Carla at a college and applied for her student visa via the endless contacts the Scaleras seem to have. She's geared up to start her degree in political science. We might have entered the US with fake passports, but these brothers have connections who will backdate and officially make us enter the US as ourselves when we're ready.

There's a knock on the door, and Tasha leans in. "The photographer is here."

Great. Wedding photos are a must apparently, to make this marriage look real under any Homeland Security officer's scrutiny. They might use the photos to leave as a breadcrumb trail to lure Franco Fiore to Boston. I'm not sure exactly what they're planning, but Matteo's apartment has been busy with a revolving door of people. I know the types. I've watched them coming and going all my life. To think it's come to this.

I steel myself. It's just photos, and in an hour, this will all be over. After the ceremony we'll have a family dinner, and that's it. Better than Tasha's wedding from what she's told me: a late night, clandestine, money-under-the-table affair that happened in a small back room at the City Hall. This is all above board.

We file out of the room, and as I look down to the open space, my heart flutters as my breath catches. I've been hiding out in my room since lunch, contemplating my life choices. Then came the hairdresser and makeup artist, and I got dressed. While I was oblivious, the space has been decorated with what seems like thousands of white roses. Center stage is the dining table, set with elaborate crystal and crockery, and silverware catching the light.

"Who arranged all of this?" I ask, stunned. I didn't hear a thing, what with the soundproofing in this apartment.

"Stephano, with a bit of help." Tasha winks at me. "They did it all off site and carried it in. Honestly, it's been such fun, and I lived vicariously through you. Do you like it?"

"You lot are really sneaky," Carla says as she comes to stand next to the railing with me. "I didn't even catch a hint of this going on behind the scenes."

It pains me how this is all for show. I'm not even sure who we're trying to impress, because it's only us and the five Scalera brothers who are attending. No parents. Stephano's are both dead, too. Don Trapani is the last connection I have left to that generation.

"I'm getting to know the Scaleras one by one," Tasha says with a smile, "and I've come to realize Stephano is a real romantic."

"You don't say." I swallow hard, knowing I'm going to leave with this *real romantic* later, for his own apartment, which I haven't even seen yet. Matteo's apartment has become this weird safe haven since we arrived, and although Carla has ventured out several times, I haven't left it once.

As for my fiancé, I haven't seen much of him lately, but I know the exact moment I agreed to all of this. Stephano wasn't even there. Matteo came up to me a couple of days ago after dinner, to confirm I was happy to go ahead with the arrangement. By then I'd realized I had no choice and said yes, provided we stuck to the terms we discussed. At this he'd quirked a brow, nodded, and disappeared off to his office again.

I glance over the space. There's no sign of Stephano or his brothers, but caterers are busy in the kitchen, doing the last prep for dinner.

"Come." Tasha has me by the hand and leads me to the stairs. "You're ready."

Somehow, this woman's unwavering support has been fundamental in getting me through the past few days. I've learned a bit more about her past and how she ended up being married to Matteo. There are many gaps in her story, but the biggest ones are filled with love.

The photographer takes photos as we progress through the apartment, and I pose where he tells me to. By the time we've made our way to the doors leading to the rooftop garden, everything is quiet. It's time. The brothers must have used another exit to get out here because they are already waiting outside in the soft light of an early Boston evening.

I step outside and stall in my steps as I meet Stephano's gaze across the short stretch of burgundy carpet leading me to him. White rose bouquets line the path to my groom, and it's simply beautiful, making my heart lodge in my throat. He's gone to extremes, and it makes me fall a little...just a little bit more. For a man I promised to loathe for all eternity, his actions have been like a wrecking ball to my resolve.

Best husband I'd ever have. It's as if he latched on to those words and made them his slogan for this joint venture, and at some point, my *most horrible wife ever* idea has slipped from the radar. How could I be terrible to a man who has been nothing but caring and gentle to me from the moment I arrived in Boston? Worst of all, he held me close, and in the past few days of not seeing him, I've missed his physical presence. His touch. His hands on my body. His reassurance that it's all going to be okay.

Now he brushes his gaze over me as he holds out his hand, with a slightly tilted head and that cocked brow I've come to read as a dare.

Carla has already walked down the aisle, and as I make my way after her, I glance at the other brothers, all Stephano's best men. They're a line-up of smoldering hotness. I've never seen them all together like this, dressed in tuxedos, hair slicked back. I was surprised to learn Stephano has an identical twin. At first glance, it's almost impossible to distinguish between them. Then I started tallying up the small differences.

Stephano is slightly taller and leaner than Luca, toned and muscled under his business suits in a way that begs me to peel off all the layers and see what else he has going on under all that fabric. But it's really his eyes that give him away. Luca looks at me with indifference. The way Stephano looks at me is always intense, just like now.

"Angel," he says as I finally make it to his side. "You look stunning." He leans closer to whisper in my ear. "And petrified, like a deer in the headlights."

"It's a bit overwhelming."

"It's going to be okay." He stands closer and rests his hand on my lower back, protective, supportive.

With a slow exhale, I settle into his touch, realizing this is exactly what I need.

The ceremony passes in a blur. It's words, nothing more, each moment accentuated by the click of a camera. Stephano's hand on my back doesn't move except for his thumb, which strokes reassuring swipes up and down, hypnotizing me.

Somewhere in there, I say yes, and then my bouquet is gone, and my hand rests in Stephano's. He slips an eternity ring on my finger, wide with big diamonds. I don't even know who procured the wedding bands, but his is a simple white-gold band, symbol of a holy promise I intend to break as soon as possible.

And then, his hand slides over my collarbone and to my neck and I stare up at him, almost straining to breathe as his thumb caresses a tender line up my throat to my jaw. We've never kissed before. Not even in Cannes where his lips traversed every inch of my body they'd wanted to. It's for show, but his hold is firm and commanding as if I'd dare pull away, and gentle in the same breath as he tilts my mouth up to his.

Suddenly, I need it more than air itself, his mouth on mine, his body on mine, his cock in me. I know why. This is the unfulfilled desire and need from the night in Cannes.

He kisses me. It's soft, lingering, and has my pulse in a riot of butterflies. When he pulls away, I need to lean into his chest to keep my balance, but he has me, his arm around my waist, hugging me close. He's staring into my eyes, and a smile toys on his lips. We don't need words. That kiss said everything.

I'm in trouble. I have been for a while now. I'm falling for the last man I ever thought I'd fall for, and in the process, stitching myself back into the life I wanted to escape more than anything else.

28

STEPHANO

That's it. I'm done. The evening has dragged on long enough, what with the ceremony, couple's photos, and dinner. The two waiters are taking orders for coffees and whiskeys, and it's barely nine o'clock, but Gigi looks exhausted. I need to get out of here with *my wife*. That's going to take some getting used to.

Gigi sits next to me, an unreadable expression on her face. She's been too quiet for my liking, but Tasha, like any woman who was groomed to be the perfect hostess, made sure there was no lapse in the conversation. She's exactly what *Il Consiglio*, and Matteo in particular, needs. It's been a pleasant evening, but we're done.

I reach for Gigi's hand, and she stills where she's been twisting her champagne glass round and round.

"Let's go home," I whisper in her ear. "It's early, but it's enough."

She meets my gaze and nods. "I need to get my things."

"Already done." Earlier, I roped in Matteo's housekeeper to pack Gigi's things while we were getting married.

"What?"

"Rosalia sorted it out. You're good to go."

"Are you always this controlling?" she mutters under her breath.

"Not controlling, angel. Organized." I stand, and she follows suit. "Thanks for the evening, Matteo, Tasha. We'll be around."

My brothers' eyes all lock with mine, and with a hitched brow and a scowl, I dare them to wolf whistle or something worse.

There's no wolf whistling, and Tasha and Carla are hugging Gigi fiercely, leaving me to run the gauntlet.

Matteo's first and pulls me close.

"Bring Gigi to see her sister in the morning," he says for my ears only. "Something's up with Carla, and I don't want any surprises."

Fuck. I have no clue what he observed in the time I've been away arranging things. And if Carla has gone and done the unthinkable, like giving their location away before we're ready—

Next comes Dominic. "Congrats, brother, you do us proud." He slaps me on the back and sends me in Luca's direction, singing *Another one bites the dust* in *sotto voce.*

"Taking one for the team, as always," Luca says with a smirk. "Have fun."

And then, there's Benedict. The youngest. Observant and somewhat sly. "Enjoy wrapping up your unfinished business, bro," he says with a smirk.

There's too much fucking smirking all around.

"Your day will come, Benny," I say with a squeeze to his biceps.

If they think I'm going to go home with my bride and have an all-nighter between the sheets, they'll be sadly disappointed.

At last, we've extracted ourselves from the family and are in the elevator, going down to Matteo's private garage. Gigi still has her bouquet with her, clutching it as if it's a lifeline.

"You're supposed to toss it to the ladies," I say, wanting to cut through the tension in this box that seems to shrink with every floor we descend. She looks so goddamn beautiful. Some hair strands have slipped free and frame her face softly, and her lips...God, those lips, which I've tasted now, are plump and full and ready for the taking.

"There's no point, what with Tasha being married and Carla the only other woman there. Plus, they're too pretty to toss."

"I see."

The elevator opens onto the garage, and I guide her to the car with my hand on the small of her back. All I want is to settle it a bit lower, on the curve of her butt and hug her closer in a gentle embrace, but there are rules here. Rules I'm already planning to break.

My driver is waiting for us. I open the door and help Gigi in, then take hold of her safety belt. She can do it herself, but I want to get into her space and inhale her scent.

"How're your bruises doing?" I ask, leaning over her. Our faces are close, and I meet her gaze in the car's little interior light.

"They're much better. Almost gone, actually."

"And lower?" I ask close to her ear. With great satisfaction, I watch how her skin pops a spread of goose bumps, straight to her nipples.

She turns her face away from mine. "I think it's fine."

I bet she hasn't looked as the mere idea of going there is too much for her. I strap her in with care, as she might still hurt, and battle the urge to press a kiss to that perfect naked shoulder.

It's quiet in the car as we head out, and the drive isn't far, plus the traffic is light. I watch Gigi as she takes in the changing environs, from downtown high-rises to the more traditional redbrick rows. It's more historical, and hopefully, she'll feel at home. When the driver opens my garage and drives into the four-car space, she glances at me.

"I know. Not Matteo's place, but we're literally surrounded by *Il Consiglio's* staff." I don't need to tell her the neighboring buildings belong to us too, how some are offices and some apartments for staff. She'll read between the lines.

We take the stairs, and I reach for her hand. She doesn't pull away, and in those heels, I'm tempted to scoop her up in my arms, but don't. I've never minded, but maybe being on the fourth floor without an elevator isn't the brightest idea.

"It's spotless," she huffs as we reach the small foyer with the door to my apartment.

"We've updated the security. Lots of high tech you won't spot unless you're a professional."

Over the past few days, Dominic and I've been busy. My place is being watched now by an in-house team sitting in the basement, keeping my wife safe. We've secured the environment as best we can. The only variable is the road outside which we can't control.

I unlock the door. It's still light out, and I want her to see this apartment with the fading pink of a spectacular sunset tinting the space.

I sweep the door open and turn to her. "Mrs. Scalera."

Before she can protest, I have her scooped up in my arms and walk her over the threshold. She's giggling and wraps her arms around my neck.

"You really don't have to." She laughs as I slide her back down to her feet.

"I'm rather a stickler for tradition." And routine. It sets a rhythm to life which makes living bearable, if predictable.

Gigi takes hesitant steps inside as I close the door. For the first time since the night when we joked about getting married, we're alone.

My heart is beating in my throat, waiting for her to respond to the space.

She comes to a stop, bouquet in hand, and takes in the tall windows and the views over the park. Her gaze travels the expanse of the open-concept first floor, the tiled kitchen with the functional island in midnight blue cabinetry, up to the double-volume ceiling and the industrial look I've got going with vent tunnels and whatnot showing.

"So, this is Stephano Scalera," she says as she homes in on the art covering most of the red-brick wall. "Wow." She walks closer, then steps back again. "You have some big names here... and several Banksy."

"They're only prints."

"But they're signed."

It's a bit of a mix, but I like it. The best way to view the collection is when taking the stairs to the loft.

"You surprise me," she says as I come to stand next to her. "I didn't know you loved art."

"My mom used to paint when she was young. And she loved to paint with us."

"Imagine that. I used to paint, too. Went to study at art school and all."

"You still paint?" We don't know much about each other except what we've revealed in snippets.

"I'm not very good," she says with a deprecating chuckle. "So I went over to art history and started my own business."

I don't buy into the part about her not being very good but say nothing. "You miss it, though?"

Funny thing is she's staring at an Italian landscape Mom painted, and I can see she loves it. I'm lucky to have this one thing of Mom's that reminds me of the person she was before she got married to Don Scalera.

"I've tried not to miss it, if that makes sense? It's so calming and quiet. I used to love it. The calm in the chaos." She points at Mom's painting. "This is Palermo's Porta Felice. Heavens. I know the exact spot where the artist stood to do this painting."

"My mom painted that one."

"Really? She had real talent."

"Yes. She gave it up, though. What with having six kids, her passion fell to the wayside and then she died." We haven't spoken much about our parents, but none were at the wedding today and she didn't question it. Maybe Tasha filled her in.

"I'm sorry. How?"

"In childbirth."

She reaches for me, but I've trapped my hands in my pockets to make sure I don't touch her. Now, her fingers rest on my arm, and they burn right through the layers of my tuxedo.

"That's terrible. You'd think that type of thing doesn't happen anymore."

"He was going to kill her, with his fists or in some other way. She wasn't supposed to have more children after having had us twins. Benedict was a fluke. I'm convinced Don Scalera did something that triggered our sister being stillborn, taking Mom with her."

Her eyes are wide as my words sink in. I sigh and fist my hands tighter in my pockets. This isn't the conversation I wanted to have tonight.

"Can I pour you a drink?" We have some things to discuss now that she's here and we're alone. I take off my jacket and bowtie and hook them over the barstool by the kitchen island.

"Okay. Yes, thank you."

I groan inwardly. We were going somewhere with that conversation, but I cut the connection off.

"But first..." Gigi holds up the flowers and heads to the kitchen where she takes a tall glass from the sink where I left it earlier. She fills it with water and dunks the bouquet's stem in, then puts it on the counter to make sure it's balanced. She turns to me, without her protective shield of flowers. "I want to get out of this dress."

I've leaned against the counter as she made herself at home and stare at her as she glides her hands over her hips and sides. She's nervous.

"Let me show you around on the first floor, and then we'll go up." I lead the way to the few other rooms on this level. "My office, washroom, and safe room."

Gigi peeks into each of them and gives a shudder when I open the steel door to the safe room.

"I'll show you how this works in the morning."

"Okay."

"This way." I nod in the direction of the staircase going up to the loft.

I wait for her to go first and follow, having the pleasure of watching her sweet curves sway in front of me, those perfect ankles and calves peeking out with each step she takes. Those heels...*fuck*. When she reaches the landing, she stops abruptly, blocking my way.

"Gigi." I put a hand on her hip to urge her forward so I can get off the stairs and stand abreast with her.

She steps to the side to make space for me. "There's only one bedroom?"

"Yes."

"This wasn't the plan, Steph."

No, this wasn't *her* plan. I made my terms clear. This is going to be a proper marriage. *With no sex. No kissing.* Until she begs for it. And beg, she will.

"When you're under my roof, you're not sleeping alone. Not until Franco has been dealt with and we're sure there're no repercussions."

29

GIGI

He's played me. But not really. We were sparring when we made those stupid terms, working each other up. I've underestimated him. In the past few days, Stephano has been different. Super focused. My first impression of him holds true: he's one of the most dangerous men I've ever met. Not only because he is in such control of himself, but because he is always five steps ahead of me.

I was stupid not to think this would come my way. He did, after all, say this would be a *proper marriage.*

With no kissing and zero sex.

There's no chance that's going to last. That notion of control I'll have by denying him? I can already feel myself slipping. This isn't forever. Only until we can safely go back to Italy. The sooner, the better. I'll have to be strong.

Problem is, I've been attracted to him since the very first moment I saw him on the Cannes marina, when he caught me when I stumbled. And he's just a man. He wants me. I can see it in his eyes, in the way his gaze travels over my body. He might not have caved in on the night of the auction because he had a point to prove, but he's just playing plain dirty now, and so will I. Whatever happens next, I can't give in to him.

I take in the big room. Mirrored cupboards line one wall, doubling the space, and a door between leads to the en suite bathroom. Floor-to-ceiling windows on the far side of the room give views over the park and city scape. Two occasional chairs face a fireplace in that corner, and around it, bookshelves cover the wall, forming a reading snug. This man is full of surprises I didn't foresee. I bet his mom read bedtime stories to her kids, just as I did to Carla.

Center stage stands the one and only bed. It's big and made up in slick grey silk that I can almost feel on my naked skin.

"It's perfect," I say, because it is. It's the perfect nest of seduction, just as he planned it.

I walk deeper into the room, making my way to the windows. The view is magnificent. Wispy clouds tinged in soft oranges and pinks stretch across the sky in the last sun rays.

With a deep inhale and focus, I turn to him. He might have control over every inch of his being, but I'm used to delayed satisfaction. I know how to bide my time and play the long game. I'll wear him down by not caving in, and hopefully, by the time I can't stand it any longer, the divorce papers will be signed.

As I walk towards Stephano where he stands two feet away from the stairs, I pull the pins from my hair. It hasn't been over-styled, and now, the thick tresses cascade in soft waves to my bare shoulders.

"Can you help me with the dress's buttons?" The long row leads the eye from the middle of my back down to my butt where it widens the dress enough to slip it off. I didn't think this far, but I can't unbutton all of them without help. It is, after all, a wedding dress and needs assistance getting on and off.

"Sure." He steps up, and I turn my back to him.

He's so close, I can feel his breathing and then his soft touch to my shoulder as he sweeps my hair to the side. My body reacts to the simple, slow caress—a frisson of desire spreads over my skin to harden my nipples. And then his fingers glide down to fiddle with the silk-covered buttons, his knuckles softly kissing my skin with each one.

It's torture because it makes me feel like a true bride being undressed by her beloved, in an arousing game of seduction that's going nowhere tonight. With every inch he progresses to the last one in the row, need builds in my core, and desire wets me right where I want him to go so badly.

This isn't new. Despite everything that's passed, I've been wanting a repeat of the night in Cannes since I arrived in Boston, from the moment Stephano hugged me close at the airport and promised to take care of me.

I have no clue what it is with this promise that makes me weak. I've been independent for so long, but since this fiasco with Franco Fiore and us becoming fugitives, I've craved for someone else to help me—to hold me, even if only by my hand. I've been on alert for ten long years, and now with the real danger here, I've depleted my energy to cope with it.

I drop my head forward, overwhelmed, and Stephano's hands still, his knuckles resting gently against my skin.

God. If only he were predictable like every other man, but he's never been.

"Gigi?"

I tremble at the soft tone in which he says my name and sway unsteady on my feet. I want to lean back into him.

"I'm fine," I whisper, but I'm not.

His hand skims to my shoulder, and he makes me turn around to face him. His fingers trace a line down my arm, and every nerve in me seems to melt into a pile of wanton threads just begging for him to unknot them. I'm defenseless against his touch, and I can't afford to submit to him.

"I'll be the judge of that," he says, his voice husky. My dress isn't loose enough yet to fall forward and expose my breasts, but his eyes don't even dip there as his gaze locks with mine. "Have you been sleeping? Like at all?"

I have no idea how he picked up on it because I've done everything to hide the dark circles under my eyes. As safe as Matteo's place was, with Carla right next door at night, memories of Franco and what he'll do to me if he finds us invade every quiet hour. Now, I want to cry, and I've always been one to keep tears at bay, with a firm hold on my emotions.

"Answer me, Gigi," he says with a squeeze to my hand, and all I can do is shake my head.

He pulls me to the haven of his chest and holds me a long minute as I battle for control over my tears. My stupid vengeful heart still wants *him* to succumb to *me*, to get back at him for that night in Cannes. I want him to lose control, but I can't. My heart is more at stake with every minute I spend with this man.

"You can stop running, angel," he murmurs in my ear. "I've got you. For ten years, you've been running, but you need to stop. Let him come to you, and then I will deal with him."

His words trap a sob in my throat, but I can't contain it anymore. I break, and it feels as if this man has been poised for decades to catch me. I lean into his warmth as tears stream down my cheeks at his unexpected understanding of everything my life has been for the past ten years.

I take a couple of heaving breaths, but don't pull away. His hands are back on my dress's buttons, and this time, it's even more intimate as he works his way ever lower while hugging me close.

"Let's get you to bed. You need to sleep. Everything looks so much worse when you're exhausted."

The dress slips from my body, but Stephano catches it and helps me step out as I hold on to his arm for balance. I'm shy and not because he's about to see most of me—he's already seen it all that first time. I'm shy because he's sliced through every defense I've had in place and peered straight into my soul.

His eyes rake over my body, from my bare breasts partly covered by my hair, down to my seamless panties and lacy thigh-highs. He sucks in a breath as his eyes home in on the little tease of fabric that came with the dress and that for some idiotic reason I'd put on.

"Is that a garter, Mrs. Scalera?"

"It came with the wedding dress," I breathe. "No point in throwing it to the bachelors, because I'd rather not let them know it was there—"

"And everything is fake, and when it comes to marriage, we Scalera boys are two down, three to go?" he says with a quirked brow as he crowds me with his body, forcing me to step backwards in the direction of the bed. "Damn fucking skippy my brothers don't get to touch something that was so close to your pussy."

Oh my God. "Steph—" I break off as the back of my thighs hit the bed, and with him towering over me, I sink back to sit.

There's no fear here, just pure, undiluted anticipation of what he's going to do next as I drown in my own desire for him to touch me.

30

GIGI

"That piece of lace comes with privileges, Gigi," Stephano says as he cups my face, forcing me to look up at him. "*Husband* privileges. And you wore it as an invitation."

I blink up at him, playing innocent, but really playing with fire. A smirk toys on his lips, and before I can even think what's next, he's dropped to his haunches. His hand ghosts from my cheek down my neck, and when his fingers trace lines over the swell of my breasts, my nipples tighten painfully.

He keeps on staring into my eyes, though, and all I want is to close them and float on the feelings his touch sparks. His other hand slips off my high-heeled sandals and now glides up my leg to the treacherous garter. When he lowers his head to place a kiss on my knee, I lean back on my elbows, wanting only to open for him.

He nips and kisses and bites his way up my inner thigh, and I'm melting into the bed with need. When he reaches the garter, he tugs at it with his teeth and drags it down with such slow, deliberate intent, his warm breath kindles goose bumps all over my skin as desire seeps from my sex.

I'm a lost cause as his fingertips run along the edges of my thigh-highs and pull them off as his gaze holds mine. Only my panties remain, covering Franco's cruel signature on my skin.

Stephano stands, the garter hanging limp from his hand. He runs the lace over my leg, ever higher, stalling over my sex, letting its weight just rest there for a few seconds before he glides it to my breasts and lets it skim my nipples.

He tosses the garter to the side and leans over me, with a hand next to my head, as he cups my face with the other. Instead of kissing me as I long for, he turns my face to the side to kiss my neck and ever lower.

A hot blaze of arousal zaps through me with every kiss and suck he caresses over my breasts, my nipples, down to my belly and the edge of my panties, his hand following his mouth. Then he looks up again with a soft squeeze to my hip.

As our gazes lock, his finger burrows underneath my panties. His touch is so gentle, so intimate, I want to squirm away, but I still as he carefully traces the lines of Franco's scars.

I struggle for breath, trying not to cry. But tears seep from the corners of my eyes as I watch him swallow hard, his shattered breath flowing over my skin.

Then his fingertip finds the start of my slit, and he pauses there for a moment, seeming to war with himself.

"He'll never touch you again," he murmurs. "In fact, once I've dealt with him, he'll never touch a woman again."

I still at those words. Stephano might be Mafia and the last type of man I've ever wished to get involved with, but he is true to his word. When he hooks the crotch with his finger and eases off my panties, I drop back and close my eyes, knowing he could do anything to me now and I'd let him.

"Fuck, Gigi," he hisses, and I look at him.

He has my panties pressed to his nose. I know he knows: I'm drenched for him.

I'm so drugged with desire, I just let him do as he pleases, and it pleases my husband to lift my foot to his hip, pressing my other leg open with a hand on my knee. Like this, I'm spread wide for him, and when he brushes his fingers over my sex, I quiver.

"You're so fucking wet," he says as he circles my clit and dips a finger into my sex. "And so fucking tight."

"Please," I beg, squeezing around the paced invasion.

"Please who?" he says as he slides into me again.

I know what he wants to hear. Stephane is into this. He was into this the night in Cannes, but this time, it's different for both of us. This is a woman who can't walk away later tonight as she has with every other sexual encounter she's ever had. This is a man who is going to fulfill every promise he made earlier today.

"Please, husband."

"With pleasure, my darling, beautiful wife."

At his sweet words, I close my eyes, and with his lips back on my skin, shudders run through my body. It won't take much to tip me over the edge. His tongue works its way from my inner thigh, ever closer to my clit. His fingers fuck me, and the buildup rises from deep within my core. It will take just one little flick of his tongue—

At the last second, he pulls away, and I still, my breathing labored as I've arched into the bed, gripping the sheets, ready to fall.

"Steph," I moan, and open my eyes only to see him stripping out of his shirt.

"It's our wedding night, angel. I'm not rushing."

I drag in a shaky breath. "We're not supposed to be having sex at all," I protest, too weak with lust to stick to my own resolve.

"I see you have a misunderstanding of the concept. This isn't having sex, angel."

God, he's high-handed. And I love it and hate it at the same time. Never mind his words—his naked chest has diverted all my attention. I knew he was built. Everything about Stephano Scalera screams *man in his prime*, but watching him unwrap his muscled chest and abs leaves me breathless. I was expecting more tattoos, but bar the one on his forearm, which I still haven't deciphered yet, his skin is smooth with no ink. There are scars, though, several with origins I can't place in the low light.

He's busy with his belt, and my gaze magnetizes to the bulge battling his fly. I want it. I've wanted it for weeks. He loosens his belt and pulls down the zipper, and when he palms his cock and frees it from all constraints, I blink. *Holy...fuck.* Every cell in my body quivers at the visual, twisting tight with an intense craving to be stretched and filled with him.

"Scoot up, angel," he says, and I oblige, keeping my eye on the prize.

As soon as I'm higher up, he kneels onto the bed, and I reach for him. He catches my hand, though, and a warning flashes through his eyes.

"This is me taking care of my wife as I've promised to do, but I don't expect you to return any favors here."

"Steph—"

"Hush, angel," he says as he traces my lips, zipping up any further protest. "I've got us both."

He reaches for some pillows. Every movement catches the flex of his muscles in the last of the evening light, and I can only stare, so much so, I'm caught off guard when he tucks two pillows under my butt and presses my legs open and up. I've never felt this exposed before, but the way he looks at me, as if he's about to worship a goddess, swells my heart.

"I want to fuck this sweet little pussy so bad," he grunts as he drives his fingers into me again, hard and with purpose this time as he jerks his cock. "But she said *no sex*."

But she's regretting it now.

"You're a control freak," I hiss back, my orgasm rounding up again from all corners of my body at the visual of him pleasuring himself.

"Fuck, yes, angel, that I am, and if nothing else, I'll stick to the terms and conditions of this arrangement."

I want to stall my peak, keep myself from crashing into bliss, but he dips his head and licks and sucks on my clit, and it's all too much. I shatter.

And shatter more with a gasp as he curls his fingers, pressing that secret spot inside me. He drags out my orgasm as he hits every swollen nerve deep within me. My legs are shaking and my body trembles with release as he straightens and spills his own, right over every scratch Franco's made on my skin, as if he could erase it with his cum.

We still, the moment passing in slow motion as we catch our breaths. Stephano lets go of my legs, but I'm too weak to close them up. Instead, I watch as he zips his pants and buckles his belt. That was it. The only bit of Stephano I'm going to see out of control tonight.

"Come," he says as he eases the pillows away and scoops me into his arms. "Let's get you cleaned up."

31

STEPHANO

I let her stand at the twin basin and reach for a face cloth. "Do you want to shower?" I ask as I open the faucet, getting ready to wipe her clean.

She still smells of perfumed bride with a touch of freshly fucked. If we'd had proper sex, she would've smelled only of freshly fucked, and I bet that's going to be my favorite scent if I ever get to smell it.

"I'm so tired, I'll just deal with my makeup," she says as she eyes me wringing out the face cloth.

I lower to my haunches and wipe away the evidence of us *not* having sex. Finally, I'm getting a closer inspection of those cuts that have been haunting me since I saw them the first time. They're healing, and not in the way they should if someone had it done for body art. The lines are scabbed and will leave a scar, but Franco Fiore will be displeased at the result. She'll have to get a tattoo or more scarification to disguise it, but she might not be into that. Her skin is beautiful with no other markings.

"What does your tattoo say?" she asks as I straighten again.

Her eyes are on my forearm as I toss the cloth to the laundry basket. "It's in your blood."

"What is?"

She meets my gaze, and I work my jaw as I take her in. In this moment, she isn't on guard. She's naked and as vulnerable as a woman can be. *Trusting.* But I could wrap her neck with one hand and choke her to death in minutes. I could work her body to a pulp, break her ribs and splinter them into her lungs, and nobody would be any the wiser when she wore clothes. *Just like Mom.* Physically, she's no match for me. A stick to snap. A bug to crush.

These thoughts revolt me, and I swallow the bile pushing up my throat. Something about talking about Mom and her paintings is pushing me to open up to this woman. I don't know what it is, but I'll probably regret it later. "Don Guiliano Scalera is in my blood."

"Your dad?"

I nod.

"What did he do to you that you inked those words on your skin? As an oath or a reminder of sorts?"

Nobody has ever asked that question as directly as she just did, and it throws me. I battle for a long moment with telling her about that night decades ago, wanting to flay myself open and keep my secrets at the same time. I bet she has a similar story somewhere. Mafia princesses often witness and are subjected to things no human should be subjected to. Mafia princesses don't run like Gigi has without reason or having lived through some shit.

"I woke up one night. There were noises coming from their bedroom." I flex and fist my hands at the familiar itch that hits me whenever I revisit this memory. "Once Don Scalera realized I was in their room, too petrified to move, he locked the door. He made me watch and then he dragged me closer and forced me to take punches at her too. According to him, this was what he expected of me, because it was in my blood, just like it was in his. Like father, like son."

I'm trembling now, the horror of that night creeping under my skin and rippling in waves through me. He would have done so much worse if Mom hadn't stopped him. To this day, I know the Don would have forced me to touch her with my dirty fucking hands in places no son should ever touch his mother. But she'd gone at him, probably for the first time in her life, retaliating. It was the only time we'd ever seen Don Scalera walk around with a bruised eye.

In the end, she'd paid for it, though, with her life. And I never walked around at night again when I heard noises coming from their side of the house. Instead, I quivered in my bed, haunted by what I'd done. I'd failed to protect the first woman I've ever loved. I was weak. I bowed to his tone and command and did as he asked, too fucking scared to defend her. Instead, I participated, and the shame of it made me ink my skin. I'm reminded every fucking day of what I did.

"Oh my God," she whispers, her eyes wide and worried. "How old where you?"

"Seven."

An age which holds a lot of blurry memories for most people. Mine don't fade; they're crystal clear. I never felt so helpless and out of control of my own body in my life. Then she died eight months later. To think she was pregnant at the time he'd gone at her.

Tears are streaming down Gigi's cheeks as she reaches for me, wraps her arms around my neck, and pulls me close. Her soft body molds to mine, her naked skin warm and comforting.

"I'm so sorry," she whispers into my neck.

Now she'll know why I got triggered that afternoon in Cannes, when she told me to get my dirty Mafia paws off her. All I want to do is touch her, kiss away every mark Franco Fiore made on her skin, and possessively make sure no man ever touches her again. Love isn't needed in this equation. She is my wife now, and I will protect her till death do us part.

"Have you ever spoken to anybody about what happened?" she asks as she leans back to look me in the eye.

Her expression is serious, but her question makes me smirk. "Angel, I'm a Scalera. I don't do shrinks. We don't do therapy. My brothers deal with their shit in their own way. *I* beat that psycho out of my system every day."

Her hands slide down my arms to where my hands are resting on her hips. She's going to peel them from her body, disengage, and walk away. Wise woman. Chills spread over my skin at the thought of her rejection when I've opened to her in a moment of stupid trust.

Instead, she wraps her hands around my own and bring them to her lips. She places kisses on each of my knuckles, her hair draping and hiding her face.

"My dad was the same. Not Don Trapani. He's my stepdad. My biological dad. I saw him flip so many times, being all placid and then the next minute...raging."

I drag in a shaky breath. "Did he ever hit you?"

"When he got hold of me. I learned to run from an early age. To steer clear of him when he was in a mood. To hide. As a grown woman...Franco was the first."

And her last. I pull my hands free to cup her cheeks. They're wet from tears.

She leans into me, her hands on my chest. "But because I know how men can be, I've never slept... I mean stayed the night with a man before."

She's never *slept* with a man before. "No? Why?"

"I'm too scared he'd be human one moment, and a monster in the next. I...I risk having sex but leave right after."

I gave her exactly what she'd wanted that night in Cannes, but her words give me pause. Every encounter alone with a man, with sex or not, is a risk for her. *Fuck*. The lives women lead, and I've seen it firsthand.

"You don't trust any man, do you?"

"No." It's barely a whisper as she shakes her head. "I don't."

I tilt her chin up, forcing her to look at me. "Do you feel safe with me?"

"Yes."

"Why?"

She swallows and dips her gaze, but when she looks up at me again, there's honesty in her eyes.

"There's a lot you can learn about a man in the way he..."

"Say it," I press her as I run my thumb along her jaw.

"In the way he *fucks* a woman. Or controls himself and *doesn't* fuck her."

A blush spreads over her cheeks, and if her words weren't so crass, she'd be downright adorable right now.

"Is that so? And what did you learn about me, angel?" I slide my hand lower to her neck, and she shivers at my tender touch.

"In Cannes, you never lost control. You never caved in and took without thinking of the woman in the equation as any other man would have. If I'd said no to anything, you would have stopped."

Yes. I would have stopped. I'm in control of myself every second of every day. But I also know the flip she talks about. I've been there, but never with a woman. "Then trust me, too. Trust me to protect you and keep you safe."

She bites her lip and nods, and in this moment, I want to kiss her more than ever before. But she has her stupid terms which I've been bending tonight. Kissing is more defined than mere sex.

"You're more your mother than your father," she murmurs. "You just never see it that way."

Gigi squeezes my hand and walks away, leaving me standing in the bathroom, whiplashed. I look like Don Scalera, not a carbon copy, but I'm physically his son in every way. I grip the vanity, listening to how she unzips her suitcase and rummages through her things in the bedroom. My heart hammers in my chest.

I'm standing frozen, the idea that I'm my *mother's* son pounding in my head when Gigi comes to stand in the bathroom door, dressed in the old-fashioned nightgown I bought for her.

Fuck. She probably thinks it's the demurest of them all, but her shape shows through the delicate cotton, the darker shade of her nipples barely visible where the fabric is gathered at the bodice. Already, I want to crumple the soft material up and stroke her naked ass, fall to my knees and press her pussy to my tongue.

I look away. This is going to be the longest fake marriage of my life. I don't plan another one. I brush my teeth and wrap up my own bedtime routine while she packs her things out on the vanity.

"I'll give you space."

I close the door behind her and stare at the bed. She's never slept with a man before. In this way, she's almost virginal, and the notion pleases me more than it should.

I go downstairs to switch off the lights and get a gun from the safe. Wedding day and all, I'd boosted the bodyguards so I could forego the usual weapons. Irrespective of Dominic's security upgrades, though, I'm not sleeping without a gun within arm's reach. By the time I head upstairs again, Gigi is finished in the bathroom and hovers by the window, taking in the city lights.

I pad over to her and take her hand. "Come, angel."

I lead her to the bed and open the covers for her. It would be the decent thing to make up a story about having work to do, or a few calls to make. A nightclub or ten to go boss over. Anything really to give her time to fall asleep alone.

But I'm not a decent guy. I'm the guy who wants to spoon my wife's ass and fondle her breasts as I watch her drift into sleep. So instead, I strip and slip under the covers right behind her.

32

GIGI

My husband is a professional cuddler. He's pulled a pillow closer and has stretched his arm out for me to rest my head on. Now, he's nudged my hips right into his, and I can feel him harden as he bundles up my gown to my thighs so he can have his hand on my bare skin. I hate how I love this so much, how I literally want to melt into his arms and die right there.

"Ignore that," he whispers in my neck.

"It's hard to ignore," I whisper back, and we both chuckle at the innuendo.

I can't help wondering how different the night in Cannes would've been if I hadn't insulted him in the first place. His demons and mine are matched, married in a way I've never thought possible. He's done so much for us since we arrived in Boston, and I don't know how any of this is going to pan out. I've not been let into any of the Scaleras' plans on how they're going to deal with Franco Fiore, but I've never felt as safe and treasured as I have in this moment.

He presses a soft kiss below my ear. "Sleep tight, angel."

At this rate, there's not going to be any sleeping involved. Wisps of desire are tugging at my sex, wanting more...wanting all of him. I can't be so weak and cave in on our first night. I know it's just sex, and I might be physically safe, but my heart has never been in bigger danger before. Something about him is worming its way into all my empty places that are longing for moments like this.

His erection is distracting, and I bet he wants to nestle it between my butt cheeks, but it will only make me want it inside me. "This isn't going to work, Steph," I say into the dark.

"No?" he says as he innocently rocks into me, a smile in his voice.

He's playful too. Of course he is. All the signs were there that night in Cannes.

I'm still surprised he told me about his past earlier in the bathroom. It broke my heart. We're just Mafia kids grown into Mafia adults, fucked up in so many ways. Even though he doesn't know it or trust himself, this man will never hurt a woman. I have no idea if Stephano has it in him to kill a man. Not with the brutality Franco will unleash if he gets to him first.

At the thought, I swallow at the tightening in my throat. The last thing I need is to become teary now.

"Turn around, husband," I whisper as I do the same, nudging him onto his side so I can spoon him instead.

Deep inside this man, there is a boy who suffered abuse at his father's hand, still seeking forgiveness for the things he was forced to do and didn't understand. I press the softest kiss possible to his back as he complies, hoping he won't feel it.

When I wake up, the bed next to me is empty, and light streams in through the tall windows. Good heavens. By the height of the sun, it's way past ten o'clock in the morning. This bed...this man...his arms. We might have fallen asleep with me holding him, but at some point, he'd cradled me. I haven't slept like this for years.

I curl up and press my nose to his pillow which is indented with the shape of his head. I inhale slowly and suppress a curse. I might be developing a problem. Also known as a crush on my fake husband.

A crush is fine. Those come and go. It's the deeper feelings I need to steer clear of. As I sit up and stretch, voices sound from downstairs. A female's and Stephano's. I sneak out of bed and pad over to the railing to peek down, just in time to see him squeeze a blonde by the arm as he opens the front door for her.

She turns and smiles at him. So pretty. Thick blonde hair. Toned arms in a sleeveless top. Skin-tight jeans and heels that are a bitch to walk in, but which she does with ballerina grace. She slips a file into a tote bag as another woman comes to stand in the open door. This one is as stunning as the first, but a redhead. Smiles and hugs between the two women and then the new one steps up to Stephano and he hugs her close.

Unnecessary jealousy spears through me. *No, no, no.* I can't. I rush to the bathroom where I close the door quietly and lean against it.

My crush is obviously further along than I anticipated.

I take a shower, forcing myself not to think how my husband had two—maybe even more—women in his apartment before lunch. I force my focus to my business, which is the one thing that will never deceive or cheat on me. There, I'm the one in charge, and if I'm not careful, I'll get a bad rep if I don't get back to it soon.

I left things hanging when I went to Lake Como, and the first thing I did when I got that laptop from Stephano was to put my out-of-office on with no specific return date. At least it's summer in Europe and business slows down significantly, but I can't afford to ignore the emails in my inbox for much longer. I'll have to check with Stephano if I should even answer them.

Who knows what the ripple effect could be from a few answered client emails.

By the time I'm dressed and head downstairs, Stephano is stepping out of his office with the redhead. I freeze, but it's too late. She's already spotted me, and it hits me he has some pimping thing going.

My stomach revolts at the idea. Virgin auctions, brothels, sex trafficking. It's all in the realm of usual Mafia fare, and I don't know why I didn't see this through the smoke and mirrors of Matteo's classy, über-luxury apartment. It's so easy to forget where the money is coming from if you don't have to think about it.

Having these women in his apartment, right under my nose, is like a backhanded slap across the cheek.

The woman drops her gaze as something in my expression must have spooked her.

"I'm glad you've moved on, Steph," she says, her words clearly audible in the double volume of the apartment. "It's what we've all hoped for." Before I can say anything, the redhead makes for the front door, and Stephano is there to see her off. "Same place, same time next month. Unless something comes up?"

"Yes."

He closes the door behind her and meets my gaze where I'm still waiting on the stairs. Waiting for what? To see how my knight in shining armor is a villain like the rest?

As if he can sense my mood from what he reads on my face, he just shakes his head. "Here we are again. I wouldn't jump to conclusions if I were you, my angel."

My angel. He's the devil in disguise.

"Enlighten me, then?" I hack back. "If those two women aren't prostitutes working for your seedy little Mafia operations, then I don't know what they are."

"Prostitution? Unless it directly affects our business, what they do in their spare time is none of my concern," he bites back, but there's an angry tremor in his voice. "For your information, none of our girls need to turn to that as a last resort."

"No?" I'm taking the stairs again, not keen to shout this conversation across the expanse of his apartment. "*Our girls*. I know what that means. No need to sugar coat it, Stephano."

"Do you wake up like this every morning?" he asks as he tracks my steps to the kitchen.

The closer he homes in, the faster my heart beats.

"And how is that? In an empty bed with my *husband* hosting an orgy in his office?"

I've gone too far. This is childish. He's a man, and this marriage is fake. *No sex* and *no kissing* are my rules. If this drags on for months and he chooses to take a mistress or fuck one of those girls, I should be happy, not furious.

I've reached the kitchen island, but he doesn't stop. Stephano keeps coming at me and traps me against the cold marble. His one hand is on my hip as the other slips to my ponytail and he twists it around his palm. Every movement is measured, controlled, and does nothing but spike my pulse and spread lust to the last corner of my being. This is the problem. And it's a big one.

"Are you jealous, Mrs. Scalera?" he asks as he manipulates my head back with my ponytail, forcing me to look at him.

"No, I'm not."

He stares into my eyes, and I see the amusement flashing in his own. His gaze consumes my face, and I swear the only thing he wants to do is kiss me. Hard. Possessively.

"You're a bad liar. Let's set a few things straight, shall we?" He leans closer to my ear, and his words are soft but crystal-clear as he runs his lips along the shell. "Firstly, if you want to keep this as a *marriage on paper* only, don't walk around with that please-fuck-me look in your eyes."

Goose bumps spread and pebble my nipples as wet heat invades my sex. *Oh, God.*

"Secondly. Don't insult me by suggesting I'd fuck a prostitute in my office while my wife is upstairs, sleeping like the angel she is." He lets go of me, and I firm my grip on the island to keep up straight. He steps away and heads for the front door. "I'm going out. Tony is here to look after you and drive you to see Carla if you want."

He opens the front door and at the last second turns back to me. "Rest assured, Gigi. What happened this morning won't happen again."

He's gone. I drop my head back and take a deep breath. The double entendre in his last words is clear. Either he's never meeting women again in this apartment while I'm sleeping upstairs...or I won't wake up alone like that again.

Butterflies stir in my stomach at his idle promise and delicious threat.

33

STEPHANO

I've warmed up on the treadmill, and now I'm going at this punching bag as if it's his face. Sweat drips into my eyes and blinds me, but I don't stop. I hate how Gigi Trapani always thinks the worst of me. This is what it means to be born into a Mafia family. Nothing can scrub you clean.

Her choice of words baited me to retaliate, but seeing the spark of jealousy in her eyes was like seeing a lighthouse in the dark. She cares. She sees those other women as competition or a threat—*as if*—and I hate how it made her doubt me.

And then, I had to taunt her by not telling her how things stand between me and the women who work in our clubs. It's the first thing I'm going to tell her when I get home. In that moment where I really only wanted to fuck her on the kitchen counter, I had to leave to come beat out the age-old rage our conversations last night about Mom and Don Scalera unearthed. If it weren't for those standing appointments I had this morning, I would have been at the gym hours ago.

Everything from last night felt undeserved. From her feeling safe with me, to her holding me and pressing that kiss to my back. Actions speak for themselves. It's as if she knew what I needed more than I knew myself. In the night, when she stirred in anguish, I held her close. I bet she doesn't know she has nightmares and whispers *Carla* and *Franco* in her sleep, getting more agitated at the mention of his name.

"You're sparring today? With a human?"

The gym's general manager has been eyeing me from a distance ever since I stalked in here an hour ago, too pumped for human interaction.

"Not a good idea, don't you agree?" I huff back. When I'm in this mood, I'm dangerous. The flip. Fuck. Gigi even has a name for it.

"Two regulars are here, who've both been wanting your blood for days now. You've been a bit absent the past two weeks. You can fight both and walk out of here with a clear head."

And a clear conscience, for what it's worth. I wipe at my mouth with my gloved hand. "Fuck. Why not."

When people know you, they *know* you. This manager has overseen my gym since it opened seven years ago. He gets me. And the guys who sign up to fight me know what they're getting into. No holds barred.

———

Two hours later, I'm about to take the stairs to my apartment, my head clear. I'm aching all over, having pushed my limits today, but that's what happens when you fight the best. I'm going to have bruises, but it comes with the territory. The security detail we've installed to watch the street signals to me, and I nod. A package arrived, and it's been verified. *Good.*

It's not one package, but several in different sizes. As instructed, the delivery guy didn't ring the doorbell, and Gigi must be home, unaware. Tony must be there too; I did let him in earlier as I walked out. I wade through the boxes to the door and open it wide, then pull the packages in one by one. It's only when I look up that I notice Gigi sitting by the dining room table, her face buried in her hands, and Tony hovering by her side like a helicopter mom.

"Tried to phone you, boss," he says. "She's been like this since she opened her laptop."

Fuck. I haven't checked my phone since I stripped my suit jacket in the gym. "What's happened?"

Gigi sniffs and glances in my direction, then shakes her head as she sobs again into a fold of tissues.

As I walk over, I indicate to Tony, and he gets the message to see himself out.

"Angel." I touch her shoulder, and she sags back.

"They've come for me, Steph. They've come for my business." She faces her laptop screen to me, and I sink into a chair. "Read it. Shit. It's in Italian. Do you read Italian?"

"Sort of." I pull the laptop closer, glancing through the lines, trying to make out the gist of the situation even though my reading Italian is at the level of an eight-year-old. Once Mom died, we read it less and less at home.

"There're articles on several UK sites as well. Accusing my business of selling forgeries. It's all fabricated, but I'm done for. They've basically killed everything I've worked for overnight with a few choice articles. I can't fight this now. Not from here and not while I'm in hiding. You know I can't."

She shoots up and paces the room, caged. I toggle through the tabs she's got open on her laptop, and my heart sinks. Each article is damning and clearly an orchestrated attack designed to make her retaliate and reveal herself.

This is good. They still don't know where the Trapani women have fled to.

"God!" she cries out, her hands in her hair. At some point, she lost the ponytail because she's tugging at her loose strands as if she'd pull it all out. "I worked so hard to get out, to get away, and this is what this sick life does. It pulls you back in and destroys everything good and pure and honest, then it just fucks you over until you die."

I get up and pull her into my arms. She fights me, but as if she knows it's futile, she almost collapses against my chest and fists my shirt as she presses her face tight into me. There're so many words I can throw out there to appease her, but I say nothing because they're meaningless.

I cup her head and hold her close as she weeps for a life she must realize now is long gone. She left it behind the night she chose to flee with her sister, and there's no going back. In reality, it was ripped from her when Franco Fiore chose to make her his wife—she just didn't know it.

"My inbox is flooded with emails from clients who want to know if the accusations are true. A few even suggested they will get professional evaluations done to check that I haven't sold them fakes." She sobs into my chest. "I buy from Christie's, for fuck's sake! And all the other reputable auction houses in Europe. They're going at me as if I run my own bloody crime ring."

Not a bad idea, but I keep it to myself. Every word she says is true. This life sucks you in and spits out nothing but your bare bones at the end of it. If you're lucky enough to dodge the acid pit. Or the promession plant in Matteo's basement.

"Have you responded to anybody?"

"No. I opened my inbox wanting to see what's been going on. I don't even know if I should have done that? If he could track me?"

That depends on how good they are. We'll see. "Don't respond. Log out of everything. I know it hurts. I'm not going to make you any empty promises. You've got to let it go."

"No!" she says as she stubbornly pushes away from me. "I'm not letting it go. I've worked hard for this, and I refuse to let Vincenzo or Franco rip my reputation apart—"

"Gigi—"

"Don't you get it? This was the only thing I had that was mine. Mine alone. Clean, untarnished. And they've now gone and sprayed Mafia sewage all over it. Nobody is going to trust me again."

"Angel. I get it, but now is not the time. If these allegations are false, it will be easy to prove."

She turns to me, so many emotions playing out on her face. "But when? I want to go home! I don't want to be trapped here and watch from afar how they burn my world down. No response is an admission of guilt."

"It's going to have to wait, Gigi. You can go back once we've dealt with Franco. This whole farce will be over then." She's too distraught to see clearly, but her common sense will kick in. "Our priority is to keep you safe. You won't prove any of those articles wrong if you're dead."

I can't even stomach that thought.

"God." She cups her hands to her face and shudders as she tries to suppress a sob.

"Here," I say as I pull her close again. "One thing at a time."

I bet she's still in shock of sorts. She's been good at pretending everything is fine. I bet she wouldn't have had this outburst in front of Carla. She'll even protect her sister from this.

"You showered," she eventually mumbles against my chest. "Was it to wash off those wome—"

"Don't say it, angel," I cut in, gentle but firm. "I went to the gym. As I do every day."

She takes a minute to digest this, then pulls away to look up at me. She is a mess of smudged mascara and red eyes and broken dreams. I want to kiss it all away.

Instead, I say, "Now if you would stop jumping to conclusions, I can explain why I have our clubs' exotic dancers come to my house on random weekday mornings."

She shudders out a little breath. “Exotic dancers? Like in *strippers*?”

“Some of them do, some of them don't. Depends on the club they're working at. They make good money, Gigi. And this is what they choose to do. We offer a safe environment, and I do financial planning for them on the side.”

“Financial planning?” She stares at me in disbelief. “Like in investments?”

“Yes. Some of these women have kids, and they want to send them to college. Some hope to retire earlier. None of them want to be in the industry forever.” I squeeze her hips. “And none of them work for us as prostitutes. In fact, they're regular employees on our payroll like anybody working in our offices. *Il Consiglio* doesn't do that type of shit. Not since we started cleaning up our operations as Matteo took over more and more of the businesses as our father got older.”

“Okay. Whatever.” She peels away from me, and I let her go. “What are your businesses then, because all I know is they can't be above board.”

“A lot of them are. Luca and I run the clubs, and we have some e-commerce things on the side. Dominic is in security.” I groan inwardly. Here it comes. “Matteo is in the import and export business. And Benedict is a hacker.” Amongst other shady online ventures.

“Import and exports. I see.” She gives a snarky laugh. “And hacking. Nice.”

“It's rather clean in comparison to a lot of things. And very profitable, like real estate. *Il Consiglio* owns several buildings in the city. Don Scalera acquired them, riding the wave of the real estate market like a pro surfer, so...” I won't lie, but she can read between the lines. Don Scalera might have started his real estate empire with laundered money, but decades down the line, it's all legit.

She throws up her hands and slumps back into her chair,

shaking her head as she presses her laptop's start button until it switches off. She closes the screen slowly, but the tears are back. "The only thing I wanted for us was to get out. To get away and have a different life. I promised my mom I'll look after Carla, and now this."

I, too, made promises to my mom. To be the antidote to the poison. Gigi is my fulfillment of that promise. "We'll figure it out, angel."

For a moment, heavy silence hangs between us. It's not only a promise, but also a future—our future. Something we'll figure out.

"What's all this?" she asks, and waves to the boxes I've dragged in.

"It's for you." I walk over and pick up a big rectangle. "I didn't know what scale you work at, so I got a starter pack. There's something of everything in here." I rip the paper off to reveal a canvas. "There's paint and turps and brushes. Uhm... Oils and acrylics and watercolors." Basically, *one of each* was my instruction this morning. "I might have gone a bit overboard."

I wanted to do something for her. Something that would make her happy. I don't buy in to her not being a good artist. She has passion and an eye for art. What with being prepared to run at any given moment for the past ten years, the one thing she's never had before was a quiet time and space to just paint and explore.

"Why on earth?" She slides a finger along the edge of the canvas.

"You need to find calm in the chaos, Gigi." This situation is either going to implode quickly, or it's going to drag on for months. Only time will tell, but with this forgery scandal, Franco showed his hand. He isn't shy about pulling out all the stops to get this woman and her money. "It's the only way to stay sane."

34

GIGI

It's late afternoon, and somehow, I've ended up at Tasha and Matteo's apartment. Stephano insisted I come see Carla. I can't explain to him how I need a break from my sister. When I'm with her, I have to keep up the façade that everything is okay. I must be strong for both of us as Carla, typical for her age, believes someone else is going to sort out the mess while she just cares for herself. By magic, everything is going to come right.

After Franco's attack on my business, things won't go back to what they were. If I were in England, or anywhere in Europe, I would have fought these allegations in the open. I would've scrambled to get lawyers in place and fight him through the legal system, but when it comes to the Mafia and staying in hiding, common law doesn't govern.

"What did you do today?" Carla asks.

We're sitting on her bed, where she was watching a movie on her laptop before I arrived.

The list is long, so I keep it short. She doesn't need to know. "I painted."

"Painted?" She leans forward and hugs her legs to her chest. "What did you paint?"

"A small canvas as a warmup. Toying with colors and so on."

To think Stephano got up this morning, ordered a whole art store of supplies for me, helped some staff with their personal finances, then went to the gym for almost three hours, only to come back and be the perfect husband by surprising me with his thoughtful gift. And this after I accused him of entertaining prostitutes.

And after the intimacy last night... I feel like a real fishwife, living up to my promise to be the most horrible wife ever. I'm swimming against the tide. I don't want to be that anymore, not with him giving me space to find calm in the chaos, talking to me, and showing me who he is.

"Sounds like fun," Carla says as she rocks herself.

"And you?"

"Nothing much, mostly looking into the course I'll be taking and so on."

"That's good." I can keep pretending, but there's no guarantee Carla will be going to university. I hope this situation can come to a head before her classes start. "How're you feeling?"

"I'm fine. Better than last week."

She looks fine. I don't know what stomach bug she caught, because I've been fine. She looks smaller here in this room, and I don't know if it's the weight loss from last week or the trauma in general that gives her this fragile air.

"Maybe you should still see a doctor? Just for a check-up. You've been through a lot."

"The last thing I want to do, Gigi, is to see a doctor. I'm fine. I'll be fine. It's been intense."

I lift my hands up and capitulate. "Okay."

There's no point in pressing her.

"Are you staying for dinner?" she asks.

"I don't know." The men are in Matteo's office, and who knows what they're discussing.

Stephano and I haven't made dinner plans. I bet Matteo wants his wife all to himself. Imagine being newlywed with house guests staying indefinitely. If there were space at Stephano's apartment, I would have insisted Carla come live with us. His place is too open concept, though, an exclusive bachelor's pad to the last brick, and Carla needs her space, which she has here. I'd love for her to get her own studio or something, but what with my cashflow cut off and the uncertainty and safety concerns, there's no way I could even suggest we look at places.

There's an awkward silence between us, and I have no clue how to crack it. It's been like this with her for months now. During our escape here, things were better, because we were each other's lifelines, but now, it's as if we're back in our own corners, cuddling our secrets.

"How was last night?" she asks, a blush staining her cheeks, and I exhale softly.

"It was fine." I don't want to discuss my fake marriage. "Is there an update on Papa?"

If there were, Stephano would have told me. I want to steer the conversation away from me, but Carla's bottom lip trembles, and she bursts into tears.

"No. There's been no word from anybody! What if he's dead? What if we indirectly killed him?"

I rub at my brow, not knowing what to say. "Time will tell, Carla, keep faith. Vincenzo won't—"

"You don't understand—"

A knock on the door makes her clam up, and after another knock, Tasha opens the door. "Are you staying for dinner? We've got so much leftover wedding food."

"I'm going to take a shower," Carla says as she gets off the bed.

She doesn't notice the pile of used tissues crumbling like a tower to the floor in her wake. She's been hiding those from me. I didn't see them when I arrived, because she literally sat down on them when I walked in.

"Have you checked with Stephano?" I ask Tasha as I stand. Something's up with Carla, and for the life of me, I can't pinpoint it.

"He said to check with you." She smiles, but it's forced as she arches an eyebrow at the pile of tissues on the bed.

I walk out of Carla's room and reach for Tasha's arm as she closes the door. "Has she spoken to you at all? Because she isn't speaking to me."

"No, I'm sorry. It seemed like she was coping, but she spent the whole day locked up in her room. I'm glad you came to see her."

"What does it help if I come see my sister, but she doesn't open up to me?" I feel lost, unfit to mother my younger sister. Something that's become harder with each year she gets closer to adulthood. It's as if she's saved face until the wedding was over and then basically caved in. "She needs to see a therapist. Talk to someone."

"I'll ask Matteo," Tasha says, but shakes her head as she tugs at my hand. "Come. I hate standing here."

"Why? It has such a view over the first floor. All the flowers from yesterday—"

A shiver runs through her. "Let's just say, I've seen things from this exact spot when Matteo held me captive...things that can't be unseen."

"What?" We're making our way to the stairs.

"I shouldn't have said anything, but I'm keen for us to move out of this apartment, and Matteo is working on it."

Oh my God. She saw someone being killed here, didn't she?

"Whoever it was, please tell me he deserved it," I say softly.

"Totally." She meets my gaze, and the particular understanding for this life, for what Mafia men get up to and how it affects us, passes between us.

I swallow, knowing the lay of the land. "Don't bother talking to Matteo. We both know no Scalera is going to allow us to talk to outsiders, even a shrink under oath of confidentiality."

She squeezes my arm. "I'm sorry."

"It's okay. Let me see if Stephano wants to stay for dinner."

"How was last night?" Tasha asks as we descend the stairs.

Honestly. Can everybody stop poking their noses in our business already? "It was fine."

"I can't help feeling there's something brewing between you two. The way Stephano kissed you yesterday—"

"There's nothing going on between us." Never mind sex, kissing is the last thing on the agenda, even though he made my knees weak with his kiss when we sealed our marriage. I couldn't deny him that one so we'll have a photo as proof should Homeland Security ever come poking around our fake marriage.

Matteo's office door opens as we take the last stair, and Stephano's eyes catch mine across the expanse of the room. My heart skips a beat, and my stomach flutters with butterflies as if on cue. I can feel Tasha's gaze burning on me as a blush spreads like wildfire over my cheeks.

"I know *nothing* when I see *nothing*," she says with a suppressed smirk.

I can't stay a minute longer than needed in this apartment, being scrutinized like a bug, and pretending I'm fine. "We won't stay for dinner. Thank you all the same."

"You good to go home, Gigi?" Stephano asks as he closes in on us, probably having read my expression.

"Yes." I don't need to sound so desperate, but suddenly, all I want is to be home, alone, with my husband. The one person in this world who knows everything. I bet he's told Matteo what happened today. Now that the initial shock has passed, I'm exhausted.

"Let's go."

He takes my hand, and I don't have it in me to protest. Honestly, he could guide me into Hell right now, and I'd follow him blindly. I can't pinpoint what changed my opinion of him like this. All I can hope is that it will last.

We say our goodbyes, and eventually, we're on our way back to his apartment. It's quiet in the car. I'm too tired to make small talk, and Stephano seems deep in thought. We both stare out of our respective windows as the driver navigates Boston's rush-hour traffic.

"How's Carla doing?" he asks when we're almost home.

"I don't know. She didn't talk much, and I sense something's off, but I don't know what."

He searches my face and then sighs. "You can't protect her from everything, angel."

A fact I'm not ready to acknowledge.

He holds my hand as we scale the stairs to the apartment, and once we're inside, he takes me by the shoulders and turns me to face him. "Do you trust me, angel?"

"You asked last night."

"Yes, but I ask you again. Do you trust me?"

I swallow at the knot in my throat. His stare is so intense, it's as if he wants to strip away every layer that ever was between us. "Why do you ask again?"

He skims his hands down my arms and catches my fingers with his. "Because there's going to come a time where you'll doubt everything. In that moment, I need you to come back to this one and remember that you *trust* me."

"I... I..." My voice breaks, and I'm in his arms.

"Say it, angel. Say the truth now."

"I trust you," I whisper as I look up at him.

He drops his head back and exhales deeply as he hugs me close. “Okay.”

“What’s going on, Steph? What’s happened? You’re scaring me. Does Franco—”

“No, not yet. But soon.” He peers into my eyes. “Remember this moment.” He leans in and presses the softest of kisses to my forehead. “I’ll sleep on the sofa going forward.”

“But...” I swallow my own protest as he lets go of me and walks to his office and closes the door, exiling me from his presence. My heart sinks, one beat at a time, to the pit of my stomach.

The one thing that kept me going was the notion that he’d be there tonight, at some point holding me close.

35

STEPHANO

I sit at my desk and send Dominic a message from my phone.

You've been monitoring Carla's laptop?

DOMINIC

Yes. Gigi's too. Why? So far, no red flags.

I huff out a breath.

Best keep an eye on what's going on there. Something's up with Carla and she won't talk to Gigi. Matty's picked up on it too.

DOMINIC

Will do. As for Gigi's business, Franco's given us the perfect starting point for our cat and mouse game.

I know. Want to comment and get this party started?

DOMINIC

I'll check with Benny and make it happen. Will keep you posted.

I got the women company-issued laptops and phones for this reason. We have simple spyware installed in what seemed like brand-new products. We can see everything they do, from the last email they sent, to the porn they watch, if any.

I groan. To think I demanded to know from Gigi whether she trusts me. Looking at everything we've put in place to keep tabs on them, she shouldn't trust any Scalera at all. It's not like their story of fleeing for their lives didn't ring true when they arrived, but we're *Il Consiglio,* and Trojan horses come in many shapes and sizes.

So far, nothing has indicated we're being set up for revenge for Randazzo's death or by anybody else. Gigi and Carla's story holds true. It seems nobody has linked Matteo and Tasha's presence to what happened in Sicily almost two months ago, but in our line of work, you can never be too careful.

I log in on my laptop to do some other work I've been neglecting, but my head isn't in it. It's because my heart is walking around the apartment behind my closed office door. Gigi is moving her art supplies or something, and I burn to tell her to leave it as it is. Make my apartment's first floor her studio.

Invade and conquer, angel, as you seem to be so good at it.

Fuck.

After we unpacked all the art supplies, she set up the easel and played for hours. I gave her the space she needed, came to hide in my office and tried to work. By late afternoon, she knocked on my open door and peeked in, a smaller canvas in her hand.

I stood as she walked in, torn between wanting to push her to my desk and fuck her senseless, and giving her the space she needs.

"It's in oil so still wet." She came around the desk and propped the canvas up against my monitor. She'd painted Palermo's Porta

Felice, a small copy of Mom's painting, but in her own style. "I made this for you...uhm... You keep on calling me your angel, but today, I've realized you're the angel here, Steph. I don't know how you do it, but you always know exactly what I need." She looked up at me, cheeks flushed and shy. "Thank you."

She went on her toes and wrapped me in a hug, and as I pulled her close, all resistance in her body seemed to deflate out of her.

That's what she'd needed in that moment: a long, warm hug.

Angel. She called me *her angel.* The last thing I needed was for her to break the final barrier standing between my heart and her. She has it now. Carries it around in the palm of her hand.

I'm so screwed. I stare at the small painting where it's propped up against a stack of books. It's fantastic, and to think Gigi thinks she doesn't have what it takes. The memory of this afternoon does things to me. My heart rate speeds up, my cock pushes against my fly, and deep inside me, I die a little. *This* wasn't the plan. Scalera boys don't get to love.

Falling in love with the woman who used to hate me, who told me I'm an angel, not knowing I'm the devil who's about to use her as a deathtrap for one of the biggest rising Mafia overlords in Europe. *I* know it's to keep her safe forever, but *she'll* think I've done it for her money when reality sinks in and never forgive me if things go wrong. If things go wrong, she'll be dead, and I won't be able to live with myself.

This afternoon, I had to get away from her body, from her sweet soul that always puts everybody else first. I stepped away from her, and I told her she needed to go see her sister.

I was grabbing at straws, but I had to see my brothers. They were all at Matteo's house already, waiting for us. While she was with Carla, Benedict led the meeting. We're all systems go.

Everything's in place. We only have to drop the first breadcrumb, and the crows will come.

I've loved before, and I've lost. Mom. Tatiana. Now Gigi. I can't lose her too. In a weak-ass attempt to protect myself from getting shredded again, I told her I'll sleep on the fucking sofa. As if that would help. I want her. And fuck knows, I need her. *You're more your mother than your father.* Her words have been eating at me, and now that she's seen me in that light, I want to prove it again and again to myself.

It's in your blood.

No, it isn't. *You're the angel here, Steph.*

I drop my face to my hands and breathe slowly, trying to calm the rising panic of being with her, before I flip into the violence always simmering in my core.

I sit for a long time, becoming calm enough to go through every single step of our plan, looking for holes and mistakes people can make. We've closed all our gaps, and Franco Fiore remains our only variable. Until he reacts to what we do, we won't know how to adjust our plans to plug the holes we don't know about yet.

By the time I've broken down every emotion, feeling numb, it's almost midnight. It's been quiet in the apartment for a long while. Gigi should be asleep, alone in the loft. I switch off all the lights and pad out of my office. I glance over the kitchen and out to the lit-up Boston skyline as I make my way to the sofa. I didn't think far enough to grab pillows and a blanket from the bedroom, but when I reach the sectional, I freeze.

Gigi is lying under our bed's duvet, which she must have dragged down the stairs. Our pillows are there, and the sofa's been stripped of its own, making it much wider, comfortable for two skinny teens, which we are not.

Baby. Angel. My love....

"Steph?" She leans up on her elbow and blinks into the dark, sounding half-asleep.

"What are you doing down here, Gigi?" I murmur, really wanting to growl at how she's played this.

"I don't want to sleep alone, and since you said you'd take the sofa, I came here." She sits up and opens the duvet for me to crawl in.

"What are you wearing?" The big windows bring in enough light so I can see it isn't one of the pieces I bought her.

She shrugs. "I dug... I'm sorry. I dug in your cupboard and borrowed a T-shirt."

She's going to kill me. So fucking slowly. Death by blue balls.

"All I want, Steph, is to hold you, and be held in return when I need it." She sucks her bottom lip. "Nothing else. Please. Just that."

She needs to be held. I knew this.

Control freak. I smirk. She called me that on our wedding night, and now, she's testing me. "Nothing else?"

"Nothing else."

"Fine." I unbutton my shirt, trying my hardest to ignore my fucking cock that's begging for everything we've agreed is off the cards.

"What happened to you?" she asks as I toss the shirt to the side, her eyes wide as they travel the expanse of my chest and sides. "You're hurt! You're—"

"Just bruised. I sparred in the gym this morning."

"*Sparred*? Steph—"

"It's fine. I'm used to it."

"Is this what you do to—"

"Yes, angel," I say as I slip under the duvet and into her arms. "This is what I do. This is me."

Raw and undiluted. Who needs tattoos if your skin is an ever-changing landscape created by battles you fight with the monsters within? I slip my hand under the T-shirt and over her butt, and sigh in frustrated relief to find she's wearing panties.

"You need to stop, Steph! It's cruel—"

"No, it isn't. I need it like Franco Fiore needs to cut into people."

She shudders in my arms. "God. Please don't compare yourself to him."

I have more in common with Franco than I'd ever admit. "Shh. Go to sleep."

She burrows her head under my chin, her hand on my chest wandering, feeling for where I'm swollen and bruised. I sigh into her hair, sinking into the feel of her gentle touch and soft curves against my harder, tougher frame.

"Whatever you do, angel, don't kiss it better."

36

GIGI

I wake up, and Steph is next to me on his side. His eyes are closed, but his fingers are playing with strands of my hair. I blink into the light.

"How did this happen?" We're not downstairs on the sofa, but in the loft and in bed.

"That sofa is uncomfortable as all fuck," he says, a hint of a smile on his lips.

Maybe we're both asleep and in a dream. "You carried me upstairs?"

"Hm-hmm."

I didn't notice any of that happening.

"I was exhausted," I murmur, but I couldn't fall asleep until he was with me.

I'm latching onto this man as if he's a drug. And it only took one hit.

The covers are pulled down to his hips, and with the morning light from the windows, I can see every punch he took yesterday. Inwardly, I wince as I can almost hear his body's resistance with each hit. "Tell me the other guy looks worse?"

"They both look worse."

Both? He fought two guys? My heart pounds in my throat at the mere thought of it.

I run my forefinger down his biceps to his pec and lower where he's bruised on his ribs.

He catches my hand as he rolls on his back. "Don't go there, angel."

But I want to go down there desperately. I'm literally thirsting for him. I get up on my elbow, lean in, and trail soft kisses on his shoulder and over his chest, kissing it better. I press my nose to his warm skin, inhaling the intoxicating scent of this man. He smells so good, I want to lick him. So I do.

He lets go of my hand, and my fingers caress his sides and the ripples of his six-pack as he contracts into my touch. "Let me go there, please, Steph."

He exhales slowly as my fingers spread wide enough to go beyond his navel, toying with his happy trail.

"Fuck, Gigi. Asking so nicely. The next thing you're going to tell me is *it isn't sex*."

"It isn't."

I giggle as I pull the duvet away from where his erection tents it. *Oh my...* No pants, no sleep shorts, no nothing. I bite my lip... I'm so going to gag on him, but even that thought is arousing. I run my tongue around my lips before I take the tip and circle it, slowly, savoring his taste and the way his cock jerks against my lips.

Stephano grunts and drives his fingers into my hair. "God, you're my perfect fantasy, you know that? So fucking perfect... And I bet you're going to take me deep, aren't you, angel?"

His words make me slow down. *His perfect fantasy*. He's never called me a whore...that was me. My words. My mind always veering towards the worst when it comes to men in the Mafia. "Is this what you thought of me? That night in Cannes?"

He fists his hand in my hair and steers me away from his cock, forcing me to look at him.

"Yes. I never thought of you as anything but a fantasy actually coming to life." He cups my face with his other hand and traces my lips with his thumb. "But you're more than that, angel. I love my wife being this strong, kick-ass woman to the outside world, but a needy, wanton goddess in bed for me, and me alone. Being weak for my cock, wanting and needing it at all hours. You're more than the perfect fantasy, angel, you're so real, and I'm the only one who knows you like this."

I swallow, his words seeming to steal their way down my body to my clit where I pulse with desire.

"And then there's more. Do you know what it does to a man to know that his wife needs him so fucking much, she can't sleep when he doesn't hold her close?"

"No?"

"It makes him want to burn down the world to protect her," he murmurs. "Now go down, take what you want, angel, and finish what you've started."

He softens his grip on my hair, and something in me shifts. I'm already his, to do with as he pleases. Maybe I am a whore, for this man only.

I hum as I close my lips around him and drive down, wetting his shaft and dragging up again.

"Good girl," he sighs as his touch turns into a caress.

I go deeper with every pump of his cock until he hits the back of my throat which is way too soon. Stephano is big, my eyes are tearing, and I haven't even taken in all of him. I wrap my fingers around the base for extra pressure and find my rhythm, sensing him tense as his hips grind up to meet me halfway.

"Fuck, angel," he hisses as he pulls my head away, sits up, and forces me to kneel. "I need to touch you."

His hands skim over my breasts to my T-shirt's hem, and he tugs it off in one sweep. He cups my face, gathering my messed-up hair away as he stares at my lips. They tingle with the need to be kissed, but instead, he homes in on my breasts, heavy with need for him to suck and toy with my nipples.

"You're so perfect," he whispers as he glides his hands down my chest, fondling my breasts as he circles his thumbs over my nipples.

I snatch in a breath at the intense desire flooding through my body at his touch, which travels ever lower until he slides his finger down my slit and right into me.

"Steph—"

"Open wider, angel," he says as he shifts to lean into me, his lips on my temple, my ear, down to my neck with slow but greedy kisses that only make me widen my knees and sink down onto his hand.

"How can a man not love his wife when she's drenched like this for him," he murmurs as he fucks me with his fingers. "Every single time, angel, when I touch you here, it's as if *this* is the only thing you've been thinking about the whole day."

I swallow as I drop my head back, too aroused at his words and the workings of his fingers deep in me to lie. "Maybe it is the only thing I've been thinking and dreaming of."

"Day and night?"

"Day and night."

"On your back, angel," he says as he extracts his hand, and this is it.

This is the moment he is going to finally succumb and fuck me raw as I've wanted from the moment we met. Break his vows and finally make me his.

"Like this, to open your throat."

He guides me by my shoulders, so my head is tipping over the edge of the bed and then he's there, standing behind me, his massive cock hovering over my lips. I suck him into my mouth, and he grunts as he pushes deep, not gentle either, testing my limits already. He holds still as his hand glides down the column of my neck, down between my breasts and all the way to where my legs are spread open in invitation.

"Good girl," he hums as he slides his fingers deep into my sex, curling them to where I feel the build-up he coaxes out of me so easily.

I caress my hands over his thighs to his butt and urge him to move in sync. He curses as he starts to piston into my mouth, his hand working me in the same rhythm. He's going so deep now, but there's space, and I dig my nails into his butt as my toes curl into the mattress.

"Fuck, Gigi," he grunts as he drives faster and harder, his free hand cupping my chin gently. "You feel so fucking good. You're good?"

I hum back, my orgasm already riding in, his palm hitting my mound with just the right pressure on my clit to break down every resistance. I moan as I come, and his fingers still as he curls them hard against my inner wall, and my muscles pulse and squeeze against his hold.

The ripples of his own orgasm ride down my tongue, and he spills into my throat, and when I swallow, he hisses something about *most perfect, most beautiful wife of mine*, but I'm so dazed, it could have been anything.

He eases out of me, first his hand, then his cock as he circles his fingers around my wrists. I struggle up, my head swaying, but he sits on the edge of the bed with me, his hands cupping my face.

"I knew that mouth would be the sweetest thing on the planet," he whispers as he slides his fingers over my lips.

I taste and smell my release as I dart my tongue out, licking his fingers where they're toying with my mouth, dipping in and out.

"We should fuck like that again," he murmurs as I open my eyes and meet his gaze.

His hand has stilled on my cheek, his thumb paused on my

lips. He's staring at me, so intently, and I know he's going to kiss me.

It's all I want. A kiss. From the man who used the words *love* and *wife* twice this morning in the same sentence, each time making my heart beat faster with a weird joy I've never felt before.

He comes closer and presses the softest, most gentle kiss to the corner of my mouth, just shy of my lips.

"I've got to get going," he says as he presses his forehead to mine. "Party's starting."

I have no clue what he means, but I stare as he walks naked to the bathroom. I blink and do a double take. Those are scratches on his fine ass, down his thighs.

My scratches, adding to the image of a broken, tortured soul painted on the canvas of his skin.

37

STEPHANO

It's been a week since Franco ripped Gigi's business to shreds with a smear campaign. It's been a week since Gigi and I started sleeping together every night, doing everything you possibly can in bed without breaking her terms. It's a challenge, and I'm on the verge of losing my goddamn mind and all control when it comes to her.

Here's the funny thing about sex. When you can't have the real thing, it's all you think of. We might do everything else, but I'm not sated. Which means I think of it all the fucking time.

To say I'm fucked is an understatement. I'm in love with my wife. The wife I've vowed to never have. The wife who plans to leave me as soon as she can be safe back in Europe. The wife I've promised to let go.

Worst thing is, she's the wife I've promised to protect at all costs now everything we've put in place is about to be tested. I read the message on my phone again.

Benedict: *Meeting at Matty's asap. Party's starting.*

I stalk out of my office as I pull on my jacket. Gigi is sitting by the window, a fresh canvas on the easel. This is the calm realm we've been orbiting in. She's painting while I'm supposedly working in my office. I'm working myself up every day with her, break myself down in the gym, battling for control over my mind and body when it comes to her. Just seeing her sit there in an old T-shirt of mine and panties is enough to make my cock rise in salute.

"I'm going to Matteo's. You want to come with me?"

She lowers the paintbrush and glances at me. "Right now?"

"Yes."

Her hair is gathered in a messy pile on her head, and it bobs as she shrugs. "Why? We were there yesterday."

"Something's come up."

"I'll pass. Honestly, I know Carla needs me, but—"

"It's fine." I've caught on that my wife is an introvert and needs her space. It would seem the two women have almost become estranged in the past weeks, which I hope they don't blame me for. I run my hand up her naked thigh and trace the line of her panties as I press a soft kiss to her temple. This is so close to a real marriage now, even I buy into it. "Go put on pants."

She rolls her eyes at me. "Tony?"

"Yes, angel, Tony."

"Does he have to be here?"

"Yep." I pocket my phone. Whenever I leave, a bodyguard stays with her. She's been hesitant to go out, and I'm surprised she hasn't gone mad with cabin fever yet. "I won't be long."

I watch as she takes the stairs until she's out of view and wait until she comes down again, this time with yoga pants on. I let Tony in and make my way to Matteo's place. By the time I walk into his office, the whole gang has gathered. It's weird how special projects like these seem to pull us together stronger with each round.

Matteo hands me a printout as I take a seat. "There've been some developments."

I glance down the pages. It's a record of someone's internet search history. Lines and lines of searches for Vito Rossi, Vittorio Rossi, then copies of emails sent into the abyss with one-liner questions. *Where are you? Are you okay?* It's all as anonymous as it can get, but one thing is clear: the messages are becoming more and more urgent.

"This is from Carla's laptop?"

"Yep," Benedict says. "She's starting to sound desperate there, don't you think?"

"Vito Rossi was her bodyguard," I say. "He helped them escape Italy, and he has no clue where they are. That's what Gigi told me."

Gigi has been slow to share the details of everything exactly as they happened weeks ago, but I've been able to put the puzzle pieces together to sketch a picture of that night. My wife is indeed a brave, kick-ass woman.

"He was going to go look out for Don Trapani after he made sure the women got to the airport. By the sound of it, Don Trapani might have been tortured that night."

"One man against Franco Fiore and his ring?" Matteo asks.

"Yeah." I sigh. "He's probably dead." A moment of silence stretches as we digest this inevitability. We might have welcomed the Trapanis into our fold, but it's not without risks. If Vito Rossi was more to Carla than her bodyguard, she would be mourning him. "That would explain her mood lately."

"And what a mood it's been," Matteo says with a grunt.

"Time will tell," Dominic says. "If there's anything new, I'll let you know."

"Do you have something similar from Gigi's laptop or phone?" I ask, turning to Benedict.

"No, nothing to raise a red flag. She's only been browsing endless art-related websites, auction houses, basically anything related to her business. She's sent no emails, hasn't even bothered to log into her account."

I nod. Ever since I bought her those art supplies, it's as if

Gigi has shut out the outside world. She's in some type of mourning, too, except she still intends to go back to Europe and pick up the shreds of what's left of her old life.

"But in other news," Benedict says, "we're finally getting traction on Franco. He's sending a scout our way."

"A scout?" I ask.

"Yes. We commented on an online article about Gigi selling fakes. Now, Vincenzo Trapani has tapped in and is coming over to see if our hint that Gigi Trapani is trying to set up shop in Boston holds true." Benedict has his laptop connected to the projector, and he throws an image on the screen. "This is Gigi and Carla's brother."

I take in the picture of a tanned man, average height, five o'clock stubble, shortly cropped dark hair, and dressed in a way I can only approve of. Nothing gives away he's Mafia, except the dark circles under his eyes. Someone isn't getting enough sleep.

"Party's starting," Dominic says with a grin.

The heat is on. Vincenzo Trapani is the loser who sold out his sisters and whose face I'm going to rearrange, for starters. Gigi will never be safe while her stepbrother is alive.

"When is he arriving?" I ask, hoping Benedict will somehow have this intel.

"He arrived this morning, got flagged by my team working on border control," he says, leaning back with a satisfied smirk. "And you are taking Gigi to the opening of an art exhibition on Friday night, at Kowalski's Fine Art. By the look of her browsing data, she's burning to go."

38

GIGI

"Are you sure it's going to be fine?"

Stephano is holding my hand where we're sitting in the back seat of his SUV. His driver will drop us off at the entrance of the high rise where the Kowalski's Fine Art exhibition space is located on the top floor. There's an adjacent wine bar and restaurant, and apparently, this is the place to be seen on the East Coast art scene.

"Yes, we have a security detail looking out for us."

The driver pulls up to the building, and Tony clambers out to open the door. Stephano holds out his hand for me and helps me out of the car. I'm wearing a long, flowing dress with a halter neck and a low back in midnight blue chiffon, with silver heels.

Getting dressed for tonight hit me with intense nostalgia. This is the first time in months I got dressed up to go somewhere, and Steph arranged for some boutique to come over with dresses and shoes for me to choose from.

When he caught me on my laptop staring at this exhibition opening tonight, he suggested we go. I was almost in tears. Not that he hasn't suggested we go out before—he always wants to take me out for dinner or to one of their clubs—but right now, I don't have it in me. This is something I can't miss. Alejandro Reyes is up and coming, and getting in with him at the start of his career is gold.

I haven't given up on my business yet. I've put it on hold. Once Franco is dead, there will be a way to prove the whole smear campaign was a scam. I will need time, and to be in Europe, so I can meet people in person.

We make our way to the elevator, and I can't be sure who is our security detail. There are other couples in suits and formal dress entering the building, creating a pile-up at the elevator bank.

"Busy night." I'm jittery with excitement I can't suppress. This is like having a slice of my old life back, except this time, it's better. I have Steph by my side.

"Yeah. You'll see there's enough space. The exhibition area is massive and very well laid out."

"You've been here before?" I ask as I shoot him a glance, but then, it sinks in. "Of course you have. To make sure it's safe?"

"To buy some art, angel, and eat at the restaurant—" He leans into my ear as he squeezes my hand. "Like normal people."

He slides his lips over my ear, and it sends a rush of goose bumps down my skin where it spreads hot desire through my body. This man... Steph has been the perfect husband in so many ways, I've stopped keeping track.

I lean closer, his solid body always there for me, and he wraps an arm around me and caresses my butt. His gun presses against my arm, and a shudder runs through me. There must always be a little reminder why we're not *normal people*.

We ride up to the top floor, and Steph has me in the corner, his body protecting me. Tony is next to us, his eyes looking lazily at the other people in the elevator, but I'm not fooled. *Il*

Consiglio is a well-run, tight ship, and Tony is taking stock of every person here. I'm safe.

I exhale slowly as we reach the top floor and file out to the foyer where a hostess greets and directs the line to either the restaurant and wine bar, or to the art gallery. Steph's hand is on my lower back, guiding me to the bigger open space. All white with perfect lighting to accentuate the art on the walls and the sculptures taking space center stage.

I rest my hand on his arm, almost giddy.

"Thank you so much for bringing me," I whisper as I glance up at him.

He covers my hand with his. "Any time, angel."

We walk the exhibit together for a while, and I'm lost in a world I've found again. Nothing can kill my joy now. Steph's comments are interesting, but I have no reason to be surprised. His love for art is displayed on the big wall in his apartment. I pull my phone out to start making notes, and Steph strays onward to the next piece.

I'm so deep in thought with my notes that I don't take stock of the suit that comes to stand close to me.

"Sorry," I say as I step to the side to make space, but an Arctic chill invades my body as I glance at the man's profile.

"Fancy seeing you here, Gigi." He steps closer and touches me on my lower back as if he would lean in and kiss me like a sister.

A frisson of disgusted loathing mixed with fear spills like a bucket of cold water over me.

"Cenzo." I falter on my heels as I step away, gripping my clutch tight as my heart starts pounding in my temple.

"So sweet to hear you call me that." Vincenzo steps closer, and it's the most threatening thing I've experienced in years. "I've missed you, Gigi."

My gaze darts over his shoulder and to the side. Steph is right there, rolling on his heels, five meters from me, unaware.

Tony is watching me, though, and would step up—but there's another man who closes in and blocks his way. God help us. Vincenzo has security here too.

"How did y-you...how did you know where to find us?"

How did he know I'd be here tonight? Fear coils in me. Since that Friday night in Lake Como, I've realized my stepbrother is a vile, dangerous man.

"Following leads. You're not the only one with friends." He reaches for my hand, and I'm too weak to pull back, frozen to the spot. "And what's this? A wedding ring?"

"I'm married. I'm no longer available for Franco Fiore."

"Are you now?" He cocks his brow with a lopsided grin as if I made a joke. "To whom?"

"Steph!" I jerk my hand out of Vincenzo's, trying to catch Stephano's attention without making a scene. He turns my way, but doesn't rush over, and panic sprints through my veins.

"Steph? That was a bit hasty, wasn't it?' Vincenzo says. "To think if you married me when you turned eighteen, none if this would have happened."

"I would never have married you," I spit out. "And to think you sold us off! Carla, so young and your own *blood* sister."

And then, Stephano is there. His hand snakes around my shoulders. "Do you know this guy, angel?"

"*Angel*?" Vincenzo mocks as his gaze jumps between mine and Stephano's. "Franco did say someone else called you that before. A lover, maybe, but never a *husband*."

He holds out his hand to Stephano as if this is a cordial meeting, but Stephano doesn't return the gesture. He gives Vincenzo the coldest stare that makes me cower.

"And you are?" he says as he reaches for Vincenzo's shoulder, gripping it with a hand that turns white with the pressure. A subtle threat.

Vincenzo shrugs him off with a wince. "Vincenzo Trapani.

Gigi and Carla's brother. I came to fetch my *soon-to-be-widowed* sister."

"Isn't that interesting," Steph says. "And here I thought we're here for a pleasant night out."

"I'm cutting this marriage venture of yours short, as my sister Gigi has been promised to another man. I'm here to take her home. Come with me now, Gigi, and it will be a clean exit."

"I see," Stephano says, staring Vincenzo down. He's at least seven inches taller than my stepbrother. "Funny thing. I don't like threats. Least of all to my wife. Touch your sister again, and I'll kill you."

"As if this is a real marriage." Vincenzo smirks. "I hate to say it, but you're in too deep."

Stephano throws his head back and laughs. "Right. Come, angel, you've seen enough?"

Tremors run through my body, and I'm clinging to Steph's biceps where I've turned into him, expecting a Mafia-style shoot-out at any second.

"Yes," I say, but my voice is small.

He has me by the hand and leads me away, but he isn't in a rush. I want to run.

"There's no way he is buying into any of this," I whisper. "He knows it's all fake! He knows, and he's going to tell Franco, and then—"

Stephano stops in his tracks outside the glass partition wall separating the gallery from the elevator bank. He stares down at me for a few hot seconds, his gaze taking in my eyes, my lips, and then he jerks me to his chest, his arm protective around me as his hand weaves into my hair that cascades down my back. He's never held me this close.

"You're worried Vincenzo will think our marriage is fake and that's the biggest factor in warding off Franco?"

"Yes, I know it sounds naive but— He's threatened to kill you!" I almost choke on the words.

When did this happen? The idea of Stephano being killed is too much, and I ache. Tears I've managed to ward off slip down my cheek, and Stephano cups my jaw, brushing them away with his thumb. I swear he can feel my heart beating against his chest. I'm faint with the shock of seeing Vincenzo here and the fact that Steph might die.

"Your biggest worry is that Vincenzo will think this is a fake marriage?"

"Yes... The idea was to make it seem real, to stop Franco, to get out—"

"It's very real, angel," he interrupts as he rakes his fingers into my hair, pulling down and forcing me to look up at him. "If only you would open your eyes to see the truth."

His mouth hovers for a second over my lips, and then he kisses me, his lips possessive and demanding. His mouth opens mine as I moan into the unapologetic way he invades me. Stephano deepens the kiss, and now, my heart is all over the place. Pulsing in my sex where I contract wantonly for him as his hands splay over my butt and squeeze. I wrap my arms around him, legs weak with the surprise and intensity of his kiss as his tongue conquers my mouth. He grips me closer and steadies me to him.

Oh, God. I've wanted this so much. I've needed this for so long. We've been so good at keeping to those terms we set out, but I know tonight, we are going to break every last vow we've made. I need us to make this real because I'm in love with my husband.

Stephano pulls away.

"Fuck," he groans. "I've been wanting to do that since the first day on your yacht in Cannes." He presses into my lower belly, making me feel the need he has for me. "Let's go," he says, his voice husky.

"Vincenzo?"

"He's being taken care of."

I glance through the glass wall to see four suited men surrounding Vincenzo, blocking him from following us. Our gazes meet, and a shudder rips through me. Another man is standing too close to a guy with a scar on his cheek; he must have him at gunpoint. Tony is standing by the elevators, mere meters from us, his lazy gaze not missing a thing.

"Has this been a set-up?" I ask as we get into the elevator.

"I told you to trust me," Stephano says as he turns his shoulder so most of my body is blocked with my back against the wall.

He reaches for my hand, and his callused fingers lace with mine. I stare down at our hands where he's holding mine close.

He didn't show an inch of fear or doubt, every movement, every word so controlled, it was as if they were rehearsed.

As soon as we're in the car and the driver pulls away, he leans closer. "Our men will take Vincenzo to an undisclosed location. There, he'll help us learn everything else about Franco Fiore that we don't already know."

My stomach turns as his words sink in. Vincenzo might not live to see tomorrow. I have no idea what Stephano is capable of. To think I doubted him when I came here—actually doubted his ability to be cruel. But this... This was something else.

I was wrong about Stephano Scalera, and not for the first time.

39

STEPHANO

I curse under my breath as we wait at a red traffic light. The need to get my wife home is compounding by the second. She's reeling from the shock of seeing Vincenzo at the gallery, but everything went as planned, and my brain has already moved south. I'm hard as fuck and heady with having kissed her.

I broke our vows and kissed my wife. And she kissed me back, riding up my cock with her body, not even aware. She's been wanting this, craving it, just like me. If there were space in the back seat, I would have gone on my knees and spread her wide, but fuck, my cock wants to bury in her so deep, it never wants to see sunshine again. I can live and die in that tight little pussy of hers and be a happy, fulfilled man.

She's sitting flush against me, her hand quivering on my thigh. Maybe seeing Vincenzo was too much for her, so soon after escaping Italy. I'm used to this rush. I've been groomed for it and then molded by it for years. *Il Consiglio* likes a clean business and a clean slate, but those don't go together in our line of work.

Gigi hasn't been in this world for years. She drops her head to my shoulder, and I press a kiss to her hair as she skims a hand up my chest to cup my jaw.

"Why didn't you tell me?" she whispers as she stares right into my soul. "Things could have gone wrong."

I don't have the time or inclination to explain how Dominic and his team secured the gallery. She doesn't need to know his team apprehended two other men who were there on Vincenzo's side, waiting to kidnap her. She doesn't need to know Vincenzo is being drugged as we sit here and will find himself locked up in the special soundproof room next to Matteo's apartment for interrogation. An interrogation which will end with his body being dry frozen and eventually fed to the fish in the string of legit pet stores we own.

I sigh. "We needed the surprise factor. If I told you, you would've refused to go. You're not a princess in a tower, angel. You can't hide forever."

"But what if...what if you'd got hurt, or worse? Been killed?" she whispers as she fists my lapel. "Steph—"

"I wouldn't have been. And I won't be. I have my brothers. Here, Franco is a loner. He might have mercenaries, or men that work for him under duress, but he doesn't have the network or backup I have."

She sniffs as she wipes at a tear. "Can't you see? That makes him ruthless, which makes him dangerous. He has nothing to lose."

I hug her close and lift her chin with my fingertip. "And I have everything to lose. I'll protect you with my life if it's the last thing I do."

"Don't say that," she murmurs, but I'm already closing the gap between us, and when we kiss, it's as if the world stops existing.

I'm gentle with her now, not only because we're in an enclosed space and it seems to shrink with our need, but Tony is in the front seat, and my driver is constantly looking in the rear-view mirror. I'm not keen on giving anybody a show.

Gigi's hand slips into my jacket and under the holster with my gun.

"Angel," I murmur against her lips. I'm not comfortable with her so close to a weapon. It's dumb, because they won't, but things could go wrong.

"Boss," my driver says, and I look up. "We have a tail."

What the fuck? I don't glance back, but meet the driver's eyes in the mirror. "You know what to do."

He accelerates and changes lanes, cautious, but putting distance between us and whoever is following us. This wasn't the plan. This wasn't even on our radar.

Gigi stares out of the back window, her eyes wide.

"Keep your head down." I pull my phone from my inner pocket and press the speed dial for Dominic's number. He answers in seconds, having been on standby in case shit hit the fan.

"All clear?" Dominic asks.

"No, we have a tail," I say as I glance back. "Luca has Vincenzo?"

"Yes. Bait and switch works like a fucking charm every single time."

I don't want to be charmed; I want my wife safe. "Why do we have a tail, then?"

"Boss, we have two now," the driver says as he swerves, tires screeching.

I wrap my arm around Gigi.

"Where the fuck did the other one come from?" I hiss.

"Slipped in from the side," Tony says, his gun shining in the streetlights as we speed past. "This isn't a normal tail."

"What the fuck's going on, Steph?" Dominic shouts into the phone.

"We're being tracked. And how the fuck did that happen?" I

growl. Gigi has shrunk into a ball next to me, hiding. "Get someone on this, Dom, like in *now*."

"Got it," he says.

I kill the call as the driver speeds onto the highway. He accelerates even more as the road clears.

I pluck my gun from its holster as I run my hand over Gigi's hip, recalling how Vincenzo rested his hand on her in greeting, and I almost lost my shit. It took everything in me not to rip at him in that moment and to let the scene play out. That fucker will never touch her again.

"Check your dress," I say as I feel her down with one hand.

"What?"

"Feel your dress for anything weird. Vincenzo might have planted a tracker on you in the gallery when the fucker touched you." Seems par for the course, given what Franco wanted to implant in her arm.

"You saw? Oh my God," she whispers, in panic running her hands all over her body.

"Of course I saw, angel. And I wanted to fuck up his face for touching you."

"Oh, my...what? Here." Her hand stops on her back and she leans forward so I can follow her hands in the dark. I freeze when I touch the small capsule-sized device Vincenzo must have stuck on her back. Between the folds of the dress and the zipper, she wouldn't have noticed it at all.

"Fuck," I hiss as I rip it off, taking some fabric with it. After giving it a quick inspection in the dark, I open the window and toss it outside. I want to keep it, but have no choice.

Gigi blinks at me. "It's similar to the tracker he tried to implant under my skin."

The cut on her inner arm has healed, but it's left a nasty scar, over an inch long and ugly. The fucker who sliced her open wasn't doing plastic surgery, that's for sure. Another reminder of what Franco did to her. Every cell in my body riots as adrenaline rushes through my blood. I feel like I'm going to flip. I drop my hand to her thigh, and it steadies me.

The driver swerves again and takes the off ramp, and Tony leans back and looks through the rear window to see whether we've ditched our tail. We take another turn and then about five others, and finally, we're in a quieter residential street. I glance around. Front and back. We're alone.

"Pull over," I say, and the driver parks the car in an open slot between a car and someone's driveway.

"What now?" Gigi asks.

"We wait."

I stare out of the black-out window to the houses lining the street. This isn't the place for a shootout, and I'm not plucking at our razor-fine truce with the local police force. The SUV's dashcams would have caught the number plates, though the best way to get info is through Vincenzo. Franco is working with someone local, and it isn't Benedict's fake gun-for-hire outfit.

"Where is Vincenzo now?" Gigi asks.

I close my eyes for a second. The last thing I want is his blood on my hands tonight. I had other plans. "Luca would have cornered him after we left, pretending to be me, and making as if to cut a deal with him. Bait and switch. We did it all the time when we were younger."

"Oh, God. Steph, are you going to... I mean..."

"Kill him? Not tonight. Well, that depends on how much he shares."

"Okay."

"Keep it to yourself. You can't tell Carla."

With a nod, she turns into my chest, and I hold her close. She's quietly crying but not fighting me. She knows how this ends, and that I don't have a choice either. Given what he's done to her, she probably wants him dead, too.

I've no idea how long we sit there in the dark, but when

Dominic's team cruises up to us in another *Il Consiglio* SUV, I know we've shed our assailants for tonight.

"You good to go home, boss?" my driver asks.

"I'm not risking it." Who knows what Franco has on us now and who he has on his team. If anybody marked me as a Scalera tonight, the best place to keep Gigi safe is Matteo's apartment. Plus, Gigi would want to be with Carla after tonight. "We'll go to Matteo's place."

40

STEPHANO

By the time we walk into Matteo's apartment, my brothers are all here, sitting in the lounge. Guns are all over the coffee table, and the boys are drinking some fine-ass whiskey. Fuckers. As if shit didn't almost go down tonight.

"Quite an afterparty you're having here."

"Yep. We started without you," Matteo says as he gives us the once-over.

Tasha already has Gigi by the hand and leads her upstairs. Carla stands by the second-floor railing, wide-eyed. We've all agreed that the less the women know, the better.

"Fuck," I mutter as I indicate we should move to Matteo's office. As we make our way, I squeeze Luca's shoulder. "Thanks for that. I owe you."

"All good. Any time."

Yeah. That's been us for ages. *All good. Any time.* Luca isn't half as fucked-up as I am. He never woke up at night when noises came from our parents' bedroom and investigated, but for years, he's looked out for me.

Once the office door closes behind us, I strip off my jacket and tie, then ditch the holster and my gun. Matteo hands me a whiskey, and I turn to my brothers.

"Who the fuck was in on it?"

"We have four guys locked up, Steph," Dominic says. "We ran the plates from your dash and rear cams. Vincenzo bought friends in the new Ukrainian faction that's trying to set up shop here. Bratva wannabees."

"Nice. Bet they didn't know who they're fucking with." I take a deep sip of whiskey. We all smirk, but it was a close call.

"They'll be eliminated," Matteo says.

"Vincenzo?" I ask.

"He's got zero balls on him," Matteo says.

Whether he means that figuratively or literally, I'm not sure. "Well, that was fast."

"Caved within minutes," Dominic says. "They don't make them like they used to anymore."

"Fucker's not going to live," Matteo says with a shrug. "But now, he knows where he stands."

"And?"

"Franco wants Gigi at all costs," he says. "He'll come for her himself if he can't count on Vincenzo."

"Good." My palms twitch. My hands fist. I smell his blood on me already. The flip Gigi talks about is rearing its ugly head. "What about Don Trapani?"

"Apparently, he's fine. Forced to sit it out in Lake Como. He's respected, and it's the only reason why he isn't dead yet."

There's a man who won't see his piece-of-shit son again. "What happened tonight can't happen again."

I hate to say it, but we were cocky and caught off guard.

"It won't," Benedict says. "Vincenzo's talking. We can manipulate everything else. He'll report that he saw Gigi and then we'll see what Franco's next moves are."

"This can't go wrong." I stand and slam my whiskey glass on the desk. "Fuck!"

The others still and stare at me as I take a desperate turn around the room.

"Cool down, Steph," Luca warns. "You can go there on Vincenzo, not here."

I strangle my hair between my fingers, taking a few deep breaths. This is what Vincenzo unleashed in me. Touching my wife. Threatening her.

"In any case, what the fuck, bro?" Luca asks. "We've already gone above and beyond for these women—"

"My *wife*," I say, my voice dangerously soft, "isn't just any woman."

Another beat of heavy silence as they all stare at me, then at each other. Matteo's gaze rests heaviest on me. He's been here, and I recall the exact moment I realized he'd fallen in love with Tasha. Now he's seeing straight through me. I sink back on the sofa and drop my head to my hands, the urge to beat something to a pulp making my hands tremble.

"Oh, boy," Matteo says. "Welcome to the husbands-only club, Fanny. Are you staying?"

"Fuck off, Matty."

This isn't what I signed up for. Divorce is Gigi's ticket out of here, and I've agreed to it—it's a term of this arrangement—but I've changed my mind. I'm not letting her go.

A knock on the door cracks the tension in the room. I look up, and when Gigi peeks around the door, I swallow hard. The idea of losing her has taken hold of me now, twisting my stomach into a knot. As I take her in, every wave of uncontrollable fury seems to retreat, leaving me holding my breath.

"I'm sorry to interrupt," she says as she steps inside, hesitant. "I want— I— Just a word...with Steph."

"Here, angel," I say, and watch as she pads over to me.

With every step she comes closer, the anger in me dies. This woman is my anchor. I reel with the sudden knowledge that I will never flip on her. Unlike for Don Scalera, my wife isn't a trigger. She's my sanity.

She's stripped off her gown and is wearing a white towel robe she must have borrowed from Tasha. My brothers' eyes are on her too, but I can feel how their gazes drop away one by one as Gigi stops in front of me.

"I—"

I reach for her hand, needing to touch her. "What?"

It's as if we both think the same thing at the same time. I pull her closer, and she sits down and curls up on my lap. I inhale her scent, and it's calming me like nothing else.

"You know I can't sleep without you," she whispers in my ear as I wrap my arms around her.

"Leave us," I say to the others without breaking eye contact with her. "I need to take care of my wife."

Gigi burrows her face into my neck, shy, and for once, all the Scalera boys file out of the room, without a word. They shoot me glances, though, and Luca holds my gaze. A mere minute ago, I was about to rip into someone if the right man presented himself. Why would they even trust me alone with her? Luca's eyes say it all. *I see how much you care for her. And we've always known you wouldn't hurt a woman. See? It isn't in your blood.*

The door clicks closed, and we're alone. I turn my cheek to rest against hers, holding on for a minute as I try to steady my head and heart.

"Steph? Are you okay?" she whispers eventually.

For the first time in my life, I might actually be okay.

"Yes, angel. How're you feeling?" I ask as I press my lips to her temple.

"Rattled." Her hand slides up my chest to play with my shirt's collar.

"It's going to be okay."

I tug the bow keeping the robe closed. As it starts to unknot,

I groan. It's way past midnight, and after everything that's happened, this should be the last thing on my mind. I'm already hard for her, and we both need this now. Something to get our minds off everything that happened; something to remind her she's mine. Something to show her I can't let go.

Gigi unbuttons my shirt, but as soon as her robe is untied, I guide her hand to rest on her hip.

"I want to unwrap you like the gift you are, angel."

The universe has given me this woman to love and to protect, at a time I needed it the most. I slip my hand underneath the robe and ease it off her shoulder, slowly revealing her breast. Her nipple pebbles, and she shakes the sleeve off, leaving her one side bare.

I skim my hand over her skin, from her shoulder to her hip, then all the way to her ankle.

"You're so soft...so beautiful," I murmur as I trail my fingers up to her hip again.

She shivers with a sigh and cups my cheek. "I'm all yours. Only yours, Steph."

Her lips are on my jaw, pressing kisses ever higher until our mouths connect and I swipe hers open with a languid brush of my tongue.

We kiss for a long time, this being a novelty in this game we've been playing. I inch my hand between her legs, and she moans as she weaves her fingers into my hair.

"Open up for me, Gigi. Let me feel how wet you are."

She complies, and as I touch her, she rocks into my hand. My cock pulses against her thigh, and there's too much fabric between us. I make her sit so her robe falls away. She's naked in my arms, and in the library's soft light, she looks like a real angel. When she peels my shirt off, I sit forward, and she shifts, pushing the robe to the floor. She straddles my lap, and I ease back. As she works my belt and zipper, I circle her sensitive nipples with my thumbs.

Her breathing becomes strained as she arches into my touch, and we both drag in ragged breaths when she slides her hand into my underwear and wraps her hand around my cock. I shift deeper into the seat and cup her ass as pre-cum drips from the tip. She teases her thumb over it, readying me for her tight little pussy.

"Steph," she murmurs.

"Take what you want, angel. Take what you need." Let her break her vows first, and then, I'll show her how it's done.

Gigi lifts, her hands on my shoulders, and I rub the tip up and down her slit before positioning it at her entrance. As she lowers down on me, she gasps, and I grunt. Fuck. I knew she was going to be perfect, so fucking perfect and tight. I grip her ass and lift her up an inch, then ease her down again, each time going deeper until I'm completely sheathed and her inner walls grip me tight.

For a moment, we stare at each other, her gaze hazed in arousal, my heart in my throat.

"Just for the record, this isn't sex," she whispers.

"No, angel, this isn't sex." I want to plunder her body, claim her as mine, but she's rolling her hips in a slow, seductive rhythm, in no rush to find release. This is it. I can stay like this forever. "*This*, angel, is making love."

41

GIGI

This, angel, is making love.

Those words… The way he said them…

I'm caving in. Against all the logic in my brain, my heart has been holding the trump card all along. I know once I go there with him, going back to Italy will be impossible. This man has managed to crawl into my heart, and I don't want any distance between us. I want to stay. I want to be his. I want this marriage to be real.

God. I've craved this. I've craved *him* from the first moment in Cannes. I've never experienced this level of intimacy before. Steph is staring into my eyes as I ride his cock, and there's no end goal for now except to be connected. He's making love to me with his hands as they ghost and skim over my body, over my back, across my sides, down to my thighs. He licks my nipples, sucks, and turns his tongue over the hardened peaks and then lets his fingers slide over them as if he's teasing my clit.

Every touch drives my desire and need to bursting point, but I don't want to come. Not yet. I don't want this to stop. I pause to keep my orgasm from crashing in and lean into him, my breathing strained. He wraps his arms around me, and our lips connect. Our kisses are slow and seemingly drunk as we dip and dance our tongues with each other. He grinds into me, and I'm so full of him, so full of love, I feel stretched to the brim.

"Hold still, Steph," I breathe. "I'm so close."

"You're a little cock tease, aren't you, my angel?" he murmurs against my mouth.

"I just want to hold on to this moment."

His hands drive underneath my ass, and he heaves me up, ripping us apart with a pop as his cock jumps free. "You liked being edged? I'll fucking edge you until you beg for it."

He drops me to the sofa and stands, staring down at me and my splayed legs, at my wet sex that wants to pulse with release. His cock bobs in front of me, and I reach for it, but he catches my hand.

"Hold on, angel," he says as he steers my hand to grip the sofa's arm rest, guiding the other hand there, as well. My one leg dangles to the floor, but he takes the other and hooks it over the backrest.

I have no idea what he's going to do next, but when he traces a line from the fold of my knee to my sex, tremors run through me. He dips two fingers into my pussy, catches my g-spot, pulls out, and repeats the motion until I'm so slick, my wet heat sounds with each thrust. At the last second, he removes his fingers, leaving me retreating again from a release that just seems to keep on building.

"Fuck," he grunts as he fists the base of his shaft and jerks at his cock while he stares at me. "I don't want to stop either."

"Just make me come already," I beg. I'm too tense, too needy to have him toy with me anymore.

With a groan, he grips my dangling leg by the knee and pushes it wide and to the side, splitting me open. He leans in and props a hand next to my head. When he thrusts into me, it's so intense, I almost immediately ripple into orgasm.

"No, you don't, angel," he says and stops, and my pussy clenches his cock in desperation. "Make me work for it a bit."

For a full minute, I squirm to rock into him, wanton and flushed with the need for release, and then he's at it again, this time pounding slow but hard. I grip his neck to pull him in for a kiss, and when our open mouths touch and his tongue licks as I suck, I can't hold back anymore. My orgasm tears through me, ripping me to shreds. It doesn't stop. Not until he hammers into me one last time and shoots his load into me.

We keep on kissing until he lifts his weight off me.

"I think we've ruined the sofa," I murmur.

"I think Matty's sofa has been here before."

"Matty?" I ask as he reaches for his pocket square in his jacket's front pocket.

"Matteo."

I giggle. "Tell me the rest of them."

To think these men have nicknames for each other curls my toes in delight.

"Matty, Nicky, Lucci, and Benny."

"Oh, God." I'm cracking up now. "And you are?"

He rolls his eyes at me as he wipes between my legs. "Don't laugh."

"Too late. Let me guess?"

He runs a finger around my sex. "Fanny."

I lean up and pull him closer for a kiss. "Because he knows how to fuck one to perfection."

"Just taking care of my wife," he murmurs, and I actually blush as I melt with love for this man. "Let's go to bed, my darling, beautiful wife. Tomorrow is going to be a rough day at the office."

He helps me into my robe, does a patchy buttoning up of his own clothes, and leads me out of Matteo's office into the dark apartment. It's really late, or rather, it's early morning. As we scale the stairs, the night's events rush through my head.

I pause on the landing. "Where's Vincenzo?"

Stephano squeezes my hand. "We're holding him."

"He isn't—" I break off.

"He'll be alive as long as he's useful."

"What's the plan?"

"I don't know. We were discussing our next steps when we got interrupted."

I drop my gaze. Oh, God.

"We're working on it, angel. I don't want you to worry about anything."

"Okay. But Carla?" She was fond of her half-brother, up until that Friday night. "How do I tell her? Or even Don Trapani when the time comes?"

Now I don't know if I can live with myself, as if I had a direct hand in his son's murder.

"Don't tell anybody anything. She doesn't even need to know Vincenzo is here, trying to kidnap you back to Italy. Just remember what he did to you, angel. He's a dead man for touching you tonight, never mind selling you out to Franco Fiore."

This is what I wanted. I fled to Boston secretly hoping the Scaleras will have it in them to protect us. Going back to Italy was always my goal, but after tonight and with Vincenzo finding his own grave here, I don't know if I can or want to look Don Trapani in the eye again.

Stephano opens the guest room door for me, and I walk inside. The bed is rumpled where I turned for ages trying to fall asleep. I remove the robe and get in under the duvet, watching as my husband disappears into the bathroom. When he comes out later, I'm still awake, staring into the dark.

"I'll organize some Plan B for you tomorrow," he says. "Unless you are on contraception already?"

I'm not on anything, but I hesitate.

"It isn't necessary," I say as he slips between the sheets. "I've got us covered."

Stephano turns to me and gathers me in his arms as he places a soft kiss in my hair. Emotion swells in me. At the end of all this, there waits a divorce. If nothing else, I might be lucky enough to be pregnant when we go our separate ways. Not that Stephano can ever know, and he'll be furious if he finds out I've deceived him, but I need something of him, of us. Something to hold close and to remind me of this beautiful man who has vowed to never marry and love a woman.

42

GIGI

It's been five days since the night at the gallery, and I've been living my fake marriage to the full. Nights with Stephano are something else, but he leaves early in the mornings to deal with Vincenzo's arrival and its consequences.

It's frustrating to be out of the loop with their plans, and I want to tear my hair out not knowing if Vincenzo is finally dead or if he's still being *useful*.

Life ticks by. I miss painting. I miss working. Tony has brought my things over from Stephano's apartment, but it isn't the same. There are too many humans around, and I want to retreat back into the world of Stephano and me alone. I'm wrung out with anxiety that abates only when my husband is home.

Worst of all is how I'm hiding what happened at the gallery from Carla, and somehow, things between us have become more strained. She still doesn't know about Vincenzo and that *Il Consiglio* is holding him. The men spun a story about what happened at the gallery, which I endorsed. Carla senses something is off, but I can't tell her the truth. I hate having this secret about her blood brother, knowing they'll kill him at some point.

It's lunchtime. I'll have to nag my sister to come eat with me, for what it's worth. She's retreated so deep into her shell, doomscrolling social media as if this is the only life she'll ever have again, that even Tasha's started rolling her eyes. There're only so many movies, TV shows, and other crap you can watch while you wait for things to come to a head.

"Sweetheart," I say as I knock on her door. "Lunch time."

"I'm not hungry."

"Please, *cara*, it's just us. Tasha left for the university, and none of the men are here." This should make it easier, for sure. When we're in Matteo's apartment, there aren't even bodyguards with us, which gives us a breather.

"I told you I'm not hungry."

For heaven's sake. I thought we'd worked through this sulky teenager stage. "Come eat, Carla. *Now*."

I glance down to where Rosalia, Matteo's housekeeper, puts a salad on the table. She's all ears for this conversation, and I blush. The bedroom door whips open, and Carla scowls at me.

"I tell you I'm not hungry. I'm not burning any freaking calories. I'm sitting in this godforsaken apartment the whole bloody day, with nothing to do." She shoves past me and heads for the stairs. "We can't go out. We can't connect with our friends. I can't get on with the life I planned for years, finally done with school, all because of *you*."

For a full ten seconds, I'm too shocked to say anything, but then, I snap. "How dare you?"

Ungrateful, spoilt brat. I make eye contact with Rosalia, and she reads the room and books it out of the living area as fast as she can.

"How dare I?" Carla snarls as she glances back at me. "If I were still in Italy, I would have had the protection of Vincenzo and Franco Fiore, and my life would've gone back to normal. Now I'm here for who knows how long because *you* chose this for us. I had zero say."

Life will never be normal again. I catch up with her, grab her arm, and yank her around to face me. She loses her grip on her phone, and it falls to the ground.

"You have no idea who Vincenzo got in bed with. Franco Fiore is a....is a—" I break off, the visual of what he's done to me and his promises of more to come too much.

"Vincenzo would have protected me." Carla shrugs me off and picks up her phone. "Papa would have protected me!"

I quiver with anger and helplessness as I follow her down the stairs. I've protected her for so long, and Don Trapani has kept his little girl safe, but now, Carla is headstrong and spoilt, unaware of this world's darkness that overlaps with ours. Yes, the Trapanis are rich beyond measure, and yes, most of our riches have a foundation in crime, but there's been more over the last forty years to elevate us above the usual Mafia. Vincenzo is jerking us down again, and it's as if I'm being stretched in both directions, slowly tearing in two. Even I can't take this much longer. If it weren't for Stephano, I would have lost my mind weeks ago.

Carla is already at the table and shoves at a chair. She sits down and stares at the salmon Rosalia prepared for us. She pushes the plate away and picks up her phone again, scrolling.

"What now?" I say through thin lips. "Put your phone away. You know the rules."

She slams her phone face down on the table and rolls her eyes.

"Is the food not good enough for you?" I ask as I pick up my knife and fork.

She glares at me. "I hate fucking salmon."

This is new, and it pushes me to boiling point. "Could you

stop insulting our hosts? Not only have the Scaleras kept us safe with a roof over our heads, clothes on our bodies, and food on our plates, they are also dealing with the maniac who cut me to plant a tracker in my arm!"

I have to keep reminding myself that Carla wasn't there in the library that night, so she doesn't know the full extent of Franco's cruelty.

"Vincenzo probably told Franco you were going to run. Because you always fucking run."

This hits home so hard, angry tears burst to the surface. "What the hell do you know about it? You with your charmed life as Don Trapani's only daughter?"

"*Pfft*. You've always been jealous. Always trying so freaking hard to be the perfect daughter. God, Gigi, you make me sick. I wish you'd left me behind!" She stands, and her chair topples. "I need to get the hell out of here before this goes too far."

We might have crossed that bridge already. We've never had a fight like this before. Things have been too tense, so I'm not sure why I'm surprised. We're close. We were close. Always. She's my last connection to Mom. She's my last real family, and she's walking out on me.

"Carla!" I call out, too rattled to stop her as she heads for the front door. "You can't—"

"I can, and I will. I'm tired of being locked up in this dumb tower. I need fresh air, and I'm going to get it."

I stand, leaning heavily on the table. "Take Tony with you." *Please*.

"As if I have a choice."

The front door slams, and the sound vibrates through me as I sink down on my seat. I cup my hands to my mouth and breathe in and out, trying to calm down. Tears are streaming down my cheeks, born out of so many things.

It's only when my phone rings for the fifth time where I left it in our bedroom that I drag my ass up the stairs to see which Scalera is trying to get hold of me. I doubt Carla is ready to talk to me, and I sure as shit don't want to hear her voice right now.

Nobody else has my new number.

43

GIGI

By the time I get to our bedroom, my phone has stopped ringing. *Stephano.* I dial his number, and he answers within two rings.

"Angel. I hear from Tony that Carla left the apartment. For a *walk*?"

I drop my head back with a sigh. "Yes. She had to—"

"Gigi, I told you to stay put."

"I know. She's had enough. She's got cabin fever." A sob rips through me as I curl up on our bed.

"What happened?" he asks, concern in his voice. "Are you okay?"

"I'm fine, but I couldn't stop her, Steph. We had a massive fight."

Muffled sounds come through his phone, and he must have covered it with his hand because I can't hear what he's saying.

"She demanded Tony stay twenty yards behind her," he says. "Where did she plan to go?"

"I don't know. Tony is with her, isn't he?" Fear dusts over me, and I sit up straight.

"Listen to me, Gigi. Carla can't be walking around Boston.

Tasha is already heading home." He takes a deep breath. "Franco Fiore landed this morning at Hanscom Field. It's one of the smaller commercial airports outside of Boston and caters for private jets. We were tracking him, but—" He grunts with frustration. "We've lost him."

"No. No-no." I'm up and pacing the room. "What now? How did you *lose* him?"

"Fuck knows. We're figuring it out. Stay at home. We're heading there now. Tony will be dragging Carla back, but if she makes it look like he's assaulting her, onlookers—"

"I don't care. I just want her safe."

"Yes." He kills the call, and I stare at the screen.

Franco Fiore is in Boston. *Carla is out for a walk.*

I rush to her room as if she'd be on her bed like every other time these past few days. My heart beats in my throat, panic seizing me.

Her laptop is on her bed, flipped open. Her inbox is on the screen, and I gasp as I see an email chain from Vittorio Rossi. She didn't even mention that Vito contacted her. I was worried sick about her bodyguard's safety that Friday night when he headed back to the house in Lake Como to look out for Don Trapani. He helped us escape, after all.

Carla was keeping to herself, but I didn't know she was keeping secrets. I'm keeping secrets too, but this? I flick my gaze over the last message.

I want to be there for you, cara. Be on standby, I'll keep you posted. Send me your phone number.

Cara? *Sweetheart.* What the hell? It's the only line in the last email from Vito, but Carla's reply is nothing but her phone number. I scroll through the rest of the email chain, starting from the top. Carla begs Vito to let her know whether he's alive, anxious for a response. She sends this message at least twice a day, but there's never a reply. And then finally, he wrote back two days ago: *I'm here, cara. I'm okay. Where are you?*

Carla responded the same day: *I'm in Boston, staying with friends. Vito, I'm pregnant.*

I sink down on the bed. Pinpricks spread over my skin as I slouch over the laptop, reading the line again and again, my hand to my mouth. *Vito, I'm pregnant.*

Oh my God. Carla is *pregnant*.

My little sister got pregnant with Vittorio Rossi, her *bodyguard*.

I glance through the rest of the message chain. Vito's responses are short and to the point, telling Carla she should get an abortion. *A fucking abortion.* After he impregnated her. The prick. And Carla's only eighteen. I see red and clench the laptop, my hands shaking. That fucking asshole. Never mind that Carla is young and in many ways innocent, her baby is even more so.

I bite my lip to stop its quivering, but I can't help the flood of emotions surging through me. Visuals of Mom when she was pregnant with Carla, of how I fell in love with my little sister the moment I held her for the first time. Mom's beautiful face as she looked at us girls, peas in a pod despite our ten-year age difference. The love I felt in that moment is a memory still as strong as if it happened yesterday. And now Carla is carrying a baby, a beautiful, gorgeous child that Vito told her to get rid of so flippantly.

Why didn't she tell me? So many things suddenly make sense. Her bouts of diarrhea, her loss of appetite and weight loss. The gaunt look on her face as the stress of this situation pressed down on her. Hiding in her room probably to hide her morning sickness.

Our fight this afternoon; Carla pushing me to my limits.

I've failed her in every possible way. I didn't see the signs, but a pregnancy was the last thing on my radar. Worst of all, she didn't trust me enough to confide in me. Tears stream down my face as I battle every rational and irrational emotion, begging our Mom for forgiveness. I didn't protect my sister. *I* gave the go-ahead for that man to come into her life, joking with her how at least he was something to look at.

But the baby—

I drag in an unsteady breath, shocked to my core. Maybe this is what she was mentally preparing for and why she was in such a state. She's going for an abortion.

She can't be doing this alone, not without me by her side. Not without me reasoning with her first. Even if Vito is here, he's left her in the lurch. He took how many weeks to contact her, whereas she's known she's pregnant for how long? If she's going to get an abortion, she can't be that far along, can she?

I close the email and scan through the rest of her inbox, desperate for more details. There are five messages, most of them about opening this new email account. She created this account when we came to Boston as we were lying low. No spam, no social media messages. I open her Sent folder. She sent over a hundred emails to Vito, asking him where he is, begging him to contact her.

Now, Franco is in Boston, and Vito wants to be there for her. I recall Carla's phone and the way she clung to it earlier, as if she was waiting for something. What if Vito flew into Boston and she was starting a fight with me to have a reason to go out? What if Franco and Vito were on the same plane... God, what if Vito became one of Fiore's henchmen to save his own skin? Who knows what happened that night after Vito left us at the Milan airport. Now, he's contacted Carla after how many weeks, nonchalantly telling her he wants to be there for her, but he is really leading her to Franco?

Dread drips through me. Something isn't sitting right. Vittorio Rossi never struck me as the type to have a liaison with a client or switch sides like this. His emails don't strike me as caring for Carla either. He doesn't even reference the night in

Lake Como where he helped us escape, looking after us—guarding us—until the last minute.

Oh my God. Steph. I need to call Steph, because my little sister has left the apartment building, pregnant and walking straight into some type of trap. I reach for my phone in my jeans pocket to dial Stephano, but I blink as a new message pops onto my screen from Carla's number.

CARLA

Don't call your husband or his brothers. I have Carla, but it's you I want. Come by yourself, and she'll live. Bring your friends, and she dies.

I read the message again and again as my fingers tremble so much, the screen blurs. Carla. He has Carla and is messaging me from her phone.

Franco?

CARLA

Why did you run from me, amorina? You didn't even give us a chance. Now I need to make you a widow so I can make you mine.

My stomach turns.

What do you want?

CARLA

I want you as a fair exchange for your sister.

Why?

I'm not even sure why I'm asking. I'm dealing with a madman. A madman who has my sister.

CARLA

You know why.

The billion euros stuck in secret Swiss bank vaults.

Leave her the fuck alone. She's pregnant!!!!!

I send the message and press the dial button. He doesn't answer the call but kills it.

Seconds later, my phone rings. It's a video call from Carla. I answer, and the camera's image comes on. I cover my mouth to muffle my scream. My little sister, the one person I've promised to protect no matter what, is blindfolded and gagged, tied to something I can't see in the dark image. Her body sways as if they're driving, but I can't be sure in what type of vehicle as it's too dark. I recognize her from her hair, her earrings, and the tiny scar on her chin where she ran into a glass door as a kid. She's moaning, making what sounds she can through the gag.

"Sweet sounds, aren't they?" Franco says, but he doesn't show his face. "Let's hope my hand doesn't slip and end motherhood prematurely."

The scalpel appears in the frame, the hand holding it tattooed with snakes, and my body locks in fear.

"You have five minutes," he says. "We'll pick you up outside the apartment building's entrance. Get into the white van without causing a scene, or my hand might slip."

He presses the scalpel to Carla's neck, and a small drop of blood leaks from her skin.

"You know what will happen to her when you're not there, *amorina*. And unlike your insignia, I won't stop until you're here. I'll cut her so much, not only won't you recognize her, but she'll bleed to death."

Over my dead body. I drop everything and run.

44

STEPHANO

The fucker gave us the slip.

Franco Fiore arrived this morning on a private jet from Naples and got stamped in with his regular passport at the airport.

It's as if he is teasing us. A sane crime overlord would have come into the country with a fake passport. This guy has been lying so low under the radar in Europe, he isn't even on Interpol's most-wanted list, which we also scoured to see where he's at. Franco Fiore isn't on *any* fucking list. In fact, he's almost a myth. He slipped out from the underworld only once Randazzo was dead.

For Gigi, he is very real, and as soon as Benedict's border control contact let us know he'd checked in, we had multiple teams out to track him down.

But now...*what the actual fuck?* He gave us the slip. Drove out of the airport terminal without anybody spotting him.

"I don't care who you have to bribe, Dominic, or how much," I hiss into the phone, "but I want all security footage from the airport to see where the fucker outwitted us."

"I'm on it, Steph, for fuck's sakes. Benedict's already hacked into airport security footage."

I kill the call. Somewhere, someone fucked up, and heads are going to roll. Our plan worked—partially. Vincenzo, while he still had all his fingers, typed up an email for Franco, telling him he saw Gigi. If he wanted her, he had to come fetch her himself as she's married, and her husband won't give her up without a fight.

Damn right. A fight that will end with Franco's brains on the floor.

But the asshole was slow to bite. He insisted on a video call to verify Vincenzo was still alive and not bullshitting him. Instead, 'Vincenzo' sent him solid proof: video footage from the gallery, where Gigi met Vincenzo, compliments of one of our security members who shot the clip. We made it look as if it had been taken by one of Vincenzo's Ukrainians. Vincenzo wasn't exactly presentable, but seeing Gigi on camera worked. There were more messages between the two men, orchestrated by us, but the only thing eluding us has been Franco's travel plans.

Now, the psycho is on the fucking loose in my city and on the hunt for my wife. I stride into Matteo's apartment, and as always, the place is eerily quiet. This high up with every noise-limiting feature in place he could install, it's like living in a vacuum.

"Gigi?" I call out when I don't spot her in the living area or kitchen. I hurry to the stairs to see if she is in our bedroom, and when it's empty, I go to Carla's. I freeze when I spot the laptop and phone discarded on the bed. That's Gigi's phone. "Fuck!"

My stomach turns as I reach for it and unlock it with the code she hasn't bothered to change.

The screen opens to her messages with Carla. Dread tsunamis through me as I glance over the last few lines.

We know Carla is pregnant, thanks to our spyware and the messages she sent to Vittorio Rossi two days ago. We were waiting for her to bring it out in the open, to tell her sister first, but not on the same day as the arrival of Franco Fiore. Talk about bad timing.

Now, the worst has happened.

"Both women are gone!" I call downstairs to Matteo and Luca who are with me. I flip open the laptop, my fingers trembling, blood rushing in my ears.

I want to be there for you, cara. Be on standby, I'll keep you posted. Send me your phone number.

I read the line again and check the time stamp. The last one was sent this morning while we were trying to intercept Fiore after he'd landed.

"Jesus Fucking Christ." I groan. We won't know about the latest calls made between Carla, Gigi, and Franco—not yet. "Franco is pretending he's Vito Rossi. He's lured Carla out, and Gigi has either gone with him or has left to save her sister." In some sick exchange.

"How the fuck?" Matteo grunts behind me. "When?"

I check Gigi's phone now, and my skin pops with chills as I notice the short video call from Carla's phone. Franco already has Carla, which means Tony is dead. And then, he phoned Gigi. Whatever he said to her, it was enough to make her drop everything and run. "Fifteen minutes ago."

"Shit. She just walked out?" Matteo says as he and Luca exchange glances.

We just missed her, and right on cue, Matteo's phone goes haywire with calls. Must be his security team in the basement trying to update him.

I don't have time. I'm already heading to the front door and the holding cell next door where Vincenzo has slowly been dying in his own sick and shit.

"Get Dominic to send you the security footage of this block. If Gigi and her sister just walked out, we'll see everything."

Their footsteps fall hot on my own, Luca already on his phone.

"Don't kill the fucker yet, Steph," Matteo warns. "He might still be useful!"

I'm ready to flip. Vincenzo will know. He *must* know. Or his cronies will. I open the secure steel door with my thumb print, and the guard stands, first wanting to block my way.

"Out. It's time these fuckers talk for real."

It's a shit show in here. The cleaner hasn't been in yet today, and the four Ukrainians we've taken on Friday night have been having the runs. Who knows what they ate before they went in for a job. The room has been hosed down a few times, but fuck it, the stench.

The five men are chained to metal chairs welded to the floor in a circle, their backs facing each other, holes in the seats and buckets underneath. They're naked and somewhat dead already. Vincenzo's head bobs as he becomes aware of us, peering at me through his swollen eyes.

I reach for his neck and choke him with my fist. "Tell me where Franco will be taking the women."

There must be an apartment or something he's bought or rented or who knows what the fuck. Vincenzo wheezes in a shallow breath and manages to shrug his shoulder.

"Think about it." I wait until his eyes bulge before I let go. I suppress the urge to punch him, but there are four more guys in the room, and these are local, for what it's worth.

"Keep your fucking cool," Matteo bites out, a warning hand on my shoulder. Unlike that time where I kicked Tatiana's assailant into the afterlife, destroying his insides in a tit-for-tat move, I have no objections to strangle these men with my bare hands.

"This is fucking war, Matteo," I snarl. "Fucking war, do you understand? With everybody who is helping that fucker. *He has my wife*!" And they still don't know what Franco Fiore is capable of.

"Don't finish them off yet, then," he says. "We'll smoke them out and eliminate them, but this isn't over until it's over."

I'm interrogating the second-last guy, now on the brink of losing my shit completely, when Luca's phone rings.

"Yeah, Benedict? You have? Send it through. We're on our way."

With a last squeeze to the fucker's throat, I turn to face my twin. "This better be good news."

Luca's phone pings a message, and he tilts his screen. "The footage is about two hours old. *This* is Franco Fiore. He disguised himself. And he's brought a woman with him. That's why we overlooked him."

Fucking rookie mistake.

I glare at the screen as the video plays, both Matteo and Luca watching, too. That could be anybody. The man in jeans and a plaid shirt with a fucking Stetson hat and cowboy boots gives zero Italian Mafia vibes. No visible bodyguards and not a tattoo in sight, even on his hands, but the woman he's holding onto gives the game away. He's walking fast, and she's lagging half a step behind, carrying a guitar case. It's her face that tells the story. She's petrified, even if she's trying to hide it.

"What the fuck," I hiss. "How did they leave the airport?"

"Took a fucking cab, like normal people," Matteo says as he reads something on his phone. "Come, Benedict is on it. He's tracing their route and will let us know where to go as he figures it out. They're not too far ahead of us."

I'm already dialing Dominic's number. His security company has cameras on every corner of all our buildings.

"Dom, I need the footage on Matteo's street," I bark as he answers.

"Already on it, Steph."

I bet Matteo already told him to keep eyes on movements from his building.

My heart is in my throat. Gigi is out there with a fucking monster on her trail. We waste precious minutes waiting for Dominic to share his screen with us. When we finally get to the salient portion—camera footage from the street—my body tightens as if fists are punching it from all sides.

Gigi, my darling, beautiful wife, is standing on the curb as a white van rolls up in front of this building. The street is busy. Suits and tourists are walking around, going about their business. It's peak tourist season in Boston. Four of our security detail are right there, guarding her, ready to pull guns and shoot.

Why the fuck didn't they notify me? I wasted precious time coming all the way up to Matteo's apartment when Gigi was probably already in the high rise's main foyer. She used the building's general entrance and not Matteo's private one, sidestepping our security guards and making sure to delay their response. Jesus. My wife thinks on her feet. She must have taken the penthouse's fucking fire escape which connects with the rest of the building on two floors, and only allows access out of the building, and not in.

And now, she'd said something to them to give them pause. Whatever it was, it was serious, because when one of the van's double back doors opens, she steps up to look inside, then turns and raises her hands to stop our guards. Something in her stance tells me she's begging. Begging again for them to do nothing.

Who knows what she sees inside the van, but I can imagine. Automatic rifles aimed into the street. Carla at the back of the van and that lunatic holding a gun to her head.

Gigi climbs inside, the door shuts, and the van pulls away.

"Track that fucker," I bark. "We're going on a road trip."

My kick-ass wife is back. She was never gone, only taking a

much-needed break after running for ten years, but now, there are innocent women's lives on the line, and of course she's going to step in and stop the worst from happening. Gigi's going to need backup, and I'm not letting Franco Fiore slip out of reach again.

"Oof," Luca groans. "The real party is finally starting."

45

GIGI

I hold my hand out to Matteo's security detail who have by some means followed me. They must have tracked my escape via hidden cameras, even if I chased down the fire escape until I could connect with an elevator to the main lobby.

"Hold off," I beg them. "I need to negotiate here." This isn't only about Carla, but also about the baby she's carrying.

When light falls into the dark interior of the van, all I see is my sister, tied up and exactly as she was on the call earlier. Now a gun points at her temple, a scalpel blinking in the little light.

"Let her out," I say. Carla has to get out of harm's way first.

"How many people do you want to die today?" Franco's voice sounds from the back.

My gaze flicks to the side, only to see another man with an automatic rifle pointing at my waist. With that half of the double door closed, he's out of view to everyone except me.

God. We're outnumbered, and the streets are busy with tourists. Kids. Moms with strollers. Normal people going about their business.

"You said this was going to be a fair exchange," I beg, knowing I've stepped into Franco's trap. *Again*.

"Not here, *amorina*. Get in, or we pull away and she's dead. Make a scene, and we shoot this street to the ground. You have five seconds."

And no choice. I hold my hands up to the guards, indicating to them to back off. "Please tell Stephano I'm sorry. I had to go. He'll understand."

I clamber into the van willingly, and the door pulls closed.

It's dark inside, and adrenaline rushes through me. Carla moans, and then someone else does. I fall back as the van drives off, and my body hits something as I crumple to the floor.

"Carla?" I manage, barely a whisper, disoriented.

A hand slaps my face from out of nowhere, and I collapse to the bed of the truck as my ears ring.

"Fucking cunt. Making me come all the way to the States. Waste of my fucking time."

His body is on mine, pressing hard as he grabs my arms and twists them painfully. He jerks me around and ties my hands as my face gets squashed against the cold metal floor. I croak out a scream, but a knee presses into my back, squeezing my lungs so hard, I can hardly breathe. He tapes my legs together, and I strain to get the biggest gap possible between them.

Once I'm tied, he forces me into an upright position, twisting me so my face collides with his chest. His smell hits me full in the face, just like in Lake Como. Whiskey and cigarettes, but the rough scratch of a beard wasn't there before.

Medical disinfectant. This scent brings back every memory of that night, and I'm dry heaving in seconds.

"Come, come, *amorina*, it's not that bad."

"Let her go, Franco," I plead. "You want me, not her."

"You're so fucking predictable. Vincenzo was right. If I want you, I need to go for your sister. Worked in Lake Como, and now, it worked again."

I can hardly breathe with the way I'm pressed to him, and

with the shock of my own stupidity. Instead of running to Carla, I should have stayed put and let Stephano and Matteo do the negotiations with this madman.

"You touch her, you die." I heave against his chest.

"Is that so?" He chuckles. "Time for you to shut the fuck up, *amorina*."

Tape rips, and before I can say anything else, it glues to my mouth, gagging me. I'm already tender where he slapped me, but now he hits me again, and I slump back. The vehicle jolts and swerves as it speeds through Boston, and I'm like a loose object, shifting with every unexpected turn. Every now and again, the ride is so rough, I collide with something softer shoved against the wall.

Franco settles in the dark, and when the flick of a lighter casts a glow in the van, I glance around, frantic. He's lighting a cigarette, and I register he's wearing a plaid shirt. Not the black suit I saw him in last.

In the few seconds of light, I spot Carla and another woman, also tied up. There are three of us now. I don't know who this other woman is, but from the raw panic in her eyes, she's in the same boat as me and Carla.

The man with the automatic rifle sits close on a small bench. I remember him from Lake Como. The executioner. How many men did Franco bring over to come and fetch me? One of his men must be driving the van, too. But it's the dead eyes of the body I've been bashing into that makes my stomach turn. *Tony*.

Oh my God. This quiet man who watched me when Steph wasn't at home, who was prepared to take a bullet for me, is dead. I can't breathe. Not with Tony's dead eyes on me.

All I know is Stephano will come for me. He'll come for *us*. And if he doesn't, I'll rather die than be this man's captive. I'll do anything to make sure Franco Fiore will never touch either of us again.

I have no idea how long we jostle along. When the vehicle slows down to a crawl, I want to cry in relief. A rolling garage door opens, and the van cruises inside.

The door rattles closed again. This is it. We could be anywhere, but my best bet is a warehouse where they plan to get rid of extra bodies. The unknown woman has turned quiet, and I can't see much, even though my eyes have adjusted to the dark.

The driver kills the engine, and Franco stands, kicks me in the butt for good measure, and opens the back doors. He jumps out, but with the executioner's gun on me, I don't move. Carla moans again, and my heart goes out to her as she sees who Franco really is. We spoke about that night in the library, what Franco did before I arrived. Nothing untoward happened, but being in the library with all those men freaked her out. She is so young. I blink at tears. *Welcome to our real world, Carla. And to think it's in our blood...*

"Come on, future wife," Franco says as he fists my hair and forces me up.

I comply, wincing and scooting until I'm sitting and can hang my legs over the edge of the van. He shoves me off, and I stumble and hop but manage to keep my balance. The executioner tosses him the rifle, and Franco swings it in my direction. The driver's door slams shut, and I also recognize him too from that night in the library. He joins us with an automatic rifle in his hand.

I look around, taking in our surroundings. We're in an old warehouse, like I thought. Light battles to shine through the dirty windows lining the top meter of the high wall; the roof is speckled with holes where rain must drip through. In several places, the tin roof has peeled away from the bolts securing it to the ceiling beams, leaving gaping holes. Barrels are stacked in one corner with random old machinery, and the floor is a patchwork of stains that could be anything from oil to blood.

The space has a pungent smell. Half mechanic workshop with oil and lubricant, but there is an acidic twang I can't place. It's abandoned, and a new layer of fear spreads over all the other layers.

What if Stephano doesn't come? Nobody is going to find us here.

The executioner roughly helps Carla down. She's still blindfolded and struggles to find her footing, but they haven't tied her legs. Franco has her by the hand and drag-walks her to stand three meters from me. The other woman comes next, and for the first time, I get a good look at her.

Her eyes are smeared with mascara, accentuating their crystal blue irises. Her thick blonde hair hangs in a messy disarray around her face. She's had the duct tape treatment, too, and Franco has her by the arm as he leans into her ear and whispers something I can't hear. I look on as tears stream down her cheeks. Our gazes meet, and then she nods at whatever Franco just said to her.

It's like déjà-vu from the day in Cannes. Here's a woman in trouble, just like Tasha was, but this time, our position is so dire, I can't see any other ending but death.

The executioner pulls a guitar case out of the van and flings it over his shoulder. Then comes another carrying case of sorts. He pokes the other woman in the ribs with a handgun, and she hustles along to a corner where he puts the case down on a barrel.

"Let me go get cleaned up for you, *amorina*. I might have flown in looking like this, but I know you prefer me to be myself."

Franco puts his gun down and starts to scratch at his cheeks, and I'm stunned as the fake beard peels off inch by inch. Then he starts to strip off his red plaid shirt, and I blink as I take in his body. He's toned and muscled, and his tattooed skin seems to ripple with every movement he makes. He is covered in tattoos of snakes which crowd around a wilting tree on which hangs one red apple, the only color on his skin.

If I could speak, I would remind him that I'm still married, with a husband I suspect has developed feelings for me as I have for him, but as if Franco reads my mind, he leers at me.

"Don't worry, *amorina*. By the time we're taking off for home, you'll be a widow."

46

STEPHANO

Il Consiglio has ruled Boston for over forty years. Don Scalera shook up the old Mafia order with merciless force, paving the way for his new regime. Then he made sure his wife gave him an army of sons—even if it killed her—to take over his reign. To say we know every back alley and dark corner in this city is an understatement. *Il Consiglio* owns them.

As we track the van towards the harbor, I can already see where it's unwittingly heading: our discarded warehouses, barely adjacent to a wharf. Five hundred yards, and a shit ton of razor wire and cement blocks separate this strip from Boston's commercial harbor. We stopped using this space years ago. Who knows who gave Franco Fiore access to our turf, but he's walked right into a trap. Franco might not have bought into my idea of hiring our men as mercenaries, but someone tipped him off that this is a good place to burn a body.

Carla's body, baby and all. Gigi is safe until the point where Franco doesn't need her anymore. And then, there's the other woman. The stranger who has been dragged into this mess.

Fuck.

We have several vehicles on the road tracking the van, but

wary that our prey might realize he's being followed, we're doing this like a lion hunt. One vehicle backs off and takes a turn as another one slips in to keep eyes on our target and fool the driver. They aren't all blacked-out new SUVs either. We have the odd battered rattle box or two to keep up pretenses. The driver hasn't picked up that he's being followed yet, as there's no panicked speeding and turning. He just drives like a fucking crazy Italian who's suddenly experiencing wide American roads for the first time.

The streets become more deserted as we head into the industrial zone, and our process becomes even more fine-tuned. We know the lay of the land. This road splits, and both are dead ends. Idiots. Two of our men on a motorbike speed past the van to park off and keep us posted where it chooses to pull in. When the van goes right, we go left and wait.

Benedict and Dominic are on their way, and we need them. Don Scalera was a sharpshooter of note, and those two inherited his skill.

A pin drops on my phone, and I show it to Matteo and Luca where they're sitting in the back.

"Well, fuck," Matteo says. "We'll get Benny and Nicky to take him out from the windows, or through a hole in the roof."

The row of warehouses will make it possible to walk along the roof right up to the one Franco chooses, without him being aware we're there. There are two access points on either side of the row, something he wouldn't have checked out.

"Too fucking easy," I grunt. I'm like a great white shark that has smelled blood. I'm pumped to end Franco, and I will.

"Fine, but we take out his men first," Luca says.

"Obviously. Gigi and Carla are in there."

"Let's hope he doesn't barrel them up to die," Matteo mutters.

I shoot him a glance. "Really? What the fuck, dude?"

"One of the Don's party tricks." He shrugs. "Personally don't care for it."

I shudder. Matteo has been places us younger lot haven't. Not that we didn't get our fair share, but still.

Benedict starts a video call, and we strategize our next move as the second confirmation comes in from one of the motorcyclists: Franco pulled into the second last warehouse. Through a small hole in the wall, the motorcyclist saw three women with two other men who are carrying automatic rifles and handguns.

I glance at my brothers. "Seem like a thin spread for such a momentous moment?"

"Arrogant fucker. You're on, boys. Go clean up what you can," Matteo says to Dominic and Benedict.

"Yes, boss," Benedict teases with a smirk. This is new for all of us. In the past, Matteo was the first-in-command henchman, but now, he's the Don. Not that we care to call him that, and he doesn't seem to give a fuck.

"Leave Franco for me," I say. "We're right behind you. We'll be blocking the street, so don't waste time."

"Got it, Steph," Dominic says. "Don't get your balls all knotted up."

Fuck. "Remember my *wife* is in there."

"As if you'd let us forget that."

Benedict kills the call, and a heavy beat of silence fills the car.

I'm trembling. My fingers are shaking so much, I have to put the phone down.

Luca reaches for my shoulder and squeezes it. "Save it. Bottle it up. You're going to need it."

It's as if my twin already senses what I need. I stretch my fingers and fist them, taking deep, slow breaths. Somehow, every trajectory in life has led me to this point.

I'm primed to perfection.

47

GIGI

It's hot in here. The afternoon sun bakes down on the metal roof, and dust motes dance in the few beams breaking through the dirt.

The executioner approaches Carla, and when she senses him, she kicks...and misses. I wince and close my eyes, not wanting to witness the repercussions.

"Sure you want to keep that dickhead's baby?" the executioner grunts. "We left him for dead in a dungeon in Lake Como after he finally caved in and gave us access to his email, sweetheart. Opening his inbox was such a...joy."

Sobs rack through Carla's body, but with a wild punch to her stomach, the executioner folds her in half, and she tumbles to the floor. With her hands bound, she can't brace her fall, and her head hits the cement floor.

Oh. My. God. She doesn't stir. I can't watch. She might be dead. Their baby...Vittorio Rossi was tortured by this man and left for dead. Probably in the wine cellar in Don Trapani's house.

Fear eats me up from the inside out, like acid. I was so ludicrously brave and arrogant, thinking running away from the

Mafia was a solution. That I would be able to free myself from this life.

Now my sister looks dead, and if not, she might lose her baby.

Tears roll down my cheeks as my nostrils flare. I can't hold my sobs in anymore, but with my mouth taped closed, they have nowhere to go. My chest burns with heartache and fear, and I sink to the floor on my knees, no longer able to stand. I watch as the executioner tapes Carla's legs together, her body wilted. He bends, picks her up with a grunt, and carries her over to the stack of barrels where he makes her sit against one. Then he proceeds to check the lids.

Oh. My. God. Not like this.

I glance to where Franco has opened the carrying case and watch in horrified fascination as he wipes the concealer from his neck, his tattoo breaking through with every swipe of the drenched cotton wool. The other woman has been jerked closer, and she nods whenever Franco pulls out a product to remove something from his skin. Now he's busy with the remains of the beard, for which there is a special solution.

God help us. She's been here to transform him. A makeup artist or a special-effects person of sorts. How the hell did she get embroiled in this mess?

For a moment, Franco pauses and picks up his phone. He glances over the screen, reading a message, then puts it down.

"There," he says with a grin as he turns to me, now shirtless and showing off his tattoo. "Like this better, *angel*?

Angel. No...*no*.

If Franco is calling me angel, does it mean—

No. I won't believe it. Not until I've seen Stephano's body with my own eyes.

"We're going to the airport. The jet is waiting," he says as he plucks a shirt from the case, black like a demon's. "We only have space for one of you girls, and we know I came for Gigi, so..."

He lets his words hang, and the other woman shakes her head, frantic. *God, no...* He's going to kill her, too.

I'm still reeling from the shock when the driver, who has been leaning against the van, keeping an eye on the warehouse door, slumps and slides down to the floor. The sound of a single gunshot seems to come late, slow to penetrate my mind, and then I spot the trickle of blood running down the man's forehead. A bullet wound.

Next, a similar popping sound, and the executioner crumbles where he's been peering into a barrel, and he tilts, banging his head on the barrel's edge as he droops to the ground.

Franco freezes on the spot and grabs a handgun. The other men had the automatic rifles, which now hang limply from their hands. He scans the space, panic flashing for a mere second in his eyes.

When the garage door rolls open, it diverts his attention, and he points the gun in that direction, but I hear something else. A shadow seems to chase over the roof, footsteps light, and then bullets come raining down. They don't hit Franco, though, but splinter the floor around him, shooting up shards of cement. Franco looks up and shoots, but it's too late. The assailant is gone.

Now, there's another shower of bullets tracing a line where he stands. Dumbfounded, he turns to follow the footsteps on the roof, his back facing the door, and in that moment, Stephano, Matteo, and Luca walk into the warehouse, automatic rifles raised. Burley and two other bodyguards file in along the walls of the warehouse, guns trained on Franco.

It's too much. This feeling in my chest wants to choke me as it tries to burst my heart.

He is here. He has come. He hasn't abandoned me.

It's only when Franco feels Matteo's gun pressing into the

back of his head that he raises his hands and drops his handgun.

And then, Stephano is there, staring down at me. He cups my cheek, and I blink when I spot his own tears. His touch is so gentle, it's hardly a breath.

"He's hurt you, angel, again," he murmurs. 'He raised his hand and hit you like that motherfucker hit her." He swallows and brushes an angry wipe to his cheek. "Fuck it, angel, I want to rip this tape off, but it's going to hurt real bad. I'll leave you to do it yourself."

Through my tears, I manage a nod.

"My brothers will look after you," he murmurs as he brushes away my tears.

Wait. What? I glance around wildly. Franco is frozen on the spot, several guns pointed at him. Why does he say it as if he won't see me again? I feel myself break, slowly, as if the world is grinding to a stop those last seconds before a tsunami hits.

He goes on his haunches and our eyes lock. "Angel, I don't want you to see this." His fingers tremble where they're pressed to my cheek. "I love you. I fell in love with you the moment you walked into that hotel room in Cannes, telling me you loved a good auction. I've never met a woman with so much raw grit and guts, who always puts others before herself. My wife who kicks ass and literally kicked my feet from under me..." He smiles, and it breaks my heart not to be able to wrap my arms around him. "Fuck, Gigi. I thought of you every single minute of every single day until you arrived in Boston. And then—" He chuckles. "I wanted to give you grief, but I wanted to marry you so bad, too. Just for once be a man worthy of a woman like you. Prove to myself that I'm a man a woman could love and respect and look up to as an honorable husband. Be anything else but what's in my blood.

"And you did. You came along and showed me that I'm nothing like *him*. You went so far as to say I'm an angel. But I'm not. I'm going to flip because there's this demon in me that I fight every day. Now everything seems like a warm-up for the real fight. Go with my brothers, my darling, beautiful wife. I'll see you on the other side."

He presses kisses to my head, my forehead, my nose, and then over my covered lips as he gently weaves his fingers through my hair. For a last second, he presses his forehead to mine. "I love you."

Stephano stands and steps away from me, giving a last command to his brothers. "Get the women out."

Benedict and Dominic rush in, sniper rifles over their shoulders. Benedict comes towards me, but Dominic runs to the far end of the warehouse.

Only now do I notice the unknown woman has dropped to the floor.

"She's wounded," Dominic calls out as he crouches by her side where she's half-hidden by the barrels and machinery. "But she's breathing," he says. "We need to get her medical attention, pronto."

Already he's pulled out his phone to make a call.

"Fuck," Matteo hisses, but doesn't lower his gun. "Burley, Carla is out stone cold, too. Get on with it."

I'm swooped up in Benedict's arms and watch as Burley carefully gathers Carla in a gentle hold. It's only once Benedict has lowered me into the car seat that I realize I might never see my husband alive again.

48

GIGI

I'm shattered. I just left Stephano. And that after he told me he loves me.

He let me go.

He forced me to leave because he was going to flip, and he didn't want me to watch him potentially die. The mere thought makes me want to break free and run back to him, but I can't. Benedict made sure to carry me, still bound and gagged, into a dead-end road that was empty. He helps me into a back passenger seat of and SUV that's parked right outside the warehouse's garage door. Nobody is going to notice what's happening here.

I glance to where Burley has carefully propped Carla up next to me and is now holding her head. She moans, but doesn't open her eyes as he straps her in.

"There's no blood, and she's coming to," he says as he flicks his gaze to mine. "Both good signs."

Benedict holds my gaze for a long second. "Don't run back inside, Gigi. Any distraction can cost him."

I nod. He cuts the ties binding my legs and wrists. I've never felt this helpless in my life. I'm free, but I can't run to the man I love. I can't protect him. I couldn't even protect my sister.

My body trembles without my restraints, and I struggle to get a grip on the duct tape covering my mouth. I rip it off in batches that burn my sensitive skin. I must give Stephano the space he needs, but I can still be there for my sister.

"Carla, sweetheart."

I reach for her hand, my heart in my throat, but she's still out of it. I meet Benedict's gaze as he leans in on that side, but everything is blurry with the tears in my eyes.

"Concussion at a minimum," Burley says as he cuts her ties.

"She could lose the baby."

"I know," Benedict says. "The doctors will do their best."

"You know about the baby?"

"It's going to be okay." Benedict gets into the front passenger's seat. "We're going to the clinic immediately."

"See you on the other side," Burley says as he closes Carla's door.

As we drive off, panic flares in my chest. Stephano said those words to me too.

"What do you guys mean?" I ask as I lean forward to touch Benedict's shoulder. "See you on the other side?"

He turns to look at me. "See you in Hell? But we aim for at home at the after-party."

Oh, God.

Those words are their final goodbye in case they get killed. A light way of saying so many things. *We're in this together. I've got your back as I know you have mine. We'll make it. And if we don't, we'll catch up in Hell. I'll find you there, and we'll carry on as normal. Remember, I love you.*

I've left my tormented angel behind to fight his own demons. I close my eyes and weep, praying Stephano will come home.

Benedict makes several calls as we head out of the industrial harbor area and back into the city. One call is to Luca. I can't make out what's happening from his one-way, one-word conversation with his brother, and when he rings off, the tension radiates off him.

"How bad is it?" I venture to ask. I'd hate for her to be dead. This unknown woman who was as much Franco's hostage as we were.

Benedict hesitates, then says, "Pretty bad, by the sounds of it. Do you have any clue who she is?"

"No, we didn't have a chance to talk. How did she get shot?"

"Could have been a bullet ricocheting, or it could have been Franco's direct hit." He drags a hand through his hair. "We'll know once we have the bullet."

I shake my head. "Franco said there was only space for one on his jet. He was planning to kill her from the start."

"Hopefully, she'll make it and get to tell us what happened."

I nod, clinging to Carla's hand in desperation. Everything could have been so much worse.

When we head into a neighborhood and then down a short, empty service road, I get nervous. "Where're we going?"

"We own a medical center for situations like this when a home visit won't cut it. Dominic will make sure the other woman gets there as soon as possible. We call in some of the best doctors in town. They'll look after Carla and this other woman until they can come home."

The best doctors are surely bought or owe *Il Consiglio* something. Mafia smooth, keeping the police and anybody else out of it.

I bite my lip to force it to still. I have zero control over any of this, and I can do nothing but blindly trust. How did they know about Carla's baby when I didn't even know? Tasha could have guessed it. Maybe Carla confided in her and she then told Matteo.

It doesn't matter now. The only thing that matters is that both women and the baby pull through.

We drive into a double garage at the back of a house. A nurse and doctor in a white coat wait for us with a gurney.

"Come have a look for yourself. Otherwise, you're going to keep worrying," Benedict says as he pops open his door.

A lot of things happen at the same time, and when Carla is finally in a hospital bed in a private room, I exhale the breath I've been holding. This is first-class medical care, and already, I'm at ease.

When Carla opens her eyes, but groans at the light that's already dimmed, I reach for her hand. What I wouldn't do to wipe this whole day from the face of our memories. "Carla... why didn't you tell me about the baby?"

She presses her hand to her head. A bump has ballooned where she hit it on the concrete floor.

"God, Gigi. How could I?" she murmurs. "With everything going on and you always so...perfect?"

"Me? Perfect?" I'm shocked my sister would even think such a thing. "I'm the furthest there is from perfect."

Carla shakes with a sob. "Do you have any idea what it's like to be coddled by this one person who you look up to, who has done *everything* right? The one person you love above everybody else but who always corrects and tells me to do things differently? I'm so sick of not being *you* that I've...that I've gone too far."

She tugs her hand from mine where I've been clutching hers ever tighter and cups both hands to her face. "Worst of all is he died for me—for us—and I'm... I'm in love with him. If I don't lose this baby, I'm keeping it. I don't care what you think or say, it's mine. The last thing I'll ever have of Vito."

"It's all right, sweetheart. I understand." Better than you'd ever know. I lean into the bed, too weak to stand. We're not so different after all. "Carla—"

She raises a hand, but it slumps back onto the bed. It's enough to cut me off.

"Your sister needs to rest, Mrs. Scalera."

I glance at the doctor in charge. It's the first time a stranger has ever called me Mrs. Scalera. "Yes, I know, but when will we know about the baby?"

"For now, we assume everything is all right," the doctor says. "She isn't too far along, and I don't want to subject her to an exam right now."

Heavens, I don't even know what that would entail, so I only nod. I need to go, but I don't want to leave her. If I lose her and Stephano both in one day, there'll be no more reason for living.

"She's going to be fine. The baby, too," the doctor says. "As soon as she's mentally able, I'll arrange for an ultrasound. If she wants you to be here, we'll make sure you are." He holds his hand out to the door, indicating I should step out of the room. "We'll let you know how she is tonight and again tomorrow, three times a day until she's ready to go home."

Home. Who knows where it will be for Carla?

All I know is, home for me is wherever Stephano is, and I never had the chance to tell him that.

49

STEPHANO

I walk over to where Matteo has Franco at gunpoint. Franco's dark gaze jumps around the room, from me to Luca, then back to me. The exact moment he realizes he's seeing double of the same person and that he's fucked, clocks on his face.

I bet somewhere out there someone is trying to take out either me or my lookalike. Probably some mercenary who didn't have time to do a proper background check. It's well known that there were six Scalera sons. What isn't well known is that two of us are identical twins. The Don always made sure this didn't become common knowledge amongst our kind, and now, it's played out to our advantage.

I strip off my jacket and toss it away. For a moment, I stare at this man who has no limits to his cruelty. Every feature on his face blurs, and I need to force myself not to see the Don in front of me.

"Franco Fiore. You hit my wife." My voice is low and menacing. "You bruised her beautiful face. You hurt her sister." I lean in and hiss in his ear. "You've cut into her flesh, leaving a mark I'll still erase. Let me show you how *Il Consiglio* deals with men like you."

I strip off my shirt as I look him in the eye.

Franco starts to mirror me while Matteo holds the gun right there.

"Fight to the death?" he sneers, and I smile as he tosses his shirt to the side.

Physically, he's in good shape, but he's had habits. Everything he's done would have weakened him. I drop my gaze to his tattooed torso. Man, this guy's committed.

"And that after I brought you someone in exchange for Gigi Trapani. Someone you can all share," he says.

Matteo stiffens, and he presses the barrel deeper into Franco's neck. "You are a sick fuck, aren't you?"

"That depends." Franco has a wicked grin on his face that I want to swipe off with my fists. "If you're into incest or not."

What the actual fuck?

My eyes flash to Matteo's where he stands behind Franco, the implication of those words slowly sinking in. Incest? Matteo's gaze wanders to the woman I can't see. Behind my back, Dominic is giving emergency care to her in the corner... *Impossible.*

I didn't get a good look at her, not that it matters, so I shake my head in annoyance.

"What the fuck are you talking about?" I bite out, hating how we are stalling.

Franco stares at me. "I'm talking about a baby sister you all took for dead."

A baby sister. We took for dead.

Luca steps up and grabs Franco by the throat. "Sick way to buy yourself some time, don't you think?"

"If you kill me, you'll never know." Franco strangles the words out between labored breaths.

Luca lets go of his throat, but I don't take my eyes off Franco's face. He is baiting us, fighting for his life with words. I don't know this guy; right now, I can't read him beyond the rage boiling in me. It's as if he knew exactly how to mess with my head. Forcing me to choose between his lie and atonement for that night decades ago where Don Scalera marked my soul. I know once I've killed this man, those memories will stop haunting me.

"If you know, others will know," I say, "and we will hunt them down."

"If she survives your bullets." He sneers again.

"I'll kill you with my bare hands," Luca spits in his face, "if it weren't a pleasure reserved for Gigi Trapani's husband. Those bullets weren't ours. You shot her."

"Fuck this shit," Matteo says as he pushes the gun into Franco's neck. "This party is over. Check his weapons so that Steph can wrap it up."

For a few tense seconds, time stops as we call him out on his bluff. Then Luca pats Franco down, pulling out two knives and another gun. Tired of playing games, he slices Franco's pants off, leaving the man standing in his boxer shorts.

Naked, we're all the fucking same; it's what's inside my head that differentiates me from this psycho. And what's inside my head supersedes what's inside my blood. I choose how this ends. Today, I'll finally take all control over my body and my mind.

I roll on my heels, cracking my neck, ready to rip him to shreds. A nod at Matteo, and he lowers his gun.

Nobody needs to ask us twice. Franco comes for me with an upper cut, but I block it and crack his jaw with a punch that has all my body weight in it. He staggers.

"Come on!" I scream as he circles out of reach. "Take it like you give it!"

I go at him, the adrenaline in my blood poison whose only antidote is to beat this guy to death.

We circle each other, slowly warming up to the fight with random punches hitting the target, but Franco soon realizes he's no match for me. Of course he isn't. Franco Fiore has demons of his own, but they aren't born out of my level of physical violence.

He manages to hold me off for a while, with the superhuman strength that surfaces when you're fighting for your life, but I'm fueled by something else. Every kick, every punch, is fueled by the need to find justice for Mom, for that night so long ago when the Don made me do shit no kid should ever do, telling me to do it harder, until I hit her with a punch that satisfied him.

When Franco finally crumples to the floor and curls into himself, I feel only warmed up. Nothing stops me now. I'm on top of him in destroyer mode.

It's only when I don't recognize his face anymore that I stop, chest heaving, blood all over me. Fuck, for a long time, it wasn't his face I was beating to pulp. It was Don Scalera's. Franco still breathes, but his chest wheezes with each labored breath. I squeeze with my thighs, and he struggles even more.

Fuck. This must end.

"The axe!" I call out. "Bring me the fucking axe."

When Matteo walks up to me, I glance up at him. Our gazes hold for a long minute, and in his eyes, there's approval for this thing we were groomed to do. For these men we've become under the Don's sick manipulation and guidance. It's in our blood, and we're only perpetuating the violence, but on our terms.

"Do it," he says. "It's like shedding old fucking skin."

Just like he shed his past when he killed Don Scalera.

I nod, knowing I will never tell a soul that my oldest brother murdered our father. "Where's Gigi?"

"Benedict took her and Carla to the clinic," Luca says. "Carla was coming to. Dominic is still with the other woman. She's unconscious."

Our little sister.

Or not.

Fuck.

I glance down at my body. I'm splattered and smeared with blood. Bruises bloom where Franco managed to get in a hit. At least Gigi isn't seeing me like this. She'll never see me like this. "If I do this, there'll be no more information from him."

"I don't care," Matteo says. "If there's any truth to his words, the woman will talk."

"If she lives." My final strike can't be the reason we're hitting a dead end.

"I have her," Dominic says as he walks past us, her body in his arms. "She'll live."

We watch him leave, then Matteo looks down at me. "If there's any truth to it, we'll figure it out some other way. Get it done, Stephano."

Matteo lowers the axe to the floor, and he and Luca step to the side. The body underneath mine drags in strained breaths, blood oozing from his lips and nose and ears. For all we know, the damage is done, and he'll never speak again.

I stand, pick up the axe, and hack off both his hands in two swift swoops of the blade.

"I promised my wife you'll never touch a woman again. I never break my promises. And it's only fair to deliver her the proof."

50

GIGI

I'm pacing the vast space that's Matteo's living room. It's almost dark outside now. Tasha is rocking herself on the sofa, knees pulled to her chest. She stares at me, and I can't help but think this situation is bringing back nasty memories for her. Matteo is out there, too, and what with this being the Mafia, neither of us have guarantees our men will come back, irrespective of the way things were when I left that warehouse.

We're alone. Benedict dropped me off and made sure I was okay, then he returned to the warehouse as backup.

My body is in a chokehold. "What if he dies?" I cry out to the void.

"He won't."

Tasha's unwavering faith seems childish to me. She doesn't know Franco.

"How do you know?"

"Matteo is there. And Luca."

"What if it was all a trap?" I can't let go of this feeling that things could still go wrong.

"Then Benedict will go blow the place up."

"God," I huff. "You're more Mafia than me."

"Don't underestimate Matteo." She hitches a brow. "And don't underestimate your husband. The first time I ever laid eyes on Stephano, he killed a man in this very room using only his steel-toed boot."

"Oh, God. This is the guy that had it coming?" I ask with a shudder.

She nods. "You see that massive square tile? I call it Execution Square."

I sink down on the sofa next to her and reach for her hand. It's easy to forget that Tasha's catapult into this family is so recent. "I don't want to know. Spare me the details."

She grips my hand and I follow her gaze to the square tile.

"Okay." Now that I see it, I can't unsee it.

The massive square tile would be so easy to clean. I recall her unease weeks ago when she said she doesn't like hanging out at the second-floor railing. I quiver inside, trying to reconcile in my head the man I love and the man who succumbs to any level of violence and brutality.

"I don't care. That asshole had it coming. Left one of the women who worked for their clubs for dead. Tatiana. She overdosed. Matteo told me what happened to her, and she couldn't live with..." Tasha trails off and starts rocking again.

I ball up next to her.

Franco had it coming too. From the moment Stephano saw Franco's cruelty on my skin, he promised revenge on my behalf. This *is* Stephano. This is *my husband*. *This* is what's in his blood, fueled by what he experienced as a child. To protect and avenge the women he loves. Not only women he loves—he'll protect all women.

Stephano can't see it for himself. I've never for a second felt unsafe with him, and in his arms, there's never been a safer place. Earlier, when he could have gone all out with Franco while we were still there, he had enough control to make sure we were gone before he started. None of us needed to witness what followed.

I drop my head to Tasha's shoulder, and for a long while, we just sit, bound in fate and in the love we have for our men.

"He said he loved me," I sob, tears welling up out of the blue. "And I never had a chance to say it back."

A soft whooshing comes from the front door, and we both look up as footsteps fall seconds later.

"Maybe you can tell him now," Tasha says, but she's already shooting up and running to where Matteo is walking into the apartment.

I'm still in shock at seeing Stephano by his side, not much worse for wear. He's wearing different clothes, but it's still a suit, still so freaking Italian. He looks so handsome, my blood rushes through my veins as a blush flushes my cheeks.

Tasha flings herself into Matteo's arms and he catches her, allowing her to wrap her legs around his waist.

"Thank God," she calls out, and then all sound is muffled as she cries into his neck.

To have Tasha's confidence...to know this thing between Stephano and me isn't fake. To know this marriage doesn't have divorce written all over it now that Franco is dead. And yes, I can see he's dead by the look in my husband's eyes.

My darling, beautiful wife. I love you.

The memory of his words rockets me out of my seat, and I fling myself at him before anything else can hold me back.

He laughs as he catches me, and my body molds to his as I wrap my arms around him, my legs hugging his hips. His hands clasp my butt in support, hitching me high enough so I can look into his eyes.

"Hey, angel."

"What took you so long?" I ask, crying openly now. I sob and hide in his neck, still struggling to believe he's alive and real and *here.*

"We waited for the cleaning crew, and then I had to clean up, too, so I went home."

"Home? Like in your apartment?"

"Home like in *our* apartment," he whispers in my ear.

I cling to him as he walks us to the sofa. Matteo and Tasha are walking up the stairs, and Matteo hugs his wife close, whispering calming words to her.

Stephano lowers down to sit and makes me straddle him. He winces, but it's barely audible.

"Where are you hurt?" I ask, sweeping my hands over his cheeks, down his shoulders and his pecs. There's a swollen bruise on his cheekbone and one by his eyebrow on the other side. I reach for his hands and inspect them. They're covered in bandages, so I can't see the full extent of his hurt. "Did you break anything?"

"No, for the first time in my life, I think...I feel whole."

I blink at him, at the raw openness in his gaze.

"God, I love you," I whisper as I lean in and kiss him.

He kisses me back, and it's intense as his hands slide to my back, and then he clings to me as if I'm as much his lifeline as he is mine. As I draw away to catch a breath, all I can do is murmur, "Thank you."

"No. No thank yous. I'll do anything for you, angel, you know that, right? I'll do what I did this afternoon a thousand times over for you. To keep you safe. To rid the world of men like Franco."

Men like Don Scalera.

My heart breaks and heals at the same time, and I nod as I lean my forehead to his. "Still."

"Just say it again."

I pull an inch away so I can look into his eyes, making sure I understand what he needs. "I love you."

He brushes my cheek with his thumb. "I love you, too. I'd go on one knee, but I'm kinda trapped right now."

"One knee? I'm hurting you?" I'm very comfortable like this, his hand on my hip, squeezing possessively.

"No, Gigi." He smiles. "I never got to ask you because I was full of shit, but I want this to be real. Marry me? Again? Just for ourselves. To make it real this time."

I swallow at the pebble in my throat. "I'll marry you a thousand times if that's what you want. If that's what you need."

He kisses me then, and I sink into his body and into his love. After a long, hot minute, I pull away, his hands already underneath my shirt, cupping my breasts.

"If it's safe, take me home, Stephano."

"It's safe, angel. From now on, it will always be safe." He smirks. "Let's go. I don't think Matteo's sofa is up to us in any case."

I giggle. That's a promise, and if there is one man in the world who keeps all the promises he makes, it's this one. *And he's mine.*

EPILOGUE

STEPHANO

I sensed something about it was off. Something about the whole situation a week ago in that warehouse was too easy. Franco Fiore picking our abandoned warehouse despite having a troop of Ukrainians looking out for him? Too easy.

At the time, we were all so focused on saving the women and getting the job done, we didn't think too far, but after the initial adrenaline rush of killing Franco, we regrouped and debriefed. Nothing was clear or made sense in retrospect, until Gigi phoned Don Trapani the next day and his first words to her were, *I assume it's been done.*

"Seems like an old man under house arrest can still pull a few strings," Don Trapani says from across the patio table.

He's suave, charming, and impeccably dressed. His grey hair, which is brushed back, and the cane—which Gigi whispered is new—are some of the few things giving away his age. He's definitely had the odd procedure or two to keep the wrinkles at bay.

He doesn't look the worse for wear after the time spent under house arrest—not that I would have a comparison—but when Gigi burst into tears and hugged him close, relief radiated off her. Apparently, he got manhandled by Franco's men, and his one knee is still in pain. This doesn't stop Don Trapani from going about his business.

Gigi, Carla, and I arrived earlier this afternoon in Lake Como, with enough security to make the Pope go green with jealousy. We just sat down for pre-dinner drinks on his terrace with fantastic views over the mountains and the lake, feeling untouchable here, but we all know it's a lie. Don Trapani's men are stationed, if subtly, on the fringes of the garden. Ours are scattered in between. I'm not taking a risk with my wife or her sister. I already know what Gigi would do if Carla is in danger, so they are a package deal and a dual safety hazard.

"How did you manage, Papa?" Carla asks.

She's clinging to a glass of water, her shoulders tense. We've been instructed not to say a word about her pregnancy. Apparently, good Catholic girls don't get pregnant at eighteen with their bodyguards who are fourteen years older than them. A bodyguard who is still unaccounted for. I didn't hold either woman back when they hit the cellar earlier, looking for Vito Rossi's body. They found nothing.

"Ah, *cara*," Don Trapani sighs. "I've been in this business from the day of my birth, born into it like all of you. In all these years, I've seen too much." He smiles wryly, but it dries up pretty quickly. "Forewarned is forearmed. Vincenzo was getting into bad company, and I made provisions for any situation. With Randazzo gone I made sure we were as ready as possible." His gaze flicks to mine, but we don't say a word; the secret of who eliminated Randazzo is still watertight.

"That Friday night caught me off guard, *cara*, and I will never forgive Vincenzo for breaking my trust like that. The plan was to brief you two girls and see that you were safe, and then he arrived with Franco in tow."

A tense silence sweeps into the space around us as Don Trapani closes his eyes.

"Bless his soul, but he is no son of mine," he mutters as he crosses himself. "But if not Franco, it would have been someone else. Cenzo was a rotten apple from the start."

We all hang our heads in feigned mutual respect for the dead. There are a few things that are never going to come out of our inner *Il Consiglio* circle. One of them is how Vincenzo died from one clean shot to the back of his head, after Dominic interrogated him about the unknown woman in our care. So far, the story of Franco eliminating Vincenzo seems to be holding up. I hope it lasts. *Il Consiglio* works on a need-to-know basis, and even though Gigi knows we killed Vincenzo, she will never talk.

Don Trapani's body shudders, and he seems to pull himself together with a deep inhale.

"You girls should both know," he says as he looks at them, one after the other, "I have people outside the Cosa Nostra that put measures in place as soon as a certain situation triggers the first domino. That Friday night was one of those domino moments." He raises his wine glass at Gigi. "You escaping with Carla was something none of us expected. Bravo, Gigi. I always knew you shouldn't be underestimated."

"Thank you," Gigi says softly, but her hand curls into a fist as she pulls it from the table to hide on her lap.

I reach for it, and she slips her fingers between mine. I rest our hands on my thigh underneath the table where nobody can see how tightly she squeezes mine for courage.

"When Vincenzo started thinking about going to Boston," Don Trapani continues, "I knew I had to steer him and his friend in the Scaleras' direction. It was just a subtle hint or two about my old school friend in Boston, and how we had a warehouse in the Boston harbor that's been standing empty for decades now. I never named names, but Franco didn't want any. Rookie mistake. In the end, you made it easy for me to clean up after Franco and Vincenzo."

Of course it's fucking clean. It's an *Il Consiglio* job with the Scaleras at the helm. Plus the whole shebang happened in the States, keeping Don Trapani's side pristine and him seemingly innocent.

Franco is busy chilling with his buddy in Matteo's promession facility, less his hands, but those have been taken care of, too. On Matteo's recommendation, I took Don Trapani a typical New England gift in the form of maple syrup in two twenty-eight-ounce designer tins, in case he wanted to shake hands with Franco one last time.

If ever he opens those cans, it would be a sticky, messy and probably a very smelly business indeed. I've still to hand him my precious little gift, but this would best be done over a tumbler of whiskey once the women have gone to bed. I might have told Franco I need proof for Gigi's sake of how he'll never touch a woman again, but I know where to draw the line.

I glance at my wife. After what happened here that Friday night, I'm not sure Gigi will be able to sleep in this house at all, and I've booked a room at a boutique hotel farther along the lake just in case. We might be sitting here on a beautiful terrace overlooking Lake Como, with the last of another warm afternoon slipping into sunset, but it's been one close call after the other. None of us is relaxed yet. We're all still on high alert and looking over our shoulders.

"Marriage seems to suit you, *cara*," Don Trapani says, breaking into a silence that's borne out of too many secrets. "I'm happy for the alliance, and it's good to have a wider network. The world is changing, and so must we. This thing with Franco —" He breaks off, clearly not over his earlier emotions. "Now with Vincenzo gone, and Franco dealt with, we need a strong leader to step in. I need a new succession plan, as my first failed."

He stares at Gigi for such a long time, the sound of the

cicadas becomes a piercing blade in the tense air. His meaning is so obvious, it sends a chill down my spine.

"Papa..." she starts, her hand growing cold in mine where she's clinging for dear life. "I don't...I—" She turns to look at me, stunned. "Please, I don't want to get involved."

"Ah, *cara*. You've seen the worst of this side of the business. You have a husband from an influential Mafia family whose roots are the same as yours. I support and am happy for your union, even if it came about under unusual circumstances. I would offer Stephano the position first, but he didn't grow up here. He doesn't know our customs firsthand like you do. The position is yours, and I want you to take it."

Fuck. This isn't what we came for. The implication of his words hits me hard. Gigi, the *Capo Crimini*. No. My darling, beautiful wife is kick-ass and gutsy, but she's too human for this type of job. Too soft. I have a whole life in Boston I've never imagined uprooting. Least of all to return to the place where Don Scalera grew up.

Or Mom. Bianca Randazzo. Her world forever captured in oil paintings that hang around her sons' apartments and houses.

Fuck.

"You're still young, Papa," Carla says. "Surely—"

"What happened cannot happen again, Carla," Don Trapani interrupts. "Know this. Without succession in place, we are as vulnerable as a newborn fawn." His eyes meet mine across the table, and he tips his head toward me. "Gigi will not do it alone. She will have you, her husband, who, from what I understand, is a good man."

Mostly. Fuck. For a week, I've had peace. No voice in my head telling me it's in my blood. I had my wife in my arms at night, her sweet kisses on my body, her contented sighs mixing with my own, our heartbeats fast where we were pressed close against each other in release.

Now, he asks me to become the one thing I loathe being the most. I know what it takes to be the Don. It takes *everything*.

"No, Papa—" Gigi protests, but Don Trapani raises his hand to cut her off.

"This is the thing, Gigi. You remember your father. You've experienced Franco Fiore. I know you want out, but it's the people who want out who we really need to keep in the organization, purely because they are not bat-shit crazy." He rubs a hand over his face. "Men like Franco Fiore, like Vincenzo, don't have limits or self-control. They rule with terror and not logic. I won't have one of them step into my shoes, and neither should you."

"Papa—"

"Hear me out, *cara*," he says, serious now. "Ten years, you've roamed Europe, and I let you, because I knew you would build valuable connections amongst the rich. I'm not interested in Randazzo's businesses, the 'Ndrangheta can fight over that between themselves. In fact, if I could put an end to it, I would. But you know how this works. Demand generates supply, not the other way around."

I swallow, sitting stiff in my chair. Yeah, there would be no need for human trafficking and any other depravity if there weren't a demand for it.

"I want you, *cara*, with Stephano, to come work with me, learn the ropes, meet our *capos*, the families, settle here to take over from me when I retire."

I hate it when someone talks sense. I know Don Trapani's type. He might be a don, but he is also a charmer, and he will get to her eventually. And I will have her back.

"Surely, Gigi isn't your only option?" I ask when the silence stretches just a few seconds too long. "What about the mole?"

Gigi shoots me a glance; Don Trapani hitches his brow. "The mole serves his purpose best as an unknown entity."

This hacks that idea off at the knees. "You know I can't just leave Boston. I have businesses I run—"

"Many of your businesses are online. You have good management in place at your clubs and other above-board businesses. You can manage," the Don says. "And Matteo can spare you. He has three more brothers to rely on. I have no sons, and you've married my daughter now. I'm welcoming you into the family, as a son. *My son*."

Fuck. The expectation is clear. This was something we never thought about when we married in a rush with divorce as an end goal. There are vows I will never break: those I made to my wife on our wedding day.

Servers appear with platters of antipasti, and we sit silent while they put them down and set the table with plates and cutlery. One server proceeds to top off everybody's wine and pours Carla some more water. With a little bow to the Don, they both wait for further instruction. Don Trapani waves them away.

"We'll have to discuss it," I say without preamble. "This isn't an easy decision, nor one that should be made lightly."

"Of course. I understand," Don Trapani says with a nod.

"I can't go back to Boston," Carla says softly.

I curse under my breath. If nothing else, that's going to seal the deal.

"Well, then," Gigi says as she reaches for a serving fork and puts some antipasti on my plate. "The Scaleras have a jet. We can fly back to Boston whenever you need to, Steph."

I grunt. The Trapanis have the yacht. And this mansion on Lake Como. And their city residences in Palermo and Rome. An apartment in St. Tropez. And a mountain hut somewhere in Switzerland for skiing. And almost a billion euros in some random unknown bank vault nobody talks about, because with Vincenzo's death, the whole inheritance now comes to Gigi and

Carla. Fuck my life. I love money as much as the next person, but this is too much.

"Well, then," I echo Gigi, somewhat resigned already. "I've always wanted to work on my Italian."

"See," she whispers as she leans in with a soft smile, her eyes however apologizing all the way. "It won't be all bad."

Fuck. And there I was planning on a cozy life in Boston with the woman I love.

There's no peace for the wicked.

Mafia business is, after all, in our blood.

MORE TO COME...

Dear Reader

Thank you for taking the time to read Stephano and Gigi's story — I hope you enjoyed the ride! Please help my visibility by swiping all the way to the end of this book and giving it a star rating — reviews aren't necessary, star ratings count!

At this point, Dominic's story is still a work in progress, and I don't have a release date. To stay up to date as to when Dominic's story will release, please follow me on social media or on Amazon.

SACRED SINS - the 3rd book in the *Il Consiglio* Mafia Series

The old Don is dead. My work is done. My brother—and the new Don of *Il Consiglio*—would never use me like our father did.

That is until Ariana Moretti crashes into our lives. Ariana looks at me with trust in her eyes and clings to my hand as if I'm her savior, making me feel alive for the first time since I was reduced to nothing but a weapon in the Don's arsenal.

She's our family's only link to a past we buried decades ago but she won't talk. Making people talk is my specialty, but I've never had to wring information out of a woman before. Never mind one who already bears scars similar to my own handiwork. Scars similar to those I have branded on my skin.

I have a duty to my family, to my brothers. A duty to make her talk. I can't be the weakest link. I can't let her crawl under my skin, and I can't cave into the desire that pulses between us. I'm the devil himself and Ariana Moretti is a slice of heaven the likes of me will never deserve.

Worst of all is I already sense, once her truth finally comes out, I'll have to kill her to save my brothers. How do I pull the trigger on the woman I love?

Follow for updates here:

ABOUT THE AUTHOR

Sophia writes sensual, emotional, and evocative contemporary romance. Some snark might sneak in. When she's not writing, she's binge-watching the latest TV series, being walked by her beagles, or planning the family's next trip into the wilds. She's ghosted Facebook, is failing at Tiktok, and has little time left for Instagram, however, she hasn't given up (yet). Check out her efforts at @sophiakarlson or @sophiakarlsonauthor

Sign up for her newsletter to get updates about new book releases and free stuff! Rest assured, you won't be bombarded! https://BookHip.com/RKDPHT

ACKNOWLEDGMENTS

Thank you to my book besties who have been fabulous in helping me write and polish this book! Amanda Holly, Meg Chronis, and Zee Monodee, you are all rockstars!

ALSO BY SOPHIA KARLSON

The Love Nests Series

The Paris Apartment - James and Mila's story

The Shrink - Stacy and Ivo's story

The Neighbor - Ruben and Marlène's story

The Intern - Bryce and Izzy's story (they pop up in HATED VOWS)

Ashleigh Lake Series - Small Town Romance

One Sweet Summer - Raiden and Georgiana's story

When I Fall in Love - Hunter and Beth's story

Standalones

Just My Type - Mark and Hayley's story

Mafia Romance

Hated Vows - Matteo and Tasha's story

Broken Vows - Stephano and Gigi's story

Perfect Series

Perfect Mistake

Perfect Obsession

Printed in Dunstable, United Kingdom

79093730R00190